NEW YORK TIMES BESTSELLING AUTHOR

Robert B. Parker's

BYE BYE BABY

A SPENSER NOVEL

BY ACE ATKINS

$9.99 U.S.
$12.99 CAN

Robert B. Parker's Bye Bye Baby

Carolina Garcia-Ramirez is a rising star in national politics, taking on the establishment with her progressive agenda. Tough, outspoken, and driven, the young congresswoman has ignited a new conversation in Boston about race, poverty, health care, and the environment. Now facing her second campaign, she finds herself not only fighting a tight primary with an old-guard challenger but also contending with numerous death threats coming from hundreds of suspects.

When her chief of staff reaches out to Spenser for security and help finding the culprits behind what he believes to be the most credible threats, Garcia-Ramirez is less than thrilled. Since her first grassroots run, she's become used to the antipathy and intimidation women of color often face when seeking power. To her, it's all noise. But it turns out an FBI agent disagrees, warning Spenser that Garcia-Ramirez might be in real danger this time. It doesn't take long for Spenser to cross paths with an extremist group called the Minutemen, led by a wealthy Harvard grad named Bishop Graves. Although Graves is a social media sensation, pushing an agenda of white supremacy and toxic masculinity, he denies he's behind the attacks. As the primary nears and threats become a deadly plot, it's up to Spenser, Hawk, and a surprise trusted ally to ensure the congresswoman is safe. This is Spenser doing what he does best, living by a personal code and moral compass that can't ever be broken.

Praise for Ace Atkins and the Spenser Novels

Robert B. Parker's Bye Bye Baby

"A crime yarn laced with tension and wit."

—*Kirkus Reviews*

"Atkins continues his very successful stewardship of the late Robert B. Parker's beloved Spenser series. . . . This fast-moving and suspenseful thriller is also laced with clever banter. . . . Spenser lives and lives well!"

—*Booklist*

Robert B. Parker's Someone to Watch Over Me

"In this latest in his continuation of Robert B. Parker's beloved Spenser series, Atkins continues to do the late author proud. . . . The talented Atkins delivers another engrossing thriller."

—*Booklist*

"Addictive . . . Atkins expertly revives the verve and muscular prose of the early books."

—*The Seattle Times*

Robert B. Parker's Angel Eyes

"Atkins does a great job making Spenser sarcastic and funny in the face of danger and keeps the plot moving along as danger seems to be around every corner."

—*The Parkersburg News & Sentinel*

"Another rock-solid addition to the Spenser case files."

—*CrimeReads*

"Atkins gets the hardest parts right—his hero/narrator now sounds indistinguishable from Robert B. Parker's. . . . Readers who've always wanted to see Spenser in Tinseltown can cross that off their bucket lists."

—*Kirkus Reviews*

Robert B. Parker's Old Black Magic

"Atkins perfectly catches Spenser's breezy voice and Parker's knack for creating vivid characters."

—*The Seattle Times*

"Atkins . . . again captures all the qualities Spenser fans love in the series: smart-ass humor, a touch of romance, plenty of violence, and, of course, Spenser's complex sense of honor." —*Booklist*

Robert B. Parker's Little White Lies

"A taut, suspenseful story line drives Edgar-finalist Atkins's sixth Spenser novel, which deepens the relationship between the Boston PI and his significant other, therapist Susan Silverman." —*Publishers Weekly*

"*Little White Lies* will keep you eagerly turning the pages to follow his latest adventures in the mean streets. And boy, will it make you hungry." —*Tampa Bay Times*

Robert B. Parker's Slow Burn

"A five-alarm thriller . . . Atkins deftly recreates the Spenser character and his Boston milieu."

—Associated Press

"Sizzling . . . *Slow Burn* rises to a blazing finish and leaves Spenser with some major decisions to make. Can't wait to find out how it goes." —*Tampa Bay Times*

"Scene-by-scene, line-by-line pleasures are authentic."

—*Kirkus Reviews*

"Atkins tosses in a surprising change to his lead's status quo, and series fans will be eager to see what he does with it in Spenser's next outing." —*Publishers Weekly*

Robert B. Parker's Kickback

"Classic Spenser—the Spenser of wry wit, tasty food and drinks, hard workouts and lethal confrontations. It's a reader's guide to greater Boston and a nostalgic trip into the noir world of guys who privately investigate all manner of wrongdoing. . . . Once again, Atkins has delivered a thriller that evokes the best of Parker's Spenser series, not least the punchy back-and-forth of the dialogue."

—Associated Press

"*Kickback* is the best one yet, with Spenser in fine wisecracking fettle. . . . Fans of the series will be gratified that both Hawk and Susan Silverman, Spenser's brilliant and beloved squeeze, get plenty of presence, along with Pearl the Wonder Dog. There are just enough bursts of violent action as Spenser untangles the whole sordid mess and at least some justice is done. Good to have you in town, Spenser." —*Tampa Bay Times*

"Another gritty and riveting Spenser novel in the best tradition of Robert B. Parker." —*The Huffington Post*

"You can always tell if you're reading a great Spenser novel because you start to read with a Boston accent. So it is with *Robert B. Parker's Kickback* written in impeccable style by Ace Atkins. . . . It's full of everything we've come to expect from the Boston private investigator—action, smart-mouthed sarcasm, the assistance of Hawk and most of all, justice." —*Suspense Magazine*

THE SPENSER NOVELS

Robert B. Parker's Bye Bye Baby (by Ace Atkins)

Robert B. Parker's Someone to Watch Over Me (by Ace Atkins)

Robert B. Parker's Angel Eyes (by Ace Atkins)

Robert B. Parker's Old Black Magic (by Ace Atkins)

Robert B. Parker's Little White Lies (by Ace Atkins)

Robert B. Parker's Slow Burn (by Ace Atkins)

Robert B. Parker's Kickback (by Ace Atkins)

Robert B. Parker's Cheap Shot (by Ace Atkins)

Silent Night (with Helen Brann)

Robert B. Parker's Wonderland (by Ace Atkins)

Robert B. Parker's Lullaby (by Ace Atkins)

Sixkill

Painted Ladies

The Professional

Rough Weather

Now & Then

Hundred-Dollar Baby

School Days

Cold Service

Bad Business

Back Story

Widow's Walk

Potshot

Hugger Mugger

Hush Money

Sudden Mischief

Small Vices

Chance

Thin Air

Walking Shadow

Paper Doll

Double Deuce

Pastime

Stardust

Playmates

Crimson Joy

Pale Kings and Princes

Taming a Sea-Horse

A Catskill Eagle

Valediction

The Widening Gyre

Ceremony

A Savage Place

Early Autumn

Looking for Rachel Wallace

The Judas Goat

Promised Land

Mortal Stakes

God Save the Child

The Godwulf Manuscript

For a comprehensive title list and a preview of upcoming books, visit PRH.com/RobertBParker or Facebook.com/RobertBParkerAuthor.

Robert B. Parker's

BYE BYE BABY

ACE ATKINS

G. P. PUTNAM'S SONS
New York

PUTNAM
— EST. 1838 —
G. P. PUTNAM'S SONS
Publishers Since 1838
An imprint of Penguin Random House LLC
penguinrandomhouse.com

First G. P. Putnam's Sons hardcover edition / January 2022
First G. P. Putnam's Sons premium edition / December 2022
G. P. Putnam's Sons premium edition ISBN: 9780593328538

Printed in the United States of America
1 3 5 7 9 10 8 6 4 2

For Team Spenser:

Joan, Mel, Luann & Jim

Forever Boston pals

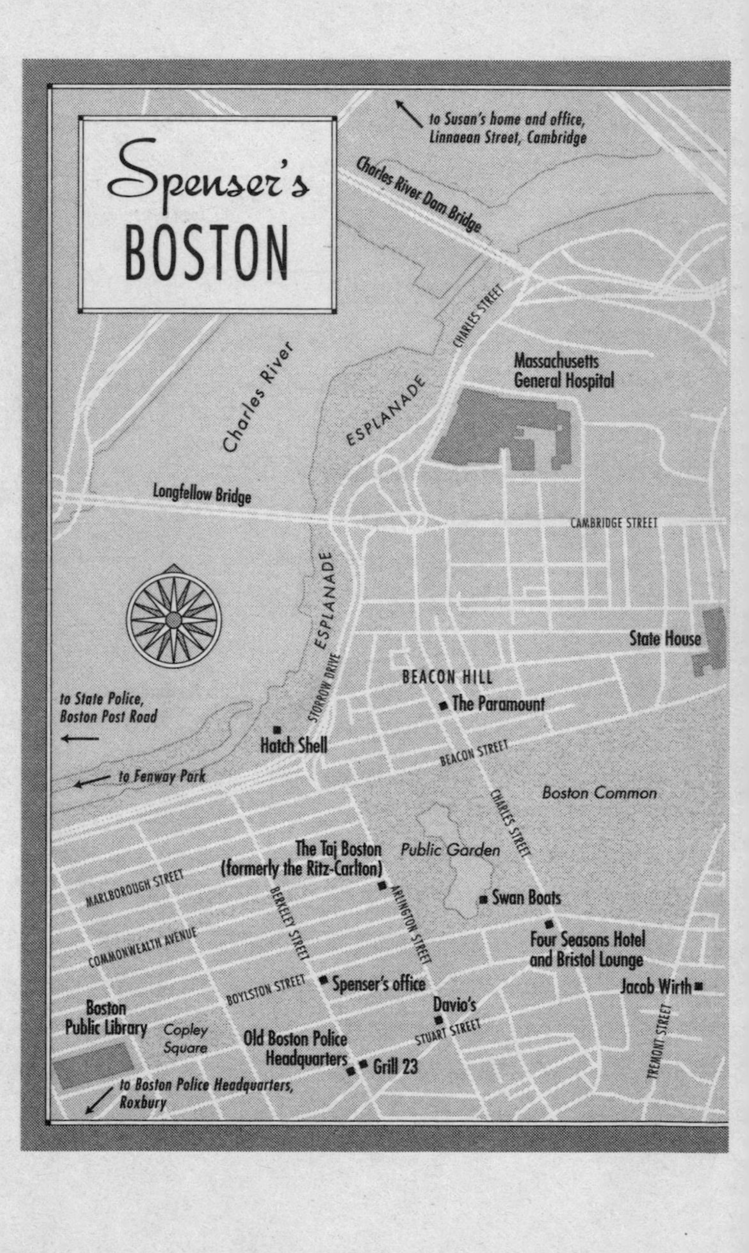
Spenser's
BOSTON
to Susan's home and office,
Linnaean Street, Cambridge
Charles River Dam Bridge
CHARLES STREET
Charles River
ESPLANADE
Massachusetts
General Hospital
Longfellow Bridge
CAMBRIDGE STREET
ESPLANADE
STORROW DRIVE
State House
BEACON HILL
The Paramount
to State Police,
Boston Post Road
Hatch Shell
BEACON STREET
to Fenway Park
Boston Common
CHARLES STREET
The Taj Boston
(formerly the Ritz-Carlton)
Public Garden
MARLBOROUGH STREET
BERKELEY STREET
ARLINGTON STREET
Swan Boats
COMMONWEALTH AVENUE
Four Seasons Hotel
and Bristol Lounge
BOYLSTON STREET
Spenser's office
Jacob Wirth
Davio's
Boston
Public Library
Copley
Square
Old Boston Police
Headquarters
STUART STREET
Grill 23
TREMONT STREET
to Boston Police Headquarters,
Roxbury

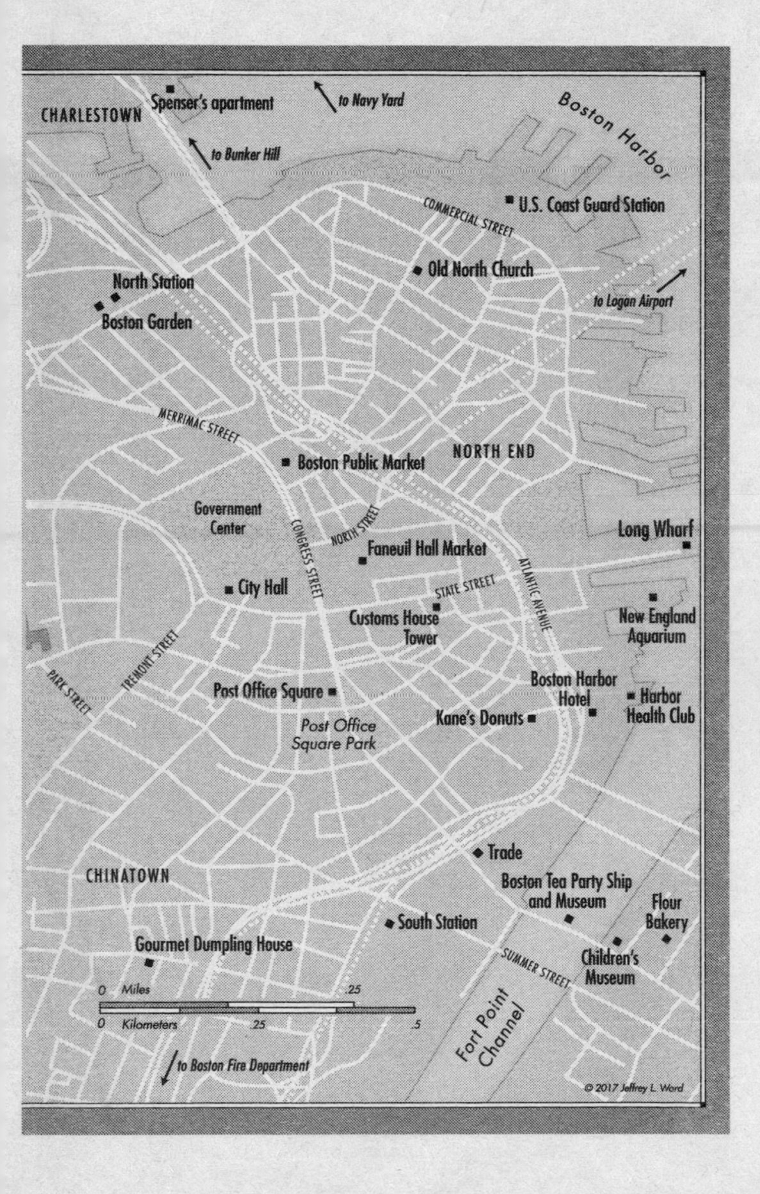
CHARLESTOWN
Spenser's apartment
to Navy Yard
Boston Harbor
to Bunker Hill
COMMERCIAL STREET
U.S. Coast Guard Station
Old North Church
North Station
Boston Garden
to Logan Airport
MERRIMAC STREET
NORTH END
Boston Public Market
Government Center
CONGRESS STREET
NORTH STREET
Faneuil Hall Market
Long Wharf
ATLANTIC AVENUE
City Hall
STATE STREET
Customs House Tower
New England Aquarium
TREMONT STREET
PARK STREET
Post Office Square
Boston Harbor Hotel
Harbor Health Club
Kane's Donuts
Post Office Square Park
Trade
CHINATOWN
Boston Tea Party Ship and Museum
Flour Bakery
South Station
Gourmet Dumpling House
SUMMER STREET
Children's Museum
0 Miles .25
0 Kilometers .25 .5
Fort Point Channel
to Boston Fire Department
© 2017 Jeffrey L. Ward

Robert B. Parker's

BYE BYE BABY

1

The reelection headquarters for Carolina Garcia-Ramirez was deep in Roxbury at the corner of Proctor and Mass, wedged between an all-night liquor store and a Honduran restaurant that advertised the best *pollo frito* in Boston.

That afternoon, I was dressed appropriately for the dog days of summer. A lightweight khaki summer suit, white linen shirt, and polished wingtips sans socks. I caught a glimpse in the office window and thought I might give George Raft a run for his money.

"May I help you?" the receptionist said.

Despite my stunning entrance, the woman had yet to look up from her computer screen.

"Can you vouch for the Honduran place on the corner?" I said. "Is the *pollo frito* really the best in the city?"

"I don't know," she said. "Never been there."

"Seems worth investigating."

"Soul food joint down on Blue Hill's much better," she said. "If you're into that kind of thing."

The woman was of a plus size, with long black cornrows and large brown eyes. I smiled, offering half-wattage so as not to distract her from her duties. She had on a white silk top with blue polka dots, a nifty little bow at the neck.

She hadn't smiled since I walked in the door. Women usually swoon or fall onto the floor with convulsions when I appear.

"Are you here to see someone?" the woman said. "Or just strolling around asking random-ass questions?"

"Might as well do both," I said. "The congresswoman is expecting me."

"The congresswoman isn't here," she said. "Is there something else I can help you with?"

"My name is Spenser," I said. "Kyle Rosen arranged a meeting."

"Spenser?" she said. "Is that your first name or last?"

"Last."

She asked me my first name and I told her. The woman stopped clicking the keyboard and picked up the phone, speaking so quietly I could barely understand what was being said. After a few moments, she nodded and pointed out a group of vinyl chairs that looked to have been swiped from a Ramada Inn lobby.

"Gonna be a minute."

I took a seat by a large plateglass window. The chair's split seams had been repaired with silver duct tape.

As I waited, a staff of a dozen or so milled about secondhand desks and wobbly chairs. The paneled wood walls brightened with posters of Congresswoman Carolina Garcia-Ramirez looking as bold and confident as Che Guevara. CHANGE, NOW and FOR THE PEOPLE written in block lettering. It sounded like most of the staff was cold-calling potential voters about next month's primary.

One exasperated young man kept repeating the congresswoman's name before finally relaying the sad news: Tip O'Neill had died long ago.

Fifteen minutes later, I spotted Kyle Rosen through the plateglass window. We had never actually met, but I'd seen his picture and read his profile in the *Globe*.

I watched him crawl from a black SUV and hold the door open for another passenger. I stood as Carolina Garcia-Ramirez stepped out, dressed in a black pantsuit, hair in a tight bun, with a phone firmly clamped on her ear. She was tall, black, and striking. Even if you didn't know who she was, she looked like somebody.

Another man, small and thin, with hair bleached nearly as white as Tedy Sapp's, followed from the front passenger seat, carrying a very large leather bag. He struggled to get ahead and open the door.

I looked to the receptionist. She smiled and nodded in their direction.

"Mr. Spenser," Rosen said. "I'm sorry we're late. The flight from D.C. was delayed twice."

Rosen was a young guy, late twenties or early thirties, with wild, frizzy brown hair and black-framed glasses that hadn't been hip since Buddy Holly died. He was medium height and skinny, wearing jeans and an oversized black T-shirt that said BE THE CHANGE.

I followed Rosen into a private conference room filled with floor-to-ceiling boxes and large stacks of posters. A long oval table was cluttered with coffee cups and fast-food containers, a few legal notepads and office supplies. A sign on the wall read I'M NOT YOUR MOTHER, KIDS. PLEASE CLEAN UP YOUR DAMN MESS.

"Thank you for coming," Rosen said.

"Any friend of Rita's."

"I met Miss Fiore at a fund-raiser last month," he said. "What a dynamite lady. She told me there's no one better at what you do."

"Besides having a pair of million-dollar legs, she also happens to have a top-notch legal mind."

The mention of Rita's legs caused Kyle to flush. Although tough and sexy as hell, she was probably the same age as his mother.

"Please excuse our offices," he said. "When you have a reelection every two years, no one wants to sign a long-term lease."

"I once had an office in the Combat Zone."

"Really?" he said. "I've heard stories."

"Grown men still weep recalling the Teddy Bare Lounge."

Carolina Garcia-Ramirez walked into the room and stopped cold before tucking her cell back into her purse. When Rosen introduced me, she seemed a bit confused.

"I thought we covered this," she said.

Rosen held up a hand to ask her to let him speak. He got as far as opening his mouth.

"I do not want, nor do I need, a bodyguard."

"Carolina."

"Damn it, Kyle," she said. "I'm exhausted. Our schedule is backed up for the rest of the week. And I don't have the time."

Rosen took in a long breath and seemed to be seeking a moment of Zen. He offered me a reassuring smile as he himself appeared to be slightly less assured.

I smiled back. Good ole friendly Spenser.

"Mr. Spenser does a lot more than just security."

"I'm also a song-and-dance man," I said. "May I serenade you with a bit of 'Bewitched, Bothered, and Bewildered'?"

The congresswoman offered a sour expression. "No," she said. "I'd rather you didn't."

The congresswoman was tall and athletic, with light coppery skin, a delicate bone structure, and a longish neck. She was what many would call pretty if it were not offensive to judge a lawmaker solely based on her appearance. Her black pantsuit was stylish and neat, an American flag pin on the collar. She wore gold jewelry subtle enough that even Susan Silverman would approve. The toes of her pumps were pointed enough to strike fear in cockroaches everywhere.

"I really think you need to hear us out," Kyle said.

"I've heard all of you and I said no."

"Well," I said, shrugging. "It's been a delight."

"Carolina, please," Rosen said. "If you're going to win this thing, you need to focus on the damn issues and quit having to look over your shoulder every five minutes."

"How am I supposed to explain personal security to my donors?" she said. "That's an extravagance we can't afford right now."

"We will work it out," he said.

"And, damn it, it makes me look weak," she said.

Rosen wrapped his arms tight around his body and screwed up his mouth to show it was tightly shut. He looked to me and then to Carolina. I looked back and forth to both of them. I felt like a kid standing between feuding parents. I leaned against the wall and felt into my suit pocket for a silver coin to flip. George Raft would've brought a coin.

"I don't make sales pitches," I said. "But perhaps you might tell me a little more about the issue at hand?"

"Can you help a country deeply divided by sexism, homophobia, and systemic racism?" Carolina said.

"It's all on the business card."

"I hire someone that looks like you and I look like I'm running scared."

"And what exactly do I look like?"

"Like a leg-breaker from Southie."

"If it helps, I live in Charlestown with my German shorthaired pointer, Pearl," I said. "Sometimes I reside in Cambridge with my significant other. Usually the weekends."

Carolina leaned in to the table, the conference room

hushed and quiet. She seemed unfazed by the mess as she took a sip from a stainless-steel water bottle.

"I've had haters on me since I announced my candidacy," she said. "They more than doubled when I got enough signatures to be on the ballot and went off the charts when we actually won. I've been called a wetback, a nigger, a dyke bitch, a whore, and a communist. What I'm saying is that I don't care. I don't worry about the threats, because this bitch is too damn busy getting work done."

"People are threatening to physically harm you?" I said.

The congresswoman started to laugh so hard she nearly did a spit take with the water.

"Physical harm?" she said. She looked over to Kyle Rosen and shook her head. "Are you fucking kidding me? They want to kill me in so many different ways. Shoot me. Electrocute me. Poison me. Hang me and then rape my corpse. Come on. I knew what I was getting into."

"So why now?" I said. "Why does this feel any different?"

Carolina stared at me while Rosen stared at her. She slowly nodded and Rosen turned in my direction. "Some recent threats show some inside knowledge of Carolina's schedule in Boston. That's worrisome."

"You think it's someone on her staff?" I said.

"We don't know," he said. "We think maybe our computers have been hacked."

Carolina Garcia-Ramirez continued to stare at me,

looking me up and down. Her face had a slight sheen of sweat. The dog days of summer were upon all of us.

"May I see the messages?" I said.

"I can print out the emails," Rosen said. "They were sent direct to the congresswoman's private account. We had a tech guy from MIT take a look, but they've been bounced around to different accounts under different names. But they're always the same. Written in the same style and asking the same thing."

"And what's that?"

"For Carolina to drop out of the primary or they'll kill her," he said. "The emails are a reminder each day of what an easy target she is."

"Do you have protection of any kind?" I said.

"It depends on where we are," Rosen said. "She has full protection of the Capitol police in D.C."

"But back in Boston," I said, "you're pretty much on your own."

Carolina had yet to speak since she ran down all the offered methods of her assassination. She continued to stare at me in a way that would make most mortal men uncomfortable. I stared back. After a while, I widened my smile.

She couldn't help herself. The congresswoman smiled.

"Okay," she said. "What exactly can you offer?"

"Personal protection," I said. "And when I'm not doing that, I can offer my sleuthing services."

"Excuse me for asking," she said, raising an eyebrow. "But how can you investigate threats sent from an unknown person from unknown sources and sent in a way even a kid at MIT can't figure it out?"

"'Faith, it does me,'" I said. "'Though it discolors the complexion of my greatness to acknowledge it.'"

"Are you shitting me?" the esteemed congresswoman said. "Shakespeare?"

"I also cook."

She looked over at Rosen and then back at me. She shook her head.

"I hope you're as good as you are cocky," she said.

The congresswoman watched me as if I were the center of a sprawling congressional inquiry. I felt the sudden need to lean in to a microphone.

I cleared my throat and said, "I'm even better."

2

"Well," Susan said. "You have to do it."

"Is that an ultimatum?"

"That's a fact," Susan said. "Carolina Garcia-Ramirez is the best thing to happen to Boston since the colonists tossed sacks of black tea into the bay."

Susan plucked an olive from her martini and took a bite. We were both sitting at the bar at Grill 23, drinking cocktails and patiently waiting for dinner. My martini was gin. Hers was vodka. It wasn't that I disliked vodka, I just didn't think it should be called a true martini. Susan and I had argued on the subject while the waiter refereed.

"I heard her speak at a Raising A Reader event last year," I said.

"And?"

"She appears to be committed to the cause," I said.

"I admire a woman who's small on talk and big on action."

"As do I," I said, raising an eyebrow at her.

Susan rolled her eyes. "Sometimes I think you are a thirteen-year-old trapped in a grown man's body."

"When I was thirteen, the only thing I knew about women was what I saw in my uncle Bob's *Playboy* collection."

Susan reached for my martini and took a sip. She scrunched up her face and set it back onto the bar.

"And?"

"Ick."

"The gin is handmade by British monks," I said.

"My grandmother would've called that bathtub hooch."

Grill 23 was all polished wood and brass, with leather seating and marble accents. The lighting was soft and pleasant, with the restaurant having the added bonus of being within walking distance of my office. The bartender set a filet in front of me and scallops in front of Susan. Susan looked at the filet and then looked at me. She asked the bartender to switch the plates.

He switched plates. I handed her a knife.

"I didn't realize we were sharing," I said.

"Neither did I."

Susan looked and smelled lovely sitting next to me. She had on a fitted black motorcycle jacket over a red sheath dress. Her black hair was pinned up and she wore diamond earrings along with an antique silver bracelet I'd given her for her birthday. I stared at her while she cut off a small bite of steak.

"We should save some for Pearl."

"Need I remind you that is a petit filet?" I said.

"Selfish."

Susan nodded to the bartender and asked for a glass of pinot noir. He poured her a glass and looked to me. I ordered a second martini.

"Gin?" he said, smiling.

"Is there anything else?"

Susan chewed for a moment and swallowed. She took a sip of wine. "When would you start?"

"Tomorrow," I said. "They're going to email me a schedule. It'll be early. I was told the congresswoman has an aggressive campaign schedule."

"Against that putz Tommy Flaherty."

"He wasn't a bad congressman," I said. "Served the district for many years."

"He's a chauvinist pig," she said. "I hope she trounces him in the primary."

"What's your definition of a chauvinist pig?"

"Haven't you seen the ads?" she said. "He's trying to bring back the old Boston establishment. The private men's club. I don't think he knows what year it is."

I named the year. Susan said I wasn't even close.

"Her campaign manager could be our kid."

"Hell," Susan said. "The congresswoman could be our kid. If we'd been a little reckless when we first met."

"I recall many reckless nights."

I smiled and cut into my scallops. They'd been artfully arranged with asparagus and a broiled tomato and appeared slightly larger than Gronk's fists.

"You know she refuses to take corporate money or handouts from billionaires?"

"I was told this wouldn't be a lucrative endeavor."

"I think you'll like her," Susan said. "She's like you. She has a code."

"A luxury few politicians can afford."

Susan cut into her artfully arranged asparagus. Before taking a bite, she took a sip of wine. Every movement meaningful and precise.

"Success hasn't seemed to have changed her," Susan said. "She's kept focused on those who got her elected. People of color. Lower-income neighborhoods. I read her father was a mechanic. Her mother a hotel maid. Both Dominican."

"Funny," I said. "In all my years of sleuthing, this is the first time you've been impressed with a potential client."

"I guess I admire her chutzpah," she said.

"I love it when you talk Yiddish to me."

"Play your cards right, mister, and I'll help you enlarge your vocabulary."

"I'll drink to that."

"You'll drink to anything."

"True," I said. "But some things are more cause for celebration."

3

Not so bright but early the next morning, I rode shotgun in a black SUV beside a burly bald guy from Quincy named Lou, with the congresswoman, her personal assistant, and Kyle Rosen in back.

The first order of the day was an interview at WBUR, then a photo op in Mattapan for a community center expansion, and later a meet-and-greet with Boston Fire in the Back Bay. Somewhere in that time, I hoped we might eat lunch. Fortunately, Lou had stopped by Starbucks and brought us all coffees. The coffee made the sluggish trip through Brookline a little less intolerable.

Carolina and Kyle Rosen were both talking on their cells. The cross-pattern of conversation was confusing to even an advanced eavesdropper such as myself.

"Been doing this work long?" Lou said.

"For a bit," I said.

"Were you a cop?"

"Once upon a time."

"Didn't like it?"

"I liked being a cop," I said. "Didn't care for the politics."

"You don't like politics?" Lou said. "Ha. Well, you're pretty screwed, then. That's all these people live and breathe."

"How about you?" I said.

"Fifteen years with Quincy PD," he said. "Best day of my life was when I got shot and went on disability. Got a friend who had a security company. Started driving for a few big shots and decided I liked it."

"Anyone I might know?"

"Bunch of stuffed shirts," he said. "Beacon Hill crowd. The mayor before the last mayor. Steven Tyler from Aerosmith. You know, the skinny guy who looks like a woman? He was nice. Brought some actors back and forth to some movie sets. All those fuckin' Wahlbergs."

"How long have you been with the congresswoman?"

"Since the election," he said. His eyes peered into the rearview. "She says I'm the smoothest driver in Boston. Right, Carolina?"

"Bullshit," Carolina said, not dropping her current call. "Lou tries to hit every pothole he can find."

"Haha," Lou said.

I drank my coffee as the first light hit the old Victorians and brownstones along Powell Street. Lou was taking us the back way up toward Comm Ave and the front entrance to the station on St. Paul. When Lou took a hard left turn, I noted a bulky shape on his right hip.

He noted what I'd seen and winked.

When we arrived, I got out, looked about, and, not spotting anyone with a bazooka, opened the back door for the congresswoman, her assistant, and Kyle Rosen. Rosen appeared downright dapper that morning in a black blazer over a gray Mickey Mouse T-shirt and tattered blue jeans. A pair of cheap sunglasses worn high on his head.

It was cool and breezy. You could almost taste and smell the fall out there somewhere.

We were ushered through security and into the studios, where a young woman with a clipboard greeted the congresswoman. The rest of us waited in the greenroom, where I helped myself to a bagel and orange juice, and refilled my empty coffee cup. Kyle disappeared into the hallway while Lou stayed with the SUV.

Carolina's assistant took a seat across from me. He was young and rail-thin, dressed in a fitted white dress shirt with a red bow tie, skinny navy pants, and white suede bucks. His hair was blond and stylishly cut. A large leather bag hung from his shoulder and looked to outweigh him by fifty pounds.

"Welcome aboard," the kid said.

We shook hands. His handshake was light.

"Have Gun Will Travel," I said.

"Adam Swift," he said. "CGR's body man."

"Body man?" I said.

"If I don't carry it," he said, "she doesn't need it. Lipstick, comb, bottled water, breath mints."

"Kind of like a cornerman."

Swift raised his eyebrows.

"Works the fight with the trainer," I said. "They carry the tape, the towels, gauze, and water. End-swells and icepacks."

"Does a cornerman whisper in the ear important names, dates, and pieces of legislation?"

"Not often," I said. "But there's a first for everything."

"I try to keep CGR on track."

"You call her CGR?"

"We all do," she said. "Try saying Carolina Garcia-Ramirez twenty times fast."

I tilted my head and shrugged. I took a bite of the second half of the bagel. I didn't attempt his challenge.

"I'm glad you're here," Adam Swift said.

I waited. I found it best to leave long silences in conversation to elicit nervous replies.

"We all begged her to get help," he said. "We were all scared. Especially after what happened in D.C."

"Of course," I said.

I had no idea what had happened in D.C.

"That whacko just came out of nowhere," he said. "Right on the Capitol steps. I was there. I got splattered, too."

"Splattered with what?"

He looked at me wide-eyed, shocked that I didn't know all the details. He leaned in and whispered, "The urine. The guy had peed in a cup and tossed it on CGR and me. I think Kyle got the worst of it. Although let's face it. He needs to burn most of his wardrobe anyway."

"Did they catch who did it?"

"Yeah," he said. "Some loon. The Capitol cops were on him. He'd come all the way up from Georgia. His family said he was off his meds. But I don't know. What if it had been a gun? What then?"

I nodded and walked over to the coffee urn and refilled the cup. I returned to the seat and pretended to be making small talk. I sat down, slow and relaxed. Just passing the time while the congresswoman spoke with *Morning Edition.*

"Have there been others?" I said.

Swift clenched his upper lip. He closed his eyes before taking a long breath and letting it out quickly. "If Kyle didn't tell you about this," he said, "maybe I should just shut my mouth."

"Whatever you tell me is between us," I said. "We both work for Carolina. Right?"

Swift nodded. He adjusted the bag in his lap and then looked back at the doorway where Kyle Rosen had disappeared.

"I've never met a woman more loved and hated at the same time," he said, whispering. "There don't seem to be many in the middle. They either think she's Joan of Arc or Attila the Hun. Everything, everyone, has become so polarized. I don't think of her issues as that radical. Nor do most people in our district. But get outside of Cambridge and people want to crucify her. There's one old congressman from Louisiana who told her that she was going to burn in hell."

"And why would that be?"

"He said she was anti-American and needed to go back where she came from."

"Roxbury?"

"Exactly," Swift said. "I mean, I'm from the South, too, Mr. Spenser. I've seen my fair share of racism. But the letters and emails we've received shock even me."

"How many people know about Carolina's schedule?"

"It changes on the fly," he said. "Our main scheduler is in D.C., but we have another here. You met Monique at the front desk? Of course, Kyle and me. And Steph Heller."

"And who's Steph?"

"Comms director," he said. "Big part of everything Carolina does."

"Anyone else?"

"We try and keep CGR's schedule on a need-to-know basis," he said. "I don't even tell my boyfriend where I'm going each day. Sometimes he accuses me of actually being a gay secret agent."

"Well, are you?"

Swift put his index finger to his lip and winked as Kyle Rosen walked into the room and started to pace. He made it back and forth across the greenroom twice before stopping in front of me. Sweat dappled his face and long frizzy hair.

"We got trouble," he said.

I stood up and placed my right hand in my pocket. The lights were dim in the greenroom in an effort to calm the guests. "You know trouble *is* my business."

"We have a welcoming committee at the community center," he said.

"A large gathering of adoring supporters?"

"I wish," he said. "Some real assholes, holding nasty signs and yelling nasty things. Don't acknowledge them. Don't confront them unless they make a move. These people feed off fear and hate."

"I'll do my best."

"Rita said you often settle scores with your fists."

"Only when a good hug fails."

4

I had Lou drive past the community center twice to get a feel for the reception committee that had formed. I counted a little more than a dozen men and three women. The men all appeared to be white, with most wearing white polo shirts and khaki pants. Many of them sported full mountain-man beards, while some were clean shaven. As we rolled by, they held up hand-painted signs that called into question Carolina's citizenship, ethnicity, mental acuity, and sexual preference. Although I couldn't hear what was being said, they yelled with such intensity that veins bulged from their necks.

"What should we do?" Rosen said.

"What we came to do," Carolina said. "Drop us off up front, Lou."

I spotted only four patrol cars and eight cops on the street. Rosen had spoken with the district sergeant, who promised to keep the crew back the allotted five hundred feet from the entrance. BPD had dutifully carved out a nice path, which made my job a bit easier.

"We won't be inside more than twenty minutes," Rosen said. "The center has been a passion for Carolina since before the election. She first volunteered there when she was just a teenager."

"This was supposed to be a quick photo op," Carolina said. "With local news only."

Several news trucks had set up across the street, with reporters and cameramen waiting by the front entrance. I absently felt for the .38 on my right hip, although the police seemed to have the situation in hand.

"I'll walk in beside the congresswoman," I said.

"The hell you will," she said.

"For you to do your job," I said, "you need to let me do my job."

"How about you just carry me in your arms?"

"To the top of the Pru Center and bat down airplanes?" I said. "If something happens, it might be tough to reach for my gun."

"You think you're funny?"

"Some have said they find me mildly amusing."

I turned in the front passenger seat to face her. Adam Swift grinned, but Carolina and Rosen didn't look at me. Lou slowed down, and when he stopped, I reached for the door handle and went around to get the congresswoman's door.

Carolina was up and out of the car faster than a caged jaguar. I did my best to keep up as we walked under a portico with waiting doors at the other end. The reception committee was awake now, spewing out racial and sexist epithets. None of them very clever. Bitch, dyke, several variations on her being black and Latinx.

"Just wind," I said.

"Fuck 'em," she said. Smiling through clenched teeth.

Not once did she acknowledge their presence. Nor did I.

The reception inside the center was decidedly more pleasant. A gathering of children, board members, and volunteers clapped as she entered. Carolina hugged several and stooped down to accept a bouquet of roses from a little girl. TV news crews and photographers recorded every moment. Everything was as well staged and constructed as the photo op needed to be.

"This truly is Carolina's home," Rosen said. "She volunteered here all through high school and between her summers at BU. Even when she was waiting tables at the Quincy Market and bartending, she never forgot about where she came from and about these kids. They offer legal assistance for immigrants, meals for the elderly, and Head Start for kids."

"Can you get me a list of everyone who got the press release on today's schedule?"

"That's like a hundred different outlets in Massachusetts," Rosen said. "I know you're good, but that seems like a fool's errand."

"I've been called worse," I said.

"What about the crew outside?"

"I thought you didn't want me to engage?"

"Of course."

"Did you recognize any faces?" I said. "Any repeat customers?"

"Maybe," Rosen said. "I try not to look at them. They feed off being acknowledged."

"You think you could ID a few?"

"I can try."

"What's with the white polos?"

"You didn't hear?" he said. "It's the new racist aesthetic."

We followed Carolina down a long hallway under fluorescent lights and across scuffed linoleum into a gym where kids were playing dodgeball. Before Rosen could stop her, Carolina had kicked off her shoes and joined in the game.

I leaned against a concrete-block wall and watched. The cops had stayed outside. There were four entrances to the gym, including two emergency exits. I made sure I was within fifteen feet of the congresswoman at all times.

I watched every entrance and exit. I scanned the gathering of teachers and press.

Carolina couldn't've cared less, as she was too busy slipping the balls and giving it back even harder. She didn't have a bad arm. When it got down to just her and a Latino boy about nine or ten, I watched as she purposely took the hit in the back. She laughed, her face shiny with sweat, as she walked over to pick up her shoes.

Rosen came up and stood next to me against the wall. He was chewing gun and checking his cell phone. "She's a natural," he said.

"I had the same thought."

"You see how she deeply cares for this district."

"Don't waste your breath," I said. "I'm not a registered voter."

"What good are you?"

For once, Rosen cracked a smile. I smiled back.

"I guess time will tell."

"There are some additional ground rules we need to discuss," Rosen said.

"Don't tell me I can't have the cookies and punch we were offered?"

"Worse," he said. "Carolina doesn't want you keeping watch after hours. She only agreed to you keeping watch at official events."

"No long nights?" I said. "No cold coffee?"

"You sound disappointed."

"I think it's a terrible plan," I said. "That threat could come from anywhere at any time. Whackos don't punch the clock."

"What do you recommend I tell her?"

"'The question is not what you look at, but what you see,'" I said.

"And what does that exactly mean?" Rosen said.

"That she needs full-time protection."

"I'll work on her," Rosen said. "Carolina can be very stubborn."

As Carolina said goodbye, I took a leisurely stroll across the street, by the barricade and past the gathering of miscreants. I pretended to be talking, the phone against my ear, as I snapped off dozens of photos. Most of the men were under twenty, many overweight and out of shape. Some were middle-aged, with gray in their beards. They all looked odd in the white polos. Like the Oak Ridge Boys had decided to crash a country club reception.

They were so intent on watching for Carolina, they didn't notice me. Just another white guy strolling among them.

I opened the door for Carolina and walked around to ride shotgun with Lou.

"I've seen a few of them before," Lou said. "But don't know any names."

"Got to start somewhere."

5

After I parted ways with the congresswoman and her entourage, I drove downtown and met Hawk at the Harbor Health Club for an early-evening workout. We followed a new plan that combined pounding the heavy bag, jumping rope, and multiple bodyweight exercises. As we hit the fourth round, Hawk made this set of twenty pull-ups as effortless as his first.

"Shit ain't as easy as it used to be," Hawk said.

"Speak for yourself, John Alden."

"You hard to understand," he said. "Breathing that hard."

I followed his lead and performed the pull-ups. He was right. It wasn't as easy as it used to be, but I acted as if I might perform twenty more.

"Uh-huh," he said. "What did I just tell you?"

"What would you recommend?" I said. "We take up Jazzercise?"

"We better keep up or next time we don't get up."

"Some of us only improve with age."

Hawk dropped down and cranked out fifty push-ups. His form was so exact it appeared to be mechanical. When he hopped up, I tossed him a towel to wipe off his glistening bald head. I followed with fifty of my own, trying to match the pace and precision.

Henry Cimoli eyed us from a leg-press machine, where he selflessly demonstrated his technique to two young women in sports bras and tiny yoga pants.

"Sad he doesn't pay attention to us anymore."

"He would," Hawk said. "We look like that."

"A lot of surgery would be required to make us look like that."

Hawk jumped onto the dip bar, going so low and easy you could balance a teacup on his head. Henry walked over, standing as tall and erect as Billy Barty on Viagra. A toothpick loose in the corner of his mouth.

"Little late for you two mutts."

"'A great cause of the night is lack of the sun,'" I said.

"Sometimes I think I let him stay in the ring too long," Henry said. "Got punchy."

I hopped up onto the dip bar.

"Don't go too low, Spenser," Henry said. "You might break a sweat."

Hawk had rolled into the heavy bag. I glanced at my digital watch but knew neither of us needed timing. We could feel a round down to the millisecond. I followed and we continued the program for another two rounds.

After, Hawk passed me a jug of water. We were both soaked with sweat.

"Better," Henry said. "But not great."

"Tell us, what would make us great?" I said.

Henry took the toothpick from his mouth and closed one eye. "A goddamn time machine."

Undeterred and ego unbruised, I showered and changed into street clothes, and found Hawk outside a parking deck along Atlantic. I'd slipped into a lightweight leather jacket and a Mississippi Braves cap. I wasn't sure if the tomahawk was cultural appropriation, but made a mental note to ask Sixkill sometime.

"You going anywhere for a while?" I said.

"Staying put in historic old Bah-ston."

"Might have something for you."

"Infliction or protection?"

"Protection."

Hawk had on black jeans, a black silk shirt open wide across his chest, and black cowboy boots. He looked like a bastard child of Johnny Cash.

"May have something for you, too," Hawk said. "Looking for a woman."

"You're always looking for a woman."

"A woman that disappeared long time back."

"A little quid pro quo?"

"Acta non verba."

"What's her name?"

"Dominique Fortier," he said.

"Fortier," I said. "Sounds French."

"Woman is French," he said. "Born and raised."

"You meet her over there?"

"Met her here," Hawk said. "Long time ago. Right after me and you got back from California."

"Got an old address?"

Hawk reached into his pocket and handed me a typed sheet of biographical information including date of birth and possible names of parents. As I glanced through the details, he opened his wallet and handed me an old photograph. The woman had long brown hair. She was young and quite striking. Her eyes ice blue.

"Is this all you have?"

"You being the master sleuth," he said. "Might consider it a challenge."

"Still live in the States?"

"Don't know."

"Where in France is she from?"

"Don't know."

"You don't make it easy on me," I said. "Now, do you?"

Hawk shrugged and pushed up the sleeves of his shirt. He raised a fist to pound mine. I pocketed the information and nodded.

"Same time tomorrow?" Hawk said.

"Yep," I said. "Want to tell me more about this woman?"

"Do you really care?"

"Absolutely," I said. "You care about mine?"

"Nope."

I nodded and we both walked in completely different directions.

6

Never pegged you as a political guy, Spenser," Wayne Cosgrove said.

"Most politicians we've known turned out to be creeps."

"But without the creeps, what the hell would we do for a living?"

"We could always join the circus."

We were sitting next to each other at the old Ritz bar that at one time had been the new Taj bar but now was completely something else. Despite the changes in ownership, the mood was the same. Fox-hunt paintings on the walls, a lovely view of Arlington Street, and the Public Garden beyond. And a perfect selection of nuts on a small silver platter. I had a tall scotch with lots of ice. Wayne nursed a club soda.

"Oh, yeah?" Cosgove said, taking a sip of club soda and speaking in his slight Virginian drawl. "And what would be your talent?"

"Strongman and soothsayer," I said. "Not to mention people would pay big bucks to examine me in a loincloth."

"Sure," he said. "At least a nickel or two."

Cosgrove had been a reporter covering cops and politics since Paul Revere hung two lanterns in the belfry of the Old North Church. He'd recently let his hair grow long and shaggy and had grown a scruffy gray beard. He wore blue jeans, a checked button-down shirt, and a corduroy jacket with leather patches on the elbows.

"Circuses and newspapers have gone the way of the dodo," Cosgrove said. "I'm lucky to have a job."

"Even with your immense institutional knowledge?"

"I was offered a buyout last year."

"Not ready?"

"Nope," Cosgrove said. "You?"

"No buyouts in my line of work," I said. "You work until you can't. But you'll be pleased to know I performed two hundred push-ups this morning."

"One-armed or two?"

"Two."

Cosgrove gave the meso-meso gesture over the table. I reached for my whiskey and took a long pull. I could feel the whiskey hit the bloodstream and soothe the system after a long workout. It was nearly seven and the lights were on in the Public Garden, tourists spilling through the wrought-iron gates and out onto Arlington. No matter how many times I'd seen it, the Public Garden always delighted the senses.

"So what's all this interest in Carolina?"

I told him. He listened. He drank a little more club soda and didn't comment. At no time did he gasp or clutch at his nonexistent pearls when I mentioned the threats.

"I read the stories about her first campaign," I said. "Sounds like she was a real long shot."

"I have to hand it to her," Cosgrove said. "She was young and inexperienced. But the team she put together was something else. Computer geeks. Graphic artists. Grassroots organizers. Her message resonated with a lot of people. Not to mention, she's Dominican. That accounts for a lot in this town."

"Just ask Big Papi."

"She and I have a mutual understanding," Cosgrove said. "I've never misquoted her or taken anything she's said out of context. Reciprocally, she comes to me first with any news of impending legislation. She also knows I have a realistic view of her agenda."

"Meaning?"

"Where do I start?" Cosgrove said. "Free college and healthcare for all, a living and respectable minimum wage, a green Boston with zero carbon emissions, a massive restructuring of law enforcement. All great talking points, but how much can she realistically accomplish for her district? How much money can she bring back home to fix our roads and schools, ensure safety in some of the more blighted neighborhoods, or . . ."

"Is there any harm in aiming high?" I said.

"Only if she can show results."

"Has she?"

"Some," Cosgrove said.

"Lot of people want to see her fail?"

"I'd think the majority of her detractors would come from outside Boston," he said. "A progressive and liberal agenda isn't actually something new here. From the letters we get at the paper, people hate her because she's a black woman from immigrant parents who isn't afraid to speak her mind. That makes a certain type of person's head explode."

"Any heads come to mind?"

"I've been doing this a long time, Spenser," he said. "I know a lot of weirdos. Present company included. I get letters. I get emails. Sometimes I'm dumb enough to read the comments under my stories. What they say is pretty mean and vicious. Do you know how many people write me to say they wish I'd just die?"

"That doesn't bother you?"

"Nope," Cosgrove said. "Sometimes people get up in the morning, take a shower, grab a cup of coffee, and head to an office. Other people get up out of their cages and start screwing with people. You know what? I think most of them are just lonely and sad."

"I mainly hear from adoring women," I said. "They want to know if I've ever considered stepping out on Susan."

"And what do you tell them?"

"Why go out for hamburger when you have filet mignon at home."

"Are you plagiarizing Paul Newman?"

"Only if I write it."

"I heard about the mess today," Cosgrove said. "One of our reporters was there. Hell, can't her people do better keeping these photo ops a little more private?"

"Therein lies the rub," I said. "No one was contacted outside Boston media. But Boston media includes a lot more these days besides the TV stations, the *Herald*, and the *Globe*."

"Heard they got pretty nasty."

"Like you, the congresswoman was unfazed," I said. "Even though they were saying some pretty rough stuff."

"Like what?"

I told him. He shook his head.

"On the surface, they appeared normal," I said. "Most of them had on white polos and khaki pants like they were in some kind of glee club."

"Ah," Wayne said.

"Did I fall headlong into a clue?"

"Might even be worth this club soda you're buying me."

"That doesn't come cheap at the Ritz."

"You're out of place and out of time, Spenser," Wayne said. "This hasn't been the Ritz for twenty years."

"Tell me about the shirts."

"It's the dress code for white supremacists," he said. "Their uniform and how they ID each other."

"Ralph Lauren must be thrilled," I said. "Real upgrade from robes and hoods."

"But the same intention."

"Any groups or names come to mind?"

"I can check," Cosgrove said. "See if we get any regulars that are focused on Carolina. But I'll warn you it's a crapshoot. I also get letters on a regular basis from a man in Weymouth who thinks he's Jesus Christ."

"In Weymouth."

"Yeah," Wayne said. "Who knew?"

"You think these threats could be legitimate?"

"Maybe," he said. "Hell. It only takes one person. It's just a goddamn mess to see through all the noise and bluster these days. Everyone is angry. Everyone has an ax to grind. At least in the old days, a nut had to roll a sheet of paper into the typewriter or paste together some jumbled clippings from a magazine. But now all they have to do is use a dummy email account and be done."

"The perils of sleuthing in the twenty-first century."

"So what are you going to do?"

"Stick close to the congresswoman and wait for someone to make a move?"

"Seems like a risky plan."

"Got any other ideas?"

Cosgrove shook his head. "I'm just a simple scribe," he said. "You're the high-paid investigator."

"Not this time," I said. "Susan pressured me to take the job."

Cosgrove smiled and nodded. He leaned over and picked up the check.

"Really?"

"There's a first time for everything," Cosgrove said.

7

The next morning, Susan and I took Pearl to frolic down by the Riverside Boat Club at Magazine Beach. We hoped she'd expel enough energy that she wouldn't bark and yelp while Susan was in session with her patients. The new Pearl wasn't even a year old and had more power than an Energizer Bunny on Adderall.

Along the reedy banks, a light fog rolled off the river and shifted in the wind. Early traffic trudged both ways across the River Street Bridge. There were walkers and joggers along the pathways and shells gliding effortlessly along the Charles. Susan and I sat on a park bench and took turns throwing a tennis ball to Pearl.

I'd brought corn muffins and coffee from the Dunkin' across the street.

"Too bad there's not a Flour Bakery in Cambridge," Susan said.

"Do I sense you're turning up your nose at your breakfast feast?"

"No," she said. "Simply recalling Joanne Chang's scones."

"That's not a fair comparison," I said. "Joanne's scones aren't of this earth."

Pearl trotted up on tall spindly legs and taunted me with the tennis ball. After a few attempts, I finally snatched it from her slobbery mouth and tossed it as far as I could. I thought she might rest when she returned. I was wrong.

"Do you think she'll ever settle down?" Susan said.

"Our old Pearl did," I said. "Until she didn't feel like taking walks."

"I guess I shouldn't wish away time."

"'I wasted time, and now doth time waste me.'"

"But she is a handful."

"I believe you said the new Pearl was completely bat-shit nuts."

"I recall using the term *high-energy*," Susan said. "And perhaps a little nuts."

The next time Pearl brought Susan the ball, she didn't make much of a fuss about keeping it away. She dropped it at Susan's feet, her tail wagging.

"I can watch Pearl until I get called to duty," I said.

"Will Carolina consider you might know what you're doing and allow you to set your own hours?"

"She only wants security when she's out in public," I said. "Other than that, she wishes to remain on her own. She doesn't want me to interfere with her privacy or independence."

"I completely understand," Susan said. "Having a killer after you is no picnic."

"Especially when the psychopath is a patient."

I stretched out my legs. Susan broke off a piece of corn muffin and rewarded Pearl for her dutiful fetching.

"What happened to no human food for the new baby?" I said.

"Did I say that, too?"

"I am a top-notch detective," I said. "Nothing escapes me. Absolutely nothing."

I attached the leash to Pearl's collar while Susan and I stood up. We tossed our trash and took our coffees with us as we walked toward the old Veterans Memorial pool. Pearl strained at the leash, digging her claws into the dirt. It was cool and shady under the trees and in the shadows.

"Did you ever consider a Chihuahua?" Susan said.

"I only go for German shorthairs named Pearl."

"And shrinky Jewish women named Susan."

"Brand loyal to a fault," I said.

The wind kicked up off the river and nearly knocked my ball cap off. I tugged the bill down into my eyes and followed Pearl's lead. She was tall and gangly, nose to the ground for fast-food wrappers or fossilized french fries.

"Have you studied these emails?" she said.

"I looked through a few hundred yesterday," I said. "They seemed to have a consistent theme and a stream-of-consciousness of hate."

"Anything I might help you with?"

"How much do you charge?"

"I'd be glad to trade some of my services for some of your services."

"That sounds like sexual harassment."

She leaned in to my ear and told me exactly what I might provide. My mouth went a little dry and my heart raced.

"Can I put down a retainer?" I said. "At the moment, I don't know enough to form an opinion on any suspects."

"What seems to be the dominant theme?"

"Our country was founded by straight white Christian males and should continue to be run by straight white Christian males."

"No mention of the Native Americans who were here when those people arrived?"

"Funny," I said. "They must've forgotten that part."

"And as a straight white male are you offended to see a black woman in power?"

"No," I said. "But the lovely men I saw at the community center yesterday seemed to take great exception."

"Not that those ideas are anything new, but the Internet has made things much worse," Susan said. "Whatever your prejudice or conspiracy theory, you can find others to bolster those belief systems."

"'In their thick breaths, rank of gross diet, shall we be enclouded,'" I said. "'And forced to drink their vapor.'"

"I was just about to say that very thing," Susan said.

I drank a little more coffee before Pearl pulled us both along.

"At the core, these people are scared," Susan said. "They're scared they'll be marginalized or replaced. Or those who've had personal failure seek out others to blame. It's really about their personal identity."

"History doesn't bode well for countries that coddle extremists."

"Hate and division are powerful drugs," she said. "My mother had relatives in Germany. I know you had an uncle who liberated the camps."

"He never spoke of it."

"Have you found any suspects?" Susan said.

"Nope."

"Got any leads?" she said.

"Zip."

"Planning on doing more than just poking around and annoying people?"

"Why mess with a winning formula?"

8

Over the years, many things have changed about my profession. I no longer kept an actual landline on my desk. Since no one had called it since a little past the first of the millennium, I discontinued the service.

My superhuman ability to scroll through microfilm was no longer in demand. Almost anything I needed to look up, from old news stories, to criminal histories, to vehicle records, could be found online. Although I missed my visits to the Boston Public Library, I'd accepted the long, boring hours at my desk, thinking about how many old cases I could've solved with Google.

That morning I'd gone from Dunkin' to the Starbucks across the street. I sat down in my office and pulled out a fresh yellow legal pad from my left-hand desk drawer. I hoped the contents of the right-hand desk drawer would not be needed today.

My office was clean, tight, and airy with the turret

windows open on Berkeley Street. A warm breeze blew into my office, scattering a few bills onto the floor. I let them lay where they fell while I rested my elbow on my desk, clicking and unclicking my ballpoint.

I turned on my computer to a Count Basie playlist and started to surf the Internet for racists, sexists, extremists, and nihilists. I hoped the best with this case was yet to come.

I tried to focus my search in the Boston metro area, but, given the very little I knew, tried to expand it into the Commonwealth and throughout New England. I soon found out that extremists were not limited to any one particular zip code. I wondered if nihilists had a website or a Facebook page, since they believed in nothing.

I drank some coffee and listened to Basie while I scrolled through an endless dung heap of hate and dissension. After an hour or so, I got up and stretched and wandered into the anteroom, where Mattie Sullivan had excelled at turning away visitors. Her pink Sox cap sat on the small desk as a reminder of our meeting long ago. She was now a grown woman with a college degree from Northeastern and currently training at the police academy. Ten years had gone by quickly.

I walked back into my office and sat down. I drank some coffee. I dove down many racist websites, Facebook pages, and dark, dirty corners of the Internet. I wasn't sure I was living in modern times or the beginning of Nazi Germany. Most of the YouTube videos I watched made me feel uneasy. I noted groups, associations, and people of suspicion. I tried to compare the images online with photos I'd taken of the greeters at the community center yesterday.

Although I wasn't quite Annie Leibovitz, the faces should have been clear enough for a match. The problem was that seldom did these people pose for a group photo.

I searched for any organization discussing Carolina Garcia-Ramirez.

I found many that loved her. I found many more that hated her. Most of the hate came from indeterminate people from indeterminate parts of the country.

I listed local groups. I listed names of local organizers.

I sat through a forty-five-minute video of a gathering at a bowling alley in Malden.

I didn't spot any familiar faces. Or recognize any names. The rhetoric was seismic.

My list grew to more than twenty organizations and more than forty names. I felt like I might have better luck digging a hole to China with a teaspoon.

After a while, I set the list aside and started my search through CGR's campaign staff. I ran names through a database that I often used, placing a check by those who had any criminal record. The charges were often minor drunk-and-disorderlies or traffic tickets. Kyle Rosen had three priors of resisting arrest. But resisting arrest can be a badge of honor for most activists.

At noon, I closed the computer and stretched. I was due back at Carolina's headquarters at one.

Just enough time for a drive-through sandwich and

another cup of coffee. Ah, the glamour of being a high-paid investigator.

I reached for my ball cap, phone, and gun and headed for the door.

On the way out, I stopped again at Mattie's desk and placed her cap on my hat tree. In a few weeks, she'd be a cop.

I'd been a cop once. It didn't take. Maybe it would take with her.

I turned off the light and locked the door behind me. The hallway to the stairwell was long and cavernous.

9

We were in the campaign conference room, where I sat on the table, with Carolina's Boston scheduler, Monique, standing in front of me. She folded her arms over her sizable chest and stared at me through narrow slits. The room cluttered with boxes of T-shirts, bumper stickers, and flyers. Perhaps someone might bring back the straw boaters before election night. The carpet was yellow and dingy. The cheap wood paneling on the walls was old and buckling off the studs.

"There's no damn way to keep Carolina's schedule to a few folks," Monique said. "And even if we did, how are we supposed to keep people quiet where she's headed? She's got meetings today with Longshoremen and the Iron Workers. Now, how the hell can they keep the meeting secret? You ever talk to a longshoreman? They don't shut up. The whole point of the meeting is to get the union to turn out. What would you like me to tell them?"

"Mum's the word?" I said. "Loose lips sink ships?"

"Mum my ass," Monique said. "I appreciate you. I appreciate what you're trying to do. But it's impossible."

"What about yesterday?" I said. "No one needed to know besides you, Carolina's inner circle, and maybe a few people at the community center. Trusted press."

"And which press are you gonna decide to trust?"

"Excellent point."

"Not my job, not my decision," she said. "That's Stephanie Heller. If you want to bring it up with that woman, go ahead. I'll give you her number."

"I just spoke with her," I said. "And she's been very helpful."

"Then what do you need me for?"

"Trying to plug a few holes," I said. "Keep the information to a minimum."

"You're gonna have to bring that up with Steph," she said. "Hard to be running a campaign, shaking hands and all that shit, without anyone showing up."

I shrugged, with very few points to argue. Monique's hand remained on her hip as she waited for me to finish. She had on a lightweight yellow dress that hit her at the knee, suede pumps, and a large, blocky necklace.

"Can we talk about the schedule for the rest of the week?" I said. "Can you tell me who knows about it and every outlet it's been sent to?"

"Damn," she said. "You don't quit. Do you?"

"Some consider tenacity a talent."

Monique walked around the table and sat in a chair facing me. She looked at me like a teacher would look at a slow kid in school and pushed her long braids down her back. But she spoke patiently and in great detail about Carolina's next stops. I had a master list and made notes as she told me what we should expect.

When she was done, I thanked her for her time.

"Can I go now?" she said.

"Monique," I said. "Would it be the worst thing in the world if we became friends?"

"I've got enough friends."

"Confidants?"

"Don't need that, either."

"What if I bring you hot coffee every morning?" I said. "Maybe a hot donut."

"You'd do that?"

"Only for you."

I smiled at her. The full wattage that might dim the greater Boston area.

"Hmm," she said, leveling her eyes right at me. "We'll see. You really think someone's gonna try and kill Carolina?"

"I don't know."

"But if they try?"

"I will thwart their efforts."

"Cool," she said, nodding. "I'll try and cut a few folks and keep stops on more of a need-to-know type of thing. I don't want to see that woman take any more crap. Carolina's a good person. Gave lots of people hope after years being neglected. Hell, she gave me this job."

"Anyone in the office that you don't trust?"

"Ha," she said. "That's easy."

I waited and drank some more water.

"Kyle Rosen," she said. "Shifty little bastard."

"You know Kyle's the one who hired me?"

"Just another damn reason," she said.

"It's the hair, isn't it?" I said. "Freaked me out, too."

Monique looked down at her hands and then back at the cracked door.

"He ain't from around here," she said. "Kyle's not even from Boston. He's from down in New York someplace. You know what I'm saying? He's talking about electric cars and windmills and all that while Carolina knows there are people around here without childcare. Without money to pay the bills or keep the heat on. I know what he did and how he got her elected. But I think he's taken that girl in a direction that she doesn't need to go. I've known her since she was sixteen. This ain't about politics. It's about what's right."

I nodded.

"What about the rest of the office staff?" I said. "Anyone you notice acting strange or asking too many questions?"

She tapped the long red nails on her right hand. She was thinking about it.

"All these kids are strange," she said. "Most of them living off their daddy's money while they play around down in the 'Bury."

"Anyone specific?"

Monique shrugged. I could smell her strawberry perfume from across the table. She was lovely but smelled like a jar of Smucker's. "What do you know about her driver?"

"Lou from Quincy?"

She nodded.

"Only what he's told me," I said.

"Well, hell," she said. "Mr. Detective. Maybe you oughta go and do some more detecting?"

10

The next morning, I was back in Roxbury, navigating a dozen or so cop cars parked in front of CGR's campaign headquarters. Lights were flashing. News crews parked on a vacant lot across the street. As a trained investigator, I surmised something was amiss.

"We had a break-in," Kyle Rosen said.

"The crime scene tape in the busted window tipped me off."

"I'm sorry I didn't call right away," Rosen said. "I had to make sure Carolina was safe and then reshuffle our schedule for the rest of the day."

"Since you hired me to augment security," I said, "it would be nice to be updated on any crimes against the congresswoman."

Rosen nodded. His faced turned a little pink.

I walked with him through the flashing lights to where the plateglass window facing Mass Ave had been shattered. We tried walking around the shards of glass across the sidewalk but still heard a little crunch. The staff that wasn't being interviewed continued to work on their laptops or phones. Monique sat at the front desk, tip-tapping away at the keyboard, not seeming to mind most of the front window being gone.

"I guess today's the day," I said. "Expect the unexpected."

"Mm-hm," she said. "You better get to whoever made this mess before I do. I'll kill 'em all."

"You get glass in your chair?"

"Most of it went outside," she said. "Just a few chunks fell this way."

I turned back to Rosen, who looked out the empty window and into the parking lot. He glanced down at his ringing phone and then pressed a button to send the call to voicemail.

"Besides the window," I said. "Anything else missing?"

"Couple hard drives," he said. "Three laptops and our coffee machine."

"I'd take the theft of caffeine as a personal affront."

"Tell me about it, man," he said. "Want to go next door? I haven't eaten all morning."

"Best *pollo frito* in the city?" I said. "Let me walk around first. I think it's best I earn my keep."

I examined the inside of the window and around the aluminum frame. Yellow crime scene tape crisscrossed the open window and fluttered in the wind. I squatted down to the linoleum floor and searched for clues. When I didn't spot any, I asked Monique where the thefts had occurred. She pointed to a far corner by the bathrooms. I walked back to where crime scene tape blocked two desks. Fingerprinting powder smudged the drawers and tops of both metal desks.

Outside the broken window, I saw Rosen speaking to a heavyset cop. Rosen nodded and then pointed through the window directly at me. I waved.

The heavyset cop did not wave back. He reached for the radio mic on his hip.

Nearby, I spotted one of Carolina's reelection posters on the floor. Someone had ripped the top half of her head away and written the word *Whore* in a dark red smear. Dark footprints had stomped across the image. A foul odor came from brown smears across the paper.

I turned my head, covered my mouth, and followed the damage to a narrow hall leading to the bathrooms. Graffiti with more colorful and uninventive language. *Die Bitch Die* written in at least three places. Behind the bathrooms, the hallway branched off into another hall. It was dark and I didn't see a light switch, only a crack of light from an exit door. Brooms and mops, cleaning supplies, and boxes of paper towels. Having few other ideas, I followed the light and pushed through until I was in the alley behind the strip mall.

It was bright. I reached into my shirt pocket for my Ray-Bans.

When I turned around to examine the back door, I saw the metal frame had been damaged, edges pried loose from the concrete wall. But looking closer, I noticed the dead bolt and box strike appeared undamaged.

Both were fully intact. I reached out to test the sturdiness of the frame. It held.

"Hey," a cop said. "Don't touch that!"

I turned to see a young black cop walking toward me. His cruiser was parked to block the only exit to the alley. The driver's-side door was open, with blue lights flashing. The passenger side opened and a second cop crawled out. He was white and smallish, with a round, pockmarked face and hair cut close to the scalp. He looked all of twelve.

"Just following the clues," I said.

"Yeah," the black cop said. "We're on it. You work for the congresswoman?"

I nodded and touched the bill of my ball cap. "Philo Vance," I said.

The black cop nodded back at me. He was young and fit, with a neatly trimmed beard. The name tag on his uniform read HORATIO. The smallish white cop joined us. His name tag read STANTON.

"Whoever did this ripped open the junction box and cut the power," Stanton said. "That's why we didn't get the call until this morning. When someone saw the window busted out."

"Find anything back here?"

"Nope," Horatio said. "You'd think someone would think to run a security camera in the alley."

"Busting out the front window was the last thing," I said. "Most of the glass shattered outward."

"Yeah?" Stanton said. "Kind of like throwing up a middle finger on your way out."

I nodded. "Something like that."

"Whoever did this isn't from around here," Horatio said. "No one messes with the congresswoman's space. This is neutral ground."

"Seems like a personal attack," I said.

"Ha," Stanton said. "No shit. And you get paid for this?"

"Yet to be determined," I said.

"We walked the neighborhood this morning," Stanton said. "Up and down the street. No one saw a thing."

"What time did the call come in?"

"Little after six," Horatio said.

"What time did you arrive?" I said.

"Six-thirty," Horatio said. "We were jammed up with an accident. The caller said the building was vacant."

"Did you notice anything beyond the window?"

"Just the mess," Stanton said. "What a fucking mess. I heard someone took a shit inside."

"A whole thirty minutes after the call went out?"

Stanton looked back to the opening of the alley. He and Horatio exchanged a look.

"Like I said, we were jammed up," Horatio said. "You'll have to talk to the sergeant. We got orders to clear this whole area. Okay?"

I handed them both a card. It was a new one with simply my name under a skull and crossbones. Horatio looked down at it but didn't seem impressed.

He read the card. "Thought you said your name is Philo?" he said.

"Philo is my nickname."

"What do I call you?" Horatio said.

"Spenser," I said. "With an *S*."

"Yeah?" Stanton said.

"Like the English poet."

They both shrugged and walked back to the prowl car. I continued past them and looked around the strip mall to find the restaurant to meet Rosen.

11

Once I was seated in the Honduran diner, a kind woman set a very tall coffee before me and asked if I'd like breakfast. In a gesture to support the local economy, I ordered two eggs over easy with a side of black beans with some sweet plantains.

Rosen leaned back in the booth and stared out into the parking lot. He had only a coffee in front of him. Adam Swift had joined us, sitting across from Rosen. I'd pulled up a chair. The heavy bag he carried didn't allow for much room.

"Well," Rosen said. "Crap."

"Maybe it was just some kids."

"You don't really believe that?"

"Nope." I shook my head. "'Hope is not found in a way out but a way through.'"

"Who said that?" Adam Swift said.

"I don't recall," I said. "But I promise it's someone very smart."

"Well," Rosen said. "Carolina is rattled. This is the second time we've been attacked."

"The first time being on the Capitol steps?"

"You know about that?"

Adam Swift looked away, pretending to find something urgent he needed inside Carolina's carry-all.

"We tried to keep it out of the press."

I added a little sugar to my coffee. It had been served in a very tall foam cup, already cut in half with heated milk. Steam lifted off the surface and swirled up into the air.

"The break-in happened in back," I said. I chose not to mention that the dead bolt remained intact.

"What about the window?" Rosen said.

"Just vandalism," I said.

"Did you see the graffiti by the bathroom?"

"Not exactly Longfellow," I said.

"More like Bukowski," Rosen said. "Just when I think I have things running smooth, some asshole wants to disrupt us."

"You know Carolina's giving a speech at Harvard on Thursday," Swift said.

"Harvard?" I said. "I've heard of it."

"At the Kennedy School," Rosen said.

"Might be time to boost the security."

"I won't fight you," Rosen said. "But Carolina will. Let's keep it to what we agreed on."

Rosen's hair looked as if he'd just been shocked by a live wire. He craned his skinny neck to look behind him at the gathering of cops outside. A few more news vans had showed up. They'd set up for a live shot. Swift tapped at the table with his thin hand. He looked at me and shook his head.

"Press conference?" I said.

"Maybe later," Rosen said. "Cops don't seem to know much."

"I may know a little," I said.

I cut into the eggs, the yolk spilling into the black beans and plantains. I forked off an even bite of all three. I chewed and decided to use some of the accompanying hot sauce. The hot sauce made all the difference.

"It doesn't matter anyway," Rosen said. "We'll have the window replaced by noon. I got two replacement laptops for the staff."

"Anything important on them?"

"Not really," he said. "Just donor and call lists. Some of Carolina's talking points for the primary. Nothing you couldn't find online."

"Did you tell her about what they did to her posters?" Swift said.

Kyle Rosen shook his head. "Not planning on it," he said. "Unless you think it will do any good?"

I shook my head and reached for my coffee. It was hot, strong, and very sweet. I decided to definitely return sometime for the *pollo frito.*

"Kids or real thieves would've taken a hell of a lot more than two laptops," I said. "And not taken the time and energy to deface a poster."

"Maybe the cops will come back with a match on the prints?" Swift said. He was a nice, optimistic kid.

"How long can you hold your breath?" I said.

"Don't count on it?" Swift said.

I shrugged. "Let me see what I can do."

"Maybe you can call in a favor with the police?" Rosen said. "I know you have friends within the department. Is that possible?"

"Sure," I said. "I'm owed so many favors, I don't even know where to begin."

12

I know why you're here," Quirk said. "And I got nothing to say about it."

"Even though I brought you a half dozen from Kane's?"

"Okay," Quirk said. "Then I'll give you half an answer."

"I'll take it," I said.

"Someone broke into the congresswoman's headquarters and made a fucking mess," he said. "End of story."

"Two of the selections are maple-glazed."

Quirk didn't respond. He removed his blue blazer, slipped it onto a hanger, and set it neatly on a hat tree. He rolled back his office chair, sat, and folded his large, blocky hands before him. He could crumble a walnut to dust with little effort.

"As assistant superintendent, I'm on limited time," Quirk said. "With limited patience."

"I, on the other hand, am footloose and fancy-free," I said. "With all the patience in the world."

I reached onto his desk and opened the carton. It was like opening a box from Tiffany's in front of Holly Golightly. His granite features turned into something that might've been a smile. He chose a maple-glazed.

Quirk did not offer me a coffee. Or ask if I'd like to share. He closed the box and leaned back in his seat. "Christ."

"I'll take that as a thanks."

He ate half the donut, swallowed, and reached for his coffee.

"There's not much to know," Quirk said. "Someone or several someones shattered the congresswoman's office window with a crowbar, jumped inside, and started tearing shit up."

"How'd you know it was a crowbar?"

"Because we found a fucking crowbar in the office, Dick Tracy."

"You know I've always preferred Bulldog Drummond."

"You know the rest," Quirk said. "They got a couple laptops and shit on her campaign posters. If this hadn't been a congresswoman's office, it wouldn't even make a brief in the paper."

"But it was a congresswoman's office," I said. "And it will make more than a brief in the paper. After someone scrawled some nasty threats in what appears to be blood and feces."

"What the fuck else do kooks write in?" he said. "These people don't use a goddamn feathered quill."

I stood up and helped myself to the coffeemaker on his side table. As I sat back down, I noticed I'd chosen a mug that read WORLD'S BEST GRAMPS. The words had a little crown on top of them. A true touch of class.

Quirk noted me staring. "Don't say a goddamn word."

Silent, I smiled and sipped my coffee.

"Heard you had a little run-in with Sergeant McGreevy?" Quirk said.

"Not much of one," I said, shrugging. "He hung up on me."

"He said you were being a real smartass."

"And what did you say?"

"I said you were a pain in my dick but altogether a decent guy."

"Shucks," I said. "Thanks, Gramps."

Quirk leveled his eyes at me. He picked up the back half of the donut and took a bite. He chewed, waiting for me to squirm.

"Who reported the break-in?" I said.

"You sure are asking a hell of a lot for a couple goddamn donuts."

I shrugged. I thought about reaching over for a donut. But adding a donut onto a big Honduran breakfast might've been overkill. Even for me.

"Guy working the liquor store reported it," Quirk said. "Said he heard the crash but never saw anyone fleeing the scene."

"Prints?"

"Yeah," he said. "But you know how that goes. If whoever did this had a brain any larger than a city squirrel, they would've worn gloves. They knew enough to cut the power for the alarm."

"It appears they got in and left through the back alley," I said. "The window was broken out from the inside. Almost all the glass shattered outward."

"Bulldog Fucking Drummond," Quirk said. "So if you're so fucking smart, then why the hell do you need me?"

"For one thing," I said. "The damage to the back door wasn't in the lock. The lock held."

"Someone used a key."

"Gee," I said. "I always knew you'd go far in this department."

Quirk took another bite of donut. His glower might've melted the iceberg that sank the *Titanic.*

"I want to make sure there wasn't a witness," I said. "And I want to make sure McGreevy has the prints processed."

"We always process the prints," Quick said.

I raised my eyebrow and crossed my legs, resting my boot against my left knee.

"Well," Quirk said. "Most of the time."

"Especially when the break-in is in the press."

"Is that it?" Quirk said. "Because I got eighty fucking people waiting in line to bust my balls."

Quirk nodded to the big black phone on his desk. I was delighted to see one was still in use.

"If you find a witness, I'd like to know."

"Sure, sure."

"You promise to call me?"

"My first order of business is keeping you happy, Spenser," he said. "But if I were you, I'd worry less about what we're doing and look more at who's working for the congresswoman. If what you're saying is true, you better watch her back. There's never a shortage of kooks and crazies working for politicians."

"I wouldn't know."

"Ever look in the mirror?"

"Every day."

"And what do you see?"

"A truly handsome bastard."

"Better get your eyes checked, Spenser," Quirk said. "The eyes are the first thing to go."

13

Late that afternoon, I was alone and in fine company at my office, feet propped up on the sill and staring out across Berkeley Street. The office was quiet without puppy Pearl scampering about. Or without Mattie in the anteroom, peeking in every few minutes to ask a question.

After a few moments of thoughtless staring, I opened up my laptop and decided to make a detailed list of everything I knew about Carolina Garcia-Ramirez's case.

The break-in was possibly an inside job.

Kyle Rosen is strange. Check out Lou from Quincy.

I took in a long breath. The cursor blinked and mocked me on the following line. I let out the breath.

I looked up to my set of Vermeer prints I'd bought long ago at the MFA. They'd grown a bit sun-faded and brittle in the frames. I'd thought about replacing them with an autographed picture of Carl Yastrzemski or Jane Fonda as Cat Ballou.

I returned to the document. The cursor continued to blink. Maybe I should shut down for the day. See if Hawk could meet at Henry's earlier or see if Susan was done with patients. The cursor continued to blink.

I was about to go in the opposite direction and create a list of everything I didn't know about the break-in when the phone buzzed and skittered across my desk.

I picked it up.

"Karl's Sausage Kitchen," I said.

"I did a little digging around in my personal whacko file," Wayne Cosgrove said. "I looked for anything I may have been emailed about CGR."

"You call her CGR, too?"

"Try saying that name twenty times fast."

"I'm working my way up to it."

"Well," Cosgrove said. "I'm sorry. There's a lot in the comments sections of stories about her. But mostly what I saw appeared to be anonymous. I didn't spot any names or handles that really jumped out. I asked a few of my colleagues, too. Shelley Murphy. Farragher. Not a thing. Although I did find out I was wrong about Jesus. He's from Worcester, not Weymouth."

"Duly noted."

"However," he said. "I did run across some recent developments on your employer's opponent."

"Flaherty."

"Yep," Cosgrove said. "I think you'll be very interested in what I learned. But first, what can you tell me about the break-in at the campaign headquarters?"

"A little less than nothing," I said.

"May I remind you that working with the press is a two-way street?"

"Boylston is a two-way street," I said. "I'm more of a cul-de-sac guy."

"Call me when you make it back out."

"Okay," I said. "What do you want to know?"

"I don't need you to be on the record," Cosgrove said. "But Kyle Rosen was making it seem like it was just a random break-in in a blighted neighborhood. He talked a lot about compassion and understanding until it made me want to puke. Instead of telling us what happened, he went on and on about poverty statistics."

"Did you take notes?"

"I take notes as I sleep."

"Okay," I said. "It wasn't just some kids."

"You sure?"

"Only if the kids were members of the Hitler Youth."

"In Roxbury?" Cosgrove said. "Not likely."

I rolled my chair away from my desk and returned to staring across Berkeley Street. I looked in vain for Linda Thomas, but she was long gone. As well as the advertising firm where she'd worked. Probably had kids. Maybe kids with kids. Instead, I saw a fat guy in glasses slurping on an oversized soda. He stared at me as I stared at him. He was no Linda Thomas.

"What did they take?" Cosgrove said.

"Exactly what Rosen said," I said. "No more. No less."

"Vandalism to the office?"

I didn't answer. I waved to the fat guy. He turned his back and disappeared.

"So if I were to mention vandalism would I be incorrect?"

I didn't answer. My window was slightly open and a dry, hot wind blew off the street. I rolled up my sleeves and watched as three young women walked south on Berkeley. They had on short, silky summer dresses and wore sunglasses. Two of them carried several bags that appeared to be from local boutiques. It reminded me that Susan's birthday was coming up soon. Summer dresses reminded me of so many things.

"Do you know who is now running Flaherty's campaign?" Cosgrove said.

"Excuse me?"

"I said, do you know who's running the Flaherty campaign?"

"Carnac the Magnificent."

"Not so lucky," he said. "Remember Frankie Farrell?"

"Unfortunately."

"Frankie says he's legit now," Cosgrove said. "He's been a political consultant for the last few years. Has a fancy downtown office, embossed business cards, and everything."

"He used to be in the pocket of Joe Broz."

"He most certainly was."

I thought for a moment. I turned my chair around and rolled back to my desk. He patiently waited as I typed in a second line about possible leads in CGR's case. It was the first time I'd thought of her as an acronym.

"You think he's still crooked?" I said.

"Like we say down south," Wayne said, "as crooked as a tomcat's peter."

"Really?" I said. "You guys say that?"

"Indeed we do."

"No wonder you guys lost the war."

14

Frankie Farrell and the Farrell Consulting Group had a big office in a short brick building on Cambridge Street across from Government Center and within the shadow of the Custom House Tower. It was a lot of marble and glass and looked like the kind of place people went to genuflect or spend a great deal of money. I had no plans for either as I took the elevator to the fifth floor to meet with Farrell.

The young guy at the desk told me to take a seat. He didn't look old enough to shave, wearing a gray sharkskin suit over a black crewneck. I watched as he picked up the phone, cupped his hand over the mouthpiece, and announced my arrival. I'd called ahead. Given our personal history, I knew Frankie would be thrilled to see me.

Within five minutes, Frankie Farrell wandered out. He was about my height, medium build, with a lot of silver hair and a longish face and bushy gray eyebrows. He had on a two-button blue plaid suit, a pink shirt, and a blue power tie. All Farrell needed was a ruby stickpin. Frankie was the kind of guy who could pull it off.

"Spenser," Farrell said. "Christ. When I heard your name, I about fell over. I thought you died."

"And I figured you'd be serving time," I said.

"Ha," he said. "Haha. Same ole Spense."

"Don't tell me you still hold a grudge?"

Farrell narrowed his eyes at me. "After what you said to me that night?" he said. "Yeah. I might hold a little grudge."

"Then why'd you agree to see me?"

The secretary looked as if he wasn't sure whether to jump between us or call the fire department. I placed a hand in my right pocket and smiled.

"I was curious," Farrell said. "After all these years."

"I came to talk to you about Tommy Flaherty."

"What about Tommy?"

"He's your client," I said.

"And how's that your concern?"

"I wasn't asking a question," I said. "I was making a statement."

"And what of it?" he said.

I motioned with my head to the office he'd just wandered out of. "I'd rather speak to you privately," I said. "Given the delicate nature of the situation."

"What's so delicate about it?" Farrell said. "Tommy was our congressman and will be again. Once we send that girlie back to tending bar."

"How about you invite me in and I'll share details."

Farrell's face turned a very bright red. He invited me

back, although it appeared he'd rather eat a buffet of glass than spend more time with me.

He waved toward a pair of well-crafted wooden chairs with black leather cushions. His office was dark and stately. A banker's lamp on an antique desk. A framed American flag that appeared to be an antique and many photos of Farrell with famous politicians from the Commonwealth. I was so impressed, I found it difficult to compose myself.

"A real-life political fixer," I said. "Wow. You've come a long way from working as an MC in the Combat Zone."

"Come on," he said. "Ancient history. Let's get on with it."

"I'd like to know about your work with Tommy Flaherty," I said. "You really think he has a shot?"

"Of course I do," he said. "I wouldn't invest my time if I didn't believe in Tommy."

I smiled and waited. I figured if I kept him talking and nervous, he just might crack and let me know all about how he was involved with the break-in last night. My stare shared the kind of intensity that only Ward Bond or Nat Pendleton possessed.

"Carolina Garcia-Ramirez is a tough cookie," I said. "With many adoring constituents."

Farrell's face went from concerned to confident. His face split into a smile and he leaned back into his chair. He rested his hands on his prosperous stomach and wet his lips.

"Don't tell me you're working for that crazy woman?" he said. "Are you?"

I found there was no reason to lie. I looked right at him and shrugged.

"Makes sense," Farrell said. "She's as screwy as you."

"Because she wants to keep old crooks like you out of the process?"

Farrell kept on grinning. "Haha," he said. "See what I mean? I can see your heart's bleeding from here."

"You know about the break-in last night?"

"I do," he said. "What a pity."

"And they took some laptops and hard drives that contained some pretty important information to the congresswoman's campaign?"

"I get teary just thinking about it."

It was getting easier and easier to dislike Frankie Farrell. I'd encountered many red-eyed rats along the waterfront with better personalities.

"I figured that kind of information would only be helpful to a handful of people."

"Don't even think of accusing me of that bullshit," Farrell said. "You're nothing but a bottom-feeder who looks in peepholes. I can have your license revoked with one phone call."

"Peepholes?" I said. "Yikes. I haven't heard about that in a while. The break-in just reminded me of your old pal Joe Broz. You still keep in touch with his son, Gerry?"

"I never worked for Joe Broz," he said. "Are you nuts?"

"Come on," I said. "I keep extensive records of my favorite cases. Confessions and recordings."

"Haha," Farrell said. "What a laugh."

I leaned forward in my chair. The more I leaned forward, the more he leaned back. I thought if I leaned back, then he might lean forward, creating a seesaw effect. For the moment, I stayed with a slight forward lean.

"How is Gerry, by the way?"

"How the hell should I know?"

"If you or any of your dirty tricksters have been involved in the threats against my client, I promise to pick you up by your dress heels and shake you upside down until your pockets are empty."

Farrell looked uncomfortable. His face flushed and his cheek twitched.

"We don't need to know about that woman's donors or talking points," Farrell said. "Tommy has this all in hand. Carolina's a joke in Washington. Everyone knows it. She's just a kid with a crummy degree in civics who believes she can change the world by printing off some fancy posters and making promises for some pie-in-the-sky bullshit that will never happen. Politics is about compromise. Making a deal you don't want to make because nothing might be left on the table. Her constituents are through with her song and dance. They're ready for some real leadership. It's just Flaherty's time. Again."

"Gee," I said. "Now that we have all that cleared up, I'm so embarrassed to have called on you."

"Go fuck yourself, Spenser."

"Thanks," I said. "But I'm not as limber as I used to be."

"Oh, hell."

"Boston has changed," I said. "Different people. Different rules."

"That's where you're wrong," Farrell said. "Nothing has changed. Not a goddamn thing has changed besides the fucking Greenway and Lockes. Why don't you grow the fuck up?"

"'With age comes wisdom, but for some age comes alone.'"

"Good luck with that," Farrell said, standing and offering his hand. "May the best man win."

I looked at it. And then back to Farrell.

"With a relic like you running the show, there's no doubt she will."

15

Three nights later, Carolina Garcia-Ramirez ran through her speech for the Kennedy School at Harvard while I ran through security for the event. I'd already met with the Harvard and Cambridge police. They'd offered a detail of six cops, while I'd keep close on the congresswoman. Despite my ability to leap tall buildings in a single bound and be faster than a locomotive, I could not keep eyes on an entire auditorium while watching out for a single lawmaker.

Kyle Rosen sat mid-row in the nearly empty room, continually checking his phone, while I made a list of entrances and exits, escape routes, and nearby hospitals. As I had to make plans for unknown suspects and unknown threats, not much was off the table. I'd spent the last few days running background checks on CGR's staff and several volunteers. It was slow, tedious work that so far had yielded absolutely zip.

After walking the auditorium several times, I took a seat beside him.

"You'll be where?" Rosen said.

I pointed to a short staircase up to the stage.

"And the cops will be where?"

I pointed out the four exits.

"All in uniform?"

"Cambridge PD will have a few extra in plainclothes."

"Did you meet them?"

I nodded.

"Will you recognize them?"

I nodded.

"You don't talk much while you're planning," he said. "Do you?"

"Never say anything that doesn't improve the silence."

"You always keep to that?" Rosen said.

"Yeah, but it's tough," I said. "I have so many interesting things to say."

Rosen shook his head, thumbs flickering across the screen of his phone. I noted two more emergency exits behind the stage. We would have a strong police presence outside. Still, there would be no guest list, no RSVPs to check. No metal detectors. No facial recognition. Not much of anything of value beyond vigilance.

Adam Swift sat in the front row while Carolina continued through her speech without teleprompter or amplification, speaking to a nonexistent crowd. She spoke about changing the future of the United States. About hope and the larger moment we find ourselves in. About how America has always been about the journey to bolstering the rights of others. *This Is America. The Good and the Bad . . .*

"I would feel better if we had some assistance from the Feds," I said.

"Me, too," Rosen said. "But they can't offer protection unless there has been an incident."

"What would you call what happened at the Capitol and the break-in here in Boston?"

"Incidents," Rosen said. He was slumped in his seat, a hat for the USS *Constitution* on his head. It still had the tags from the gift shop earlier that day. "They just don't see things the same way."

"Things will have to get worse before we get more help."

"That's what we've been told," Rosen said, sliding his phone back into his pocket.

Carolina's voice echoed in the empty space, speaking about social justice and how we must all pick up where the Civil Rights Movement left off. She looked down into the empty seats, raised a fist, and asked where we would all go from here.

A deeper silence hung in the room. The pause long and pregnant and seemingly waiting for an answer. Adam Swift started to clap.

She gathered the speech and handed the papers to Swift, who promptly placed them inside his giant bag. His blond hair looked almost white in the stage lights as he passed a water bottle to the congresswoman.

I stood with Rosen by the steps. Carolina walked down to meet us.

"Perfect," Rosen said. "Just perfect."

"I don't know," she said. "I kind of miss the part about the founding fathers having strong ideas but being far from perfect."

"That comes across," Rosen said.

"I'm not so sure," she said. "It feels like I don't go far enough."

"For this crowd?" Rosen said. "All you have to do is stand onstage and you'll get a standing ovation."

Carolina placed one hand on the hip of her pantsuit. It looked like every other black pantsuit I'd seen her in. I wondered if she didn't have a closet filled with them like a superhero. She looked to me, wondering aloud if she should add back in the part on the founding fathers.

"You're asking me?" I said.

She nodded.

"Not in my job description."

"You don't believe in what we're doing here?" she said.

Rosen bit the top part of his lip and dipped his head. He removed his hat and twirled it in his hand.

"What I believe or don't believe doesn't matter."

"It matters a little bit."

"What matters is that I feel you're vulnerable."

"The campus police don't think so," Carolina said.

"That's why they're campus police," I said. "What you have here is set dressing. Security without really being secure."

Carolina unscrewed the top of her water bottle and drank. Her eyes were dark and intense. She swallowed and turned her gaze to Rosen.

"I'd like to bring in some assistance," I said. "Both here and outside your home."

"My private life is private," Carolina said. "I don't need to know what you're doing after-hours."

"Probably picking up a little something at Riverside Pizza for my main squeeze."

"You call her that?"

"Sometimes," I said. "We've been together for a while. She's grown used to it."

"How long?" Carolina said.

"I thought you said our private lives are private?" I said.

She handed the water bottle back to Swift. She placed her hands on her hips. Rosen looked from her back to me.

"We'll have a half dozen cops," Rosen said. "Isn't that enough?"

"I nccd somconc good in thc crowd."

"You know someone like that?" Carolina said.

"Indeed I do."

"Someone you trust?" Carolina said.

"I'm told he's the very best at what he does."

Carolina folded her arms across her chest, chin lifted to me. "I thought you were the best," she said. "Right?"

"I've tried to explain that to him for years," I said. "Maybe one day he'll listen."

16

I walked with Hawk along the waterfront between the Long Wharf and the Aquarium. After a tough workout with weights and boxing, Hawk had twisted my arm into having two beers at Legal. The third had been all my idea. As I looked out onto the water, I saw the rough, rude sea was unable to wash the balm from an anointed king.

"Background check?" Hawk said.

"Technically you'll be my employee."

"Good," Hawk said. "I don't do background checks."

"And background checks don't do you."

"What's the job?"

"I want you to attend the speech," I said. "And blend into the crowd."

"Blend in at Harvard?"

"Harvard prides itself on its cultural diversity."

"Ain't nobody like me," Hawk said. "Never has been. Never will be."

It was nearly twilight, but the sailboats and small pleasure crafts still filled the choppy harbor. The wind was strong off the water, ruffling my hair and Hawk's scalp. We walked over to where a thick black anchor chain marked the end of the wharf. Tourists took photos of the boats, the federal building at Fort Point, and across to East Boston.

"Carolina Garcia-Ramirez might see me and lose track of what she's saying," Hawk said.

"The thought had not crossed my mind," I said.

"Maybe it should."

"Susan might find that remark to be sexist."

"Can't be sexist if it's a fact."

"The congresswoman isn't the type to lose focus."

"Good-looking woman."

I nodded. Across the harbor, I watched a large plane take off; the ferry from Logan crossed the harbor.

"She married?"

"Nope."

"Got a boyfriend?"

"I don't know," I said. "Didn't ask. She prefers to keep her private life private."

"Might be good to ask."

"For her safety or for you?"

Hawk shrugged. He had on a tight-fitting white silk T-shirt with a lightweight leather jacket casually tossed over his shoulder. The wind was intense but still warm. The setting sun spreading across downtown Boston, softening the edges of the tall office buildings, turning the mirrored windows a bright gold.

"How about Vinnie?" he asked.

"Vinnie might prove more problematic."

"More problematic than me?"

"I know," I said. "Hard to believe."

"Since Vinnie is a known criminal figure in Boston?"

"Involved in current criminal activity."

"Aren't we all," Hawk said. "Some just do it on the down low."

"You will be known to the cops," I said. "In case there is trouble. That work?"

"What kind of trouble you expecting?"

I told him more about the break-in and more about the man who'd tossed a cup of urine at the congresswoman back in D.C. I told him about the hate groups and the letters received at the *Globe*. I explained a little about Tommy Flaherty and my conversation with Frankie Farrell, who had once worked with the Broz family.

"Makes me think back to a kinder, gentler time in Boston," Hawk said. "Men yelling at children for wanting to go to a decent school."

"Farrell told me that Boston never changes."

"Neighborhoods change," Hawk said. "People don't."

"I'll stay close to the congresswoman," I said. "The cops will watch the entrances and exits. I'd feel better with you keeping watch."

"Dig it."

"You know what they say about an ounce of caution?"

"That it beats shooting someone dead?"

"Precisely."

Hawk nodded. I saw my reflection in the dark lenses

of his sunglasses. His face impassive. “This woman got threats on all sides.”

“I believe someone in her office is working with her opponent,” I said. “But I haven’t ruled out multiple threats.”

“She must get under some white folks’ skin.”

“Strong, attractive, bilingual black woman.”

“I like it.”

“That’s because you’re confident in who you are.”

“You know it, babe.”

“Susan believes the congresswoman threatens a certain kind of man.”

“That ain’t nothin’ new.”

“Nope.”

“Like the man said, ‘*Not everything that is faced can be changed, but nothing can be changed until it is faced.*’”

“I figured you’d bc in.”

“This speech gonna be enough to draw ’em out?”

“That’s the plan.”

“Okay, then,” Hawk said. “Let’s catch that motherfucker.”

17

I'm looking forward to it," Susan said.

"Just because you went to Harvard, that doesn't mean attendance is mandatory."

"Graduate or not, I wouldn't miss it."

"Even though I'm telling you there might be trouble in River City?"

"Even then."

Susan wouldn't be Susan if there was a possibility of changing her mind. I took the matter into consideration and checked her nearly empty refrigerator for beer. Pearl helped, nuzzling into a lower shelf filled with wilted lettuce, a large onion, and two soft tomatoes.

"What would you have done if I hadn't brought the pizza?" I said.

"Ordered one."

"Is that all I am to you?"

"The hunky pizza delivery guy?"

I nodded.

"Do you want to be anything else?"

"Not really," I said. "Do you want me to go back outside and knock on the door? Maybe you can tell me that you don't have any money."

"And then you'll tell me that I can pay in other ways?"

"That's the spirit."

I started to pick up the pizza. She placed a hand on my wrist.

"Or," Susan said. "We could stay here, eat the pizza, watch some TV, and then I'll slip into that outfit you bought me from La Perla."

"The one with the leather cuffs and the riding crop."

"That one hasn't arrived yet," she said.

"Any day now."

"The low-cut one with the French lace and thin shoulder straps."

I set the pizza back on the kitchen island. Pearl jumped up and placed her front paws against the island, nose in the air, sniffing the pizza fumes. I opened the box and tossed her a pepperoni.

"Or," I said. "We could go into your bedroom, make violent love, and then work up our appetites."

"But the pizza might get cold."

"The reason God invented microwaves."

"God invented microwaves?"

I nodded. "Of course she did."

Susan walked up to me, placed her hand behind my head, and laid a kiss on me so strong, I felt like stomping my foot and whinnying.

"Good?"

"The best," I said.

18

Do you want to tell me what in the hell's going on, Spenser?"

It was early morning and Kyle Rosen didn't sound happy.

"I took my dog for a long walk along Linnaean Street and then made banana-walnut pancakes with a side of bacon," I said. "After that, I drank a pot of coffee and read the sports pages front to back. I was about to dig into *Arlo & Janis.* How are you?"

"Lou Pasquale quit."

"Sorry to hear that."

"He blames you," Rosen said. "He said you were snooping into his personal life."

"To be fair," I said, "I was hired to snoop into everyone's personal life."

"You were hired to protect Carolina and find out who was threatening her," he said. "Not make trouble for our staff."

"Investigation requires asking tough questions," I said. "Lou was a cop. Surely he understands the concept."

"He fucking quit, man," Rosen said. "We have twelve campaign stops today and no driver."

"Have you considered Uber?"

"It's not funny," Rosen said. "Jesus. What did you do?"

I set down my mug and looked at my watch. It was seven-fifteen. I was still wearing a navy terry-cloth robe I kept at Susan's. I felt like the poor man's Hugh Hefner.

"Where are you?"

"Stuck on the Mass Pike," Rosen said. "Carolina is going to freak."

"And where's Lou?"

"I assume he's at home," Rosen said. "Back in Quincy. Don't tell me you're thinking about causing more trouble?"

"It's a character trait," I said. "But perhaps I can reason with him."

Kyle Rosen let out a long and very exasperated breath. I forked off a little more of my world-famous banana-walnut pancakes. In my humble estimation, they were five stars. So good, I offered a bite to Pearl. She gobbled them up off the kitchen floor and stared up at me as if she'd been starving to death.

"Okay," Rosen said. "Do you need his address?"

"Nope," I said. "Spoils of the snooper."

I finished my breakfast and my coffee and changed into a fresh pair of jeans and a short-sleeved white linen shirt I'd left at Susan's. An hour later, I was down in Quincy, driving along Sea Street in Houghs Neck. Soon

I found Lou's address. A not-so-charming cottage a block off the bay, painted a fading yellow and surrounded by a chain-link fence.

I parked and walked up to the gate. A sign warned me that the premises were being monitored by video surveillance. Undeterred, I opened the gate and walked up onto a short asphalt drive surrounded by a patchy piece of yellowed lawn.

I got halfway across the lawn when a very large German shepherd came running.

I stood still and held out the flat of my hand. The dog stopped within five feet of me, barking and growling. I spoke in cool and easy tones, singing, "*If I could walk with the animals. Talk with the animals.*"

The dog growled lower and more intently.

"*If I consulted with the quadrupeds think what fun we'd have.*"

The dog stopped growling and looked back at the house.

Lou Pasquale came ambling around the corner, shirtless but otherwise immaculately dressed in khaki cargo shorts and orange crocs. A cigarette dangled from his fingers as he yelled for King to shut the fuck up. His face looked bloated and he was sweating.

"Top of the morning," I said.

"Lucky I'm here or King would've ripped your snausage right off," he said. "What are you doing? Singing?"

"Doing my best Rex Harrison."

"Rex whosis?" Pasquale said. He took a puff of his cigarette and then bent down to congratulate the dog for nearly ripping me to shreds. Lou's large belly dropped down over the cargo shorts. "Listen, if you came to talk me out of quitting, don't bother. Rosen had no business putting you all over my ass. I don't have time for that crap."

"Not even a background check?"

Pasquale looked up. "A background check I don't mind," he said. "Calling my old sergeant is something else. If you got questions, come to me. Okay?"

"Mind if we sit down and talk?" I said. "Kyle's hoping you'll come back in time for tonight's speech."

"Fat fucking chance."

"'Hope has as many lives as a cat or a king.'"

I patted King's flank while I studied Lou. He hadn't shaved his head that morning and a black ring encircled his scalp. The puffy face and the sweat made me know he'd had a hard night with the booze.

"Not that it means anything now, but I don't think that IA investigation would disqualify you from working for the congresswoman."

"No shit," Pasquale said. "I didn't do a goddamn thing."

The Quincy PD had once investigated Louis J. Pasquale for giving a police escort to his wife's cousin's wedding. I didn't care about his time in Quincy. I only wanted to find out what had annoyed him so much about me even asking.

"I don't need the fucking aggravation."

"I did background checks on everyone," I said. "Including Kyle Rosen and the entire staff."

"Rosen is the one you should be looking at," Pasquale said. "Fucking tree-hugger. I looked him up, too. How many times did he get busted for resisting arrest? Check with NYPD."

"I did," I said. "He was involved in several sit-ins on Wall Street."

"Yeah," Pasquale said.

"Yep."

"You weren't trying to jam me up?"

"Not even a little."

"Shit," he said. "Come on, Spenser. Go around to the deck and I'll get some coffee. Don't mind King. His bark is worse than his bite."

"He seems like a true friend."

"The best fucking friend I got."

Pasquale walked up into the house and King and I continued around to the deck. It was a homemade job coated in a reddish sealant and had a half-decent view of the bay, if you squinted through two larger and more expensive houses. Lou's place looked to be the last old place standing as newer houses were taking over Houghs Neck.

I sat down at a small wrought-iron table. Pasquale slid open a glass door and asked how I liked my coffee. I told him.

It was a muggy gray morning on the bay. A light fog rolled in off the beach, scattering across Sea Street. He brought out a couple cups of coffee.

Pasquale had slipped on a faded white T-shirt with the old-fashioned logo of the Patriot about to snap the ball.

After he sat down, King stayed at his left leg. The dog panted, a lot of gray around the muzzle.

"Getting old," he said. "But he's still got it when he needs it."

"Glad he kept my snausage intact," I said. "I still use it. From time to time."

"Sorry you came out this way," he said. "You coulda called unless there's something special you wanted to ask."

"I guess I don't understand why you'd objected to a background check."

Pasquale shrugged. He rubbed the dog's neck. King's eyes clouded with cataracts. It reminded me of how my old Pearl looked in her final years, gray and arthritic. The spirit willing, but the body not able.

"How old is he?" I said.

"Twelve," he said. "King was one of our police dogs. I got him to help out not long after I got shot."

"At the robbery."

"I guess you know all of it now," he said. "I got the suspect and the suspect got me."

"And the suspect didn't live."

"You ever aim for the leg?" Pasquale said. His face flat and expressionless.

"Never."

"Raised his gun," he said. "Hit him dead center. Dead before he hit the fucking ground."

I drank some coffee. Pasquale would never get a job as a barista.

He wiped his forehead with a kitchen napkin.

"Is there more?" I said.

"More to what?"

"Why you quit."

"Christ," he said. "Are we having two separate conversations?"

"Your sergeant said you were a good cop," I said. "But had made a few small mistakes."

He shrugged.

"I made a few mistakes, too," I said. "Insubordination."

"You ever shoot someone?"

I shrugged. "Never anyone I liked."

"Me either."

We sat there and drank coffee. King settled down onto his belly and soon started to snore. We didn't speak for a long while. We just sat there and watched the fog dissipate while the sun came out. A few beachgoers parked along the road. A crew of workers hammered and drilled at a house under construction. The whole place, the whole beachfront, seeming to be in transition.

"Any way you might come back?" I said. "Might make things easier on the congresswoman."

Pasquale took in a deep breath. He looked down at King and then back at me.

"I thought you'd bust my ass about the IA thing."

"Taking your wife's cousin to her wedding?"

"Yeah," he said. "How stupid was that?"

"I'm looking for whoever wrote those emails," I said. "And broke into the reelection headquarters."

"Well," he said. "I didn't fucking do it."

"So noted," I said. "Got any ideas who might have?"

"People hate Carolina before she even opens up her mouth," he said. "How long you been in Boston?"

I told him. He nodded.

"Then you get it," he said. "Right? This may be a progressive state, but there's plenty of Neanderthals lurking around. A woman like Carolina? It's too much for their heads to process."

I nodded. We talked a little more and I finished my coffee.

"You know, at first I wasn't really into what she had to say," he said. "But after listening to her for a while, I know she's serious."

"So you'll come back?"

"I don't know."

"Carolina sent me to ask personally."

Pasquale thought about it. He rubbed King's head and looked through the narrow slot of the two buildings to the water. "Sure," he said. "I mean. What the hell."

He walked me back to his gate and we shook hands. I only believed half of what he'd told me.

19

The Kennedy School auditorium was standing room only.

Mostly students, but a lot of Cambridge types. Plenty of hemp clothing and clogs. Among them, Susan Silverman sat in the second-to-last row. Susan didn't qualify as a Cambridge type. Instead of Birkenstocks, she wore a pair of very high, very expensive heels with a black wrap dress and gold hoop earrings.

Her hair worn loose and curly down her back. No matter how many times I saw her, I felt a charge deep in my chest.

I winked at her. In return, she stuck out her tongue.

It was fifteen minutes before Carolina would take the podium set in a theater in the round. Four separate aisles facing the stage. Two local news cameras and a crew from CSPAN. Carolina waited in the hospitality room along with Adam Swift and Kyle Rosen. Lou was back in action and waiting with the SUV in a nearby parking garage.

I found Hawk seated at the end of the sixth row on the opposite side of me. He had on a white suit with a navy silk shirt and appeared as stoic as a stone figure of Marcus Aurelius.

There were cops at all three main exits. Marked and unmarked units outside.

It was crowded but manageable. An intimate space for Carolina to engage with supporters and potential voters. A venue where Harvard students could demonstrate their parents' money was well spent. Maybe there should be a grudge match to find the smartest among them.

I stood on the west side of the stage, which would be five feet from the congresswoman. I glanced about for any DON'T TREAD ON ME T-shirts or white polos. Maybe a few with buck knives in their teeth or tiki torches in hand.

What I saw was white, black, brown, male, female, young, old. Some wore campaign T-shirts, others held campaign signs. CGR FOR CHANGE. NEVER LOOK BACK. UNIDOS, NO DIVIDIDOS.

I looked for anyone who looked nervous or out of place. Anyone sweating or jittery. Besides Hawk, most seemed pleased to be in attendance.

The students giggled and talked in small groups. An older woman with curly gray hair and wearing a denim dress furtively ate a granola bar. Two young women sat at the far edge of the auditorium, switching back and forth with a baby. The child began to cry and one of the women walked to the lobby with the child.

I looked at my watch. Ten more minutes.

I looked back at Hawk. He didn't appear to have taken a single breath.

The cops talked in huddles. Campus security helped attendees to their seats.

Kyle Rosen walked out from the back room and nodded at me, his long, wild hair pulled into a ponytail. He wore a dark suit with a dark T-shirt and Converse tennis shoes.

"How are we doing?" he said.

"Looks clear."

"So did Ford's Theatre."

"You and Carolina refused a preapproved guest list."

"We wanted this to be a true open forum," Rosen said. "Can't have democracy without trust."

I nodded. I wore my J. Press blazer over a white dress shirt, a nifty paisley tie, and my chrome-plated .357 Magnum. My pants were a dark green and cuffed over my cordovan loafers.

I was ready for a night out on the town or shooting any would-be assassins. Whichever one came first. Hawk still had on his sunglasses, which would have been strange to see on anyone but Hawk.

I walked the perimeter of the auditorium. I checked in with Cambridge and the campus cops. All was going according to Hoyle as the lights dimmed and I found my place near the stage. *Something familiar. Something peculiar. Something for everyone.*

A senior fellow at the Kennedy School introduced the congresswoman. He was a heavyset older gent who'd served as an adviser to a past president. His intro was bold without being too effusive. He made sure everyone understood his delight that the congresswoman had accepted the invitation.

People stood and clapped. I stood and scanned the auditorium.

My breathing felt a little shallow. My nerves jangled a bit.

I took in a long breath and continued to watch.

Hawk was there. The cops were there. I was there.

Carolina beamed as she launched into her story. Like all great speakers, she had the unique talent of making sure her focus and energy were evenly distributed. When she turned and glanced my way, it felt like she was talking to me about how the top earners in our country didn't pay a dime in taxes, the burden pushed onto the middle class.

She told the story of two Dominicans coming to Boston for a better life, meeting in Roxbury, and getting married. She talked about growing up without much but believing in a system that she thought to be merit-based. But instead of being able to afford school with scholarships, she had put herself through Boston University waiting tables and tending bar. She claimed she made the best Bloody Mary in Boston.

I wondered how she felt about gin versus vodka in a martini.

She talked about her accomplishments, her failures, and how much was still left to be done. After, two young women walked down the aisles with microphones to assist with the Q&A.

Toward the back exit on the southern section of seats, I watched a man listen to Carolina while stroking a long, brushy beard. He had on a white shirt, a skinny red tie, and red suspenders. It had been a long while since I'd seen anyone wearing suspenders outside a fire station. He sat directly under one of the overhead lights, illuminating a severe haircut with the top longer and slicked back and the sides shaved. He had a pinched face with smallish eyes and a bulbous nose. I figured him for his late twenties or early thirties. If I'd been Spider-Man, I'd have started to tingle.

He did not look like a student. Or a Cambridge resident. He looked more like a carnival barker or a preppy survivalist.

He wore a plastered smile on his face as Carolina addressed poverty across Boston's neighborhoods. The man was sweating but didn't seem to notice or care.

Something about the man's face bothered me. Or maybe I just didn't like the Rollie Fingers mustache and the odd haircut.

When I glanced back, Carolina was taking a question on ending combustible engines and microplastics. When I looked to Hawk, he wasn't there.

I scanned each corner and saw Hawk marching down the row with a man in a dark suit. Hawk had his hand on the man's upper arm and was leading him out of the auditorium. I assumed it wasn't for putting his feet up on the furniture.

Rosen had seen it, too. He gave me a nervous nod.

I followed Hawk out of the auditorium, where a group

of cops had met Hawk at the exit. As Hawk wasn't a fan of cops, I stepped in and let them know he was with me.

"With you?" Hawk said.

"An associate," I said.

"Haw," Hawk said.

Even outside the auditorium, I could still hear Carolina speaking. It was muted and unclear but greeted with applause.

"Man's carrying," Hawk said. "That's against the rules."

"Who the fuck are you?" the man said.

"The man who makes the rules."

The man Hawk had escorted out tried to shake free from Hawk's grasp. He couldn't.

He was youngish and black, wearing a dark-colored suit. One of the Harvard cops asked if he had a permit to carry.

"I'm going to reach in my coat," the man said. "Okay?"

No one stopped him. Hawk and the cops stood on edge.

The man flashed a badge, and when Hawk's grip slackened, he shook his arm free.

"I'm a goddamn federal agent."

20

We reconvened at the nearby parking garage, where several cops and a few Feds gathered in an impromptu focus group on the fourth floor.

A well-dressed Asian man wearing a tailored gray suit and polished black wingtips stood flatfooted, arguing with a Cambridge PD sergeant I knew named Sully. The Asian man seemed both upset and exasperated. I held up my hand as Sully was about to respond in the classic Boston fashion of telling him to go have sex with himself.

Hawk looked to the man and then looked back to me. The Asian man turned to both of us, took in a deep breath, and sadly shook his head.

"Oh, no," Bobby Nguyen said.

"Oh, yes," I said.

"Someone told me you'd joined the congresswoman's team, but I thought they were screwing with me."

"Why wouldn't you be thrilled about working with me?" I said.

"Atlanta," he said.

I shrugged. "Since when are you with the FBI?"

"I've been with the Bureau for two years now."

"Congrats," I said. "Your pals at the ATF must've mourned their loss."

"It was an evolution of my professional career," he said. "I had hoped I wouldn't run into you ever again."

"But here I am."

"And Hawk, too."

"We're kind of a package deal," I said.

"Lucky me," Nguyen said.

The parking garage was nearly empty except for the patrol cars and three unmarked black sedans. Tires squealed on a lower level of the garage. The federal agents turned to make sure the vehicle wasn't headed our way.

"You might've checked with us before you made a scene," Nguyen said.

"Sloppy," Hawk said. "Spotted that gun right off."

The youngish black agent Hawk had grabbed glowered at him. Hawk met his gaze. The young man looked away.

"Didn't the congresswoman tell you she was under federal protection?" Nguyen said.

I didn't answer. It was best to be quiet when the answer might only make you look stupid.

"We take threats very seriously," Nguyen said. "We don't need help from a couple of Boston bouncers."

"Can you speed things up?" I said. "We have the late shift at Mr. Dooley's pub."

Hawk watched the much smaller man speak. He cocked his head slightly to his left.

"If Carolina knew who you were," Nguyen said, addressing Hawk, "she wouldn't want you within a hundred miles of her campaign."

Hawk didn't answer. His silence sent a wave over the agents.

"I was hired for security," I said. "Hawk's with me."

"Terrific," Nguyen said. "Just fucking terrific."

Nguyen asked if we might converse privately. I told him I needed to get back to the congresswoman but would give him a minute. He turned and I followed him out of earshot over by the elevators. He raised his index finger and pointed it directly at my chest.

"Do you have any idea how serious this is?" Nguyen said.

"I do," I said. "That's why I was taking it seriously."

"This isn't just some weirdo sending emails," Nguyen said. "Or a cranky old kook who doesn't like diversity in the voting booth."

"Wish to enlighten me?" I said. "Technically, we're part of the same team."

Nguyen looked over my shoulder at the cops and Feds. Hawk stood free of the group, leaning down and checking out a new Mercedes coupe. He appeared to be window-shopping, running a hand over the smooth curve of the trunk.

"We don't know," he said.

"Besides tossing drunks around," I said, "I also run a professional investigation service. Would you like a card?"

"I have your fucking card," Nguyen said. "And I want you to keep clear of our business. If the congresswoman decided to pay you for bodyguard services, that's on her. But you can't start snooping around our investigation."

"From past experience, you know one can benefit the other."

"And from past experience, I know your involvement can royally fuck things up."

"Didn't you get what you wanted?"

"Yeah, yeah," Nguyen said. "We got the bastard."

"Didn't I do what I said I'd do?" I said.

"Sure," Nguyen said. "But listen up, Spenser. I don't know why Carolina chose not to tell you or her staff what we're doing. But I promise you we wouldn't be involved if there wasn't something mean and nasty on the horizon. No offense, but this is a little outside your skill set. This isn't about busting heads. Or playing soldier out in the woods. This is about making a goddamn case."

"Aha," I said. "Then you're onto something."

"I didn't say that."

"You said I was in the way of you making a case," I said. "And if you're trying to make a case, that means you know who you're making a case against."

Nguyen shook his head and started to walk away. He stopped, turned back, and held up his hand, looking up at me. I was much taller than him.

"Nobody wants to see the congresswoman get hurt," he said. "You just need to keep clear and let us do our damn job."

"If someone is working the inside," I said, "I need to know."

"You think there's someone on her staff?"

"Yep," I said. "I most certainly do. Someone made a mess of the campaign office and tried to make it look like a break-in."

"Are you sure?"

"Trust me," I said. "I have solved a case or two."

With great pain, Nguyen reached into his pocket and handed me his new spiffy business card with the FBI logo. As I accepted it, I gave a low appreciative whistle.

"Fidelity, Integrity, and what's the last thing?" I said.

"Bravery."

"Oh," I said. "Always forget that one."

"Keep out of our way," Nguyen said. "Few things would give me more pleasure than charging you and Hawk with obstruction."

"Few things?" I said. "Maybe you need to find some new hobbies."

"This is my hobby," Nguyen said. "Chasing bad guys is my bliss."

Nguyen stared at me. I grinned. He rubbed the back of his neck and turned to where the agents had gathered by their black sedans.

Hawk met me at the stairwell. We briskly wound down the steps to street level.

"Little man tell you to get lost?" Hawk said.

"You know it."

"Guess he don't know you too well."

"You know," I said. "I tried to argue that very point."

21

I had lunch with Carolina the next afternoon at Maxine's on Saint James.

The soul food restaurant was in a three-story brick building next to a fluff and fold in Roxbury. The menu said they offered the best Louisiana and Southern cuisine in Boston, which was good enough for me. I ordered the fried catfish over grits and a side of gumbo. Carolina had the crab cakes with a Caesar salad.

We sat at a small table near the window. There weren't many people at a little after eleven, and no one outside our waitress seemed to recognize the congresswoman.

"We didn't get off to the best start," she said.

Her makeup and hair were immaculate. Today she had on a light blue pantsuit that was downright festive for her.

"I thought we got off to a fine start," I said.

"I told Kyle not to hire you."

"After that."

"After that, I felt you were in our way," she said. "I wasn't sure about the optics of using a hired gun."

"I'm no Alan Ladd," I said. "I'm two feet taller."

"Still."

"I quoted Shakespeare to you and told you I could cook."

"You can't cook as good as Maxine."

"Don't be so quick to judge."

"Just wait," she said. "You'll see."

I drank some ice water. The congresswoman had some iced tea.

Paintings by local artists hung on the walls. Lots of bright colors and paint splashes against the exposed brick. Ceiling fans twirled overhead. Whatever they were cooking up at Maxine's smelled wonderful.

Lou Pasquale sat outside with the SUV but I'd promised him I'd bring him back a to-go order. The wings special looked so good that I'd thought about ordering it myself.

"You like soul food?" Carolina said.

"Of course."

"It's different from what I grew up with," she said. "But that's Roxbury. A cultural hodgepodge. Caribbean, Southern, Mexican. It's a small world after all."

"But you now live in Cambridge?"

"My boyfriend lives in Cambridge," she said. "We didn't feel I needed another place when I was back."

"What does he do?"

"Trey's a graphic artist," she said. "He does all my

posters. Web design. We met during the first campaign. And where'd you grow up?"

"Wyoming."

"No," she said. "Wyoming? Really?"

"I grew up in Laramie, and when I was a teenager my father and his uncles moved to Boston."

"And your mother?"

"My mother died," I said. "My father and uncles brought me up."

"Wow," she said.

"My father heard Boston was the Athens of America," I said. "He thought it was a good opportunity for all of us."

"Any of them still living?"

"Gone for a long while."

"And did you find what you hoped in Boston?"

"That," I said. "And then some."

"My parents came here for the same reasons," she said. "Better opportunities. But we had family here. A place to live. Some jobs waiting. Not good jobs. But they were jobs."

"And they are both living?" I said.

She nodded.

The food arrived and I tried some of the hot catfish with grits. I had always been cautious about grits until I spent a fair amount of time in Georgia. Somehow I'd learned to appreciate them. Especially with a little cheese and crispy catfish. My expression gave me away.

"Good?"

"Wow," I said.

"Better than haddock?"

"Don't make me choose between catfish and haddock," I said. "Haddock and I are very close."

We both ate a little. I tried the gumbo. I soon finished the gumbo.

"And you're not married?"

"I'm pretty much married."

"Which means?"

"I've been with the same woman for a long time."

"Very modern of you."

"We try to remain relevant," I said.

"And what does she do?"

I told her all about Susan, how we met, and how we'd stayed together. About her work as a psychologist and with local philanthropy.

"Very impressive."

"She's very impressed with you," I said. "She was at your talk last night."

"And she agrees with what I have to say?"

"Very much so."

"And you?"

"I don't think that matters," I said. "My political views are irrelevant."

"Maybe they're important to me?"

I ate some more. I drank some water. I tried to steer the conversation toward what I'd learned from Agent Nguyen, who was now the special agent in charge of Boston. It was a delight to recognize another friendly face in local law enforcement.

"Have you heard any more from the Feds?" I said.

"Only what I heard last night."

"It would've been nice to know they were among us," I said. "It came as a surprise to me and my associate."

Carolina shrugged. She put down her fork and wiped the corner of her mouth. "If I'd known, I'd have told you."

"The special agent in charge said your office had been told you were under their protection."

CGR looked genuinely surprised. She shrugged. "First I'm hearing of it," she said. "We turned over some of the emails to Capitol police. I had been told they alerted the FBI. But that was pretty much the end of it."

"No one has spoken to you more about the threats?"

"I still don't know how seriously to take them," she said. "I mean, if everyone in public service cowered when someone threatened them, we'd have no one left standing up for the people."

"The break-in doesn't concern you?"

"Of course," she said. "But it doesn't change what I have to do. Nor will it change my routine in any way."

I finished the catfish. I ordered a wing plate for Lou and a cup of coffee to go.

"I'd like to put someone on your place in Cambridge."

"Nope."

"What if I insist?"

"Then I'll fire you."

"What if I do it anyway?"

"I guess I'll have to talk to that special agent in charge," she said. "What is his name, anyway?"

"Nguyen," I said. "*Bobby* Nguyen. How about just until the primary? After that, we can scale back."

"After the primary," she said, "Kyle promises you'll be gone."

"That's up to you and Kyle," I said. "But I'd hoped you'd grow accustomed to my face."

"Nice face," she said. "And such an interesting nose."

"It was reworked by several professionals."

"Surgeons?"

"Boxers," I said. "A souvenir from another time."

The waitress brought the coffee and a foam clamshell. A cook and another waitress came out of the kitchen to meet Carolina. She stood up and posed for photos. She took a tour of the kitchen and shook hands with the dishwasher and two other cooks. By the time we left, the restaurant had grown crowded, and it took some effort getting her back to the SUV.

Outside, I handed Lou his to-go order.

Carolina and I got into the backseat.

"Do you promise not to get in our way?" she said.

"Are you asking if I'll peep in your windows late at night?"

"Yes."

"I won't," I said. "Scout's honor."

She nodded. But she didn't answer either way. I took a nonanswer as a sign she'd approve of putting some people on her boyfriend's place in Cambridge.

"Susan does sound wonderful."

"Susan is the very definition of the word."

Lou started the car and circled back to the office. She had two more events scheduled for the day.

"Would you like to have dinner with me and my boyfriend sometime?" she said. "I think we'd all get on very well."

"Since I'll be attached to you full-time and Susan thinks you've hung the moon," I said, "we'd be fools not to."

22

After two campaign stops, I left Hawk watching reelection headquarters while I headed to Belmont, where Vinnie Morris ran an old bowling alley off the Concord Pike.

The bowling alley served both his legitimate and illegitimate purposes with a touch of midcentury style. The building didn't appear to have been renovated since the high times of Dean, Frank, and the boys. A blinking neon martini glass advertised a bar upstairs, tilting forward and back in a toast to good times.

When I walked into the lobby, I found a new girl working the register and counter. The girl was young and blond, with hair in a ponytail, and wearing an old-fashioned bowling shirt. Not many people could pull off the shirt, but she wore it over a thin white tank top with a certain panache. On me, it would've looked like a circus tent.

"Is Vinnie in?" I said.

"I don't know," she said. "Who's asking?"

"Fred Flintstone," I said. "I'm here about arranging a meeting of the Royal Water Buffalo."

"You're Spenser, aren't you?"

I tried to appear modest.

"Vinnie told me about a big guy with a smart mouth."

"And devilishly handsome?"

"Nah," she said. "Vinnie didn't say none of that. But you're not too bad. For an older guy."

"Shucks," I said. "You might make me blush. What's your name?"

"Darlene."

"Hello, Darlene," I said. "What happened to Sal?"

"Sal moved to New Bedford," she said. "You know. Family shit."

"Lot of that going around."

"Upstairs," she said, pointing. "You know where."

I followed the staircase with steps that appeared to be cards shuffled in midair with two quick turns. I heard the music before I even saw Vinnie. Frank singing "The Game Is Over."

Vinnie was at his impromptu desk at the edge of the empty bar. He hadn't opened the bar since he bought the place. Or bothered to buy a desk and a chair, preferring to work the countertop like a North End bookie.

"'*Gone*,'" I said, singing. "'*The days are gone now*.'"

"No fucking shit," Vinnie said. He looked up, half-glasses down on his nose, a bunch of notepads around him and an open laptop computer. He had on a lime-green polo, his hair now more salt than pepper and swept back from his tan face. A cigarette burned in an ashtray by his elbow. "What the fuck do you want?"

"Maybe I was just in the neighborhood."

"Bull crap," Vinnie said. "You wanted to shoot the shit, you would've called."

Vinnie stood up, lifted up the counter, and walked into the U-shaped bar. He clattered around in a small refrigerator and found a Blue Moon ale. He slid it down to me like in an old-time Western.

I caught it. I would've asked for an orange slice but felt that might be pushing it.

"Testing my reflexes?" I said.

"Nope," he said. "I'm testing mine."

"Much obliged, partner."

"Christ."

I drank some beer and looked around the bar. He'd added an old jukebox since the last time I'd been there, a polished silver Seeburg that advertised authentic Stereo Sound. The needle ran out on Frank and the flipper mechanism laid down a 45 of Dion doing "The Wanderer." Vinnie's head bobbed in time with the music, right hand tapping away.

"Takes me back," Vinnie said. "Beach parties on Revere Beach. Myles Connor and his boys. How about you?"

"Sure," I said. "Reminds me of hanging out with Archie and Jughead back in the day. I had a thing for Betty but there was just something about Veronica."

"Picked up the jukebox over in Mystic," Vinnie said. "Some guy named Koster had it loaded down with nothing but blues and crap eighties music. I jammed it full of all the stuff I like. Not a bad song in the whole machine."

I drank some of the beer. I checked the time. I needed to be back in Roxbury in a few hours to change places with Hawk. Hawk wasn't one that you kept waiting.

"Speaking of the oldies," I said. "I went to see Frankie Farrell the other day."

Vinnie shrugged. He kept on bobbing his head to the music. His mind somewhere back on Revere Beach. I believed he was half listening to me. I clarified.

"Political consultant?" I said. "Used to be a city councilman. Old friends with your old friend Joe Broz."

"Frankie Farrell?" he said. "The fucking fixer?"

"Yep."

"Jesus," Vinnie said. "I thought the bastard was dead."

"Still alive and still fixing."

"He was involved with that mess with the city," Vinnie said. "Right? Got all those kickbacks for road projects that never happened."

I nodded. I drank some more beer. Dion kept on singing. Vinnie picked up his dwindling cigarette and took a puff.

"You think he might still be working with the Broz family?"

"Gerry?" Vinnie said. "Saw him at his Christmas party last year. He's on his fourth wife. Half his age with a chest like a pair of zeppelins."

"He still in the life?"

"Gerry Fucking Broz?" Vinnie said. "He couldn't go legit with a gun on him. But politics and kickbacks aren't really his thing. That was more like Joe. He doesn't have the time and patience. Gerry's looking for the quick buck, not the long haul."

"What's he into these days?" I said. "Last time I saw him he was wholesaling tropical fish."

"Now it's seafood," Vinnie said. "At least that's what it says on the sign outside. You know. Import. Export. That covers a lot of fucking ground."

"Stolen goods?"

"Not stolen," Vinnie said. "Illegal. If you're not supposed to have it, Gerry probably sells it."

"Who's more into the old-fashioned rackets?" I said. "Like Joe?"

"You talking kickbacks?" Vinnie said, shaking loose a new cigarette from a pack. He cupped his hand in the airless room and lit up. "Bribery? Blackmail?"

"All the classics," I said.

"I dunno," he said. "Jackie DeMarco. Maybe the Burkes. Why are you asking about Frankie Farrell?"

"Farrell is running Tommy Flaherty's campaign."

"Flaherty's a crook, too."

"Of course he is," I said. "He's a politician."

"You want to know if Farrell's still as much of a crook as he used to be?" Vinnie said.

"Yep," I said. "And maybe who he would call on for special favors."

"Like what?"

"Like breaking into a reelection office for a sitting U.S. congresswoman."

"Saw that on the news," Vinnie said. "Didn't know you were mixed up in all of that."

"There have been threats on the congresswoman's life."

Vinnie shook his head. "Not exactly Farrell's style," he said. "He's sneaky but not mean. They like to win, but they're not going to pop some broad."

"But they might gain a certain advantage by trying to scare her."

"Yeah," Vinnie said. He ashed his cigarette into a coffee mug. "Sure. I can see that. I could see them pulling something like that."

"Thanks."

"Okay," he said. "What's in it for me?"

"Helping out a pal," I said. "A return to the glory days?"

"Glory days?" Vinnie closed one eye as he drew on the cigarette. "You're fucking witnessing it."

"This is as good as it gets."

"Better than walking behind a guy your whole life."

"Now you walk behind no one."

"You better fucking believe it."

23

Hawk sat behind the wheel of a silver Ford Fusion parked outside Carolina's condo in Cambridgeport.

"Nice to see you've decided on a sensible new vehicle," I said.

"Only thing sensible about it is that no one noticed it."

"Must have been an impulse purchase."

"Man I know impulsively stole it," he said. "Plates clean. He said drop it wherever I like."

"Efficient."

Hawk didn't say anything. It was dark. Pleasant Street was indeed pleasant, a mix of newish condos, older two-story houses, and duplexes. The car's stereo glowed as it played Waylon Jennings.

"Country?"

"I'm a little bit country," Hawk said. "You just a little bit old."

We'd been there for only a half-hour but planned to stay until Carolina left for the airport early the next morning. She'd be back in D.C. for the next three days.

When she was gone, I'd go back to Charlestown and sleep for the rest of the day. That weekend, Susan had plans for us to drive down to the Cape for long beach walks and plenty of beer. I had been having daydreams of a never-ending bucket of fried clams.

"You seen Carolina's man?" Hawk said.

"Nope."

"Look like what we used to call hippies."

"Yeah?"

"What you call 'em now?"

"Millennials."

"Damn," Hawk said. "Nothing makes sense."

"Says the black man listening to country music."

"Waylon is cowboy music."

"You a cowboy?"

Hawk nodded as Waylon sang about being "Lonesome, On'ry and Mean." We sat for a while and listened. A young skinny white guy in electric-blue shorts and a black tank top walked a Dalmatian by the car. He took no notice of us as we took notice of him. Although he didn't seem much of a threat. Assassins rarely brought their dogs to work.

Streetlamps attached to telephone poles glowed crooked and intermittently down the street toward the river.

"Trying to find out more on your mystery woman," I said.

"Mm-hm."

"Looks like her visa expired fifteen years ago," I said. "And she went back to France."

"And that's where the trail ends?"

"No," I said. "That's where the trail starts. I know a guy who knows a guy in Paris. He does similar work. He's been trying to make a connection. So far he can't find her."

"I said this wasn't gonna be easy."

"Did this woman do you wrong?" I said. "Or do you right?"

"All of it, babe," he said. "All. Of. It."

A car slid behind us, lights hard in the rearview. Hawk and I quit talking and watched as the back door opened. I lifted my hand to the handle. Hawk's eyes watching the side mirror. Two drunken women came tumbling out; one helped the other and struggled up to the lit front porch of a narrow two-story. I let out a long breath. The car pulled out and drove off along Pleasant Street.

"Congresswoman know we here?" Hawk said.

"Yep."

"She care?"

I shrugged. "She didn't say either way."

"But you worried she gonna get hit."

I nodded.

"But don't know from which direction."

I nodded again.

"That little Fed we met in Atlanta's worried."

"Bobby Nguyen is more worried about us butting out of their business," I said.

"But won't tell us why."

"Nope," I said. "And I asked so nicely."

"Feds never like us."

"Few cops like us."

"Smart cops," Hawk said. "Belson. Quirk. Lee Farrell."

"Lorraine Glass."

"She don't like you," Hawk said. "Loves me."

"Can't account for taste," I said.

Hawk pulled a phone from the dashboard and scrolled through messages. It seemed he had a different model every time I saw him. He set down the phone, crossed his arms across his broad chest, leaned his head back for a moment and closed his eyes. "Just thinking on that," he said. "Congresswoman could do better."

"A black cowboy who prefers champagne to beer?"

Hawk grinned.

"Does it matter to you that he's white?"

"What if it did?" Hawk said.

"I'd be supremely offended," I said. "Might even take it up with Thug HR."

"Ain't that he's white," Hawk said. "It's that he's soft."

"And hard is good?"

"Haw," Hawk said. "You know it."

"She's half your age."

In the darkness, Hawk grinned wider. I think it was the first time I'd ever seen Hawk to be smitten. Although I doubt he would've used that word.

"Maybe if we slay the dragon, she'll be grateful," I said.

"Mmm."

"Only we don't know the dragon."

"Only thing we have to fear is fear itself?"

"Something like that."

"You never see a coward coming," Hawk said.

"That's why they're cowards."

"Best be vigilant," Hawk said.

"That's why I changed my underwear before driving over."

Hawk looked up at the condo, down Pleasant Street, and back to the rear and side mirrors. He held the wheel with his right hand, staring straight ahead.

"Been dealing with this shit my whole life," Hawk said. "Nothing changes. New ones just replace the old ones. The old ways now the new ways."

I nodded. It was something I could empathize with, but something I could never feel. I was quiet. I let Hawk talk. I listened.

"Sometimes just being born makes you a target."

Pleasant Street stood imperfect with potholes, still and silent. A light rain began to tap at the windshield. Hawk looked again at his phone. He set it down and turned on the wipers.

"There was a man at the speech the other night."

"White dude with the Moses beard and the Hitler haircut," Hawk said.

"You saw him, too?"

"Man wasn't digging what the congresswoman had to say."

"Nope."

"Know who he is?"

"No," I said. "But I aim to find out."

Hawk stared up at Carolina's condo again. Lights still on in the upstairs window facing the street.

"Get some rest," I said.

"Don't need no rest," he said. "Read those threats you sent me."

"You want to be here when the beast is upon us?"

"Haw," he said. "Can't have you playing the white savior in this story."

24

"Are you sitting down?" Vinnie Morris said.

It was Monday and I was standing up in the kitchen of my condo in the Charlestown Navy Yard. After a long weekend with Susan and Pearl on the Cape, I'd slept late before a jog along the marina and then up to the Bunker Hill monument and back. I made coffee, cracked open two eggs with Canadian bacon, and managed to burn two pieces of rye toast.

"Would sitting down facilitate matters?"

"Cokey McMichael."

"Cokey?"

"Yeah," Vinnie said. "How the fuck you think he got that nickname?"

"Because he'd like to teach the world to sing in perfect harmony."

"Yeah," Vinnie said. "That's right. Straight through the old kazoo."

"Ah."

"Farrell and Cokey are pals," Vinnie said. "Cokey is low-level. Smash-and-grabs. Chop shops. Beat-downs for cash."

"The best people."

"Cokey also cuts Frankie Farrell's grass."

"Is that a euphemism?"

"He's Farrell's flunky," Vinnie said. "He picks up his dry cleaning and paints his fence. Probably clips his cigars and massages his feet."

"I'm about to eat breakfast," I said. "That's a mental image I could do without."

"Well," Vinnie said. "Good to know?"

"Very good," I said. "Where can I find Mr. McMichael?"

Vinnie gave me an address in Chelsea on Broadway, not far from the ScrubaDub car wash. Twenty minutes later, I had dressed and headed that way. I felt as fresh as a slightly wilted daisy.

The neighborhood in Chelsea was all industrial, cleared lots among abandoned brick warehouses. The address was for a newish building made of sheet metal with four large bay doors. I parked across the street, keeping watch through a space under an elevated enclosed walkway that linked two large warehouses. I watched cars come and go. A few transport vans. It looked like any other good old-fashioned car-theft ring. No signage. No windows.

It was gray and cloudy, the wind warm and sluggish through the open windows of my car. I was driving an older-model Mustang that year. My beloved classic Land

Cruiser had finally gone kaput on the Lynnway and I'd decided to go for something a little speedier and more reliable. It was an older Fastback with an enhanced suspension and a well-cared-for engine. A little salt damage up under the carriage, but good new tires and nice pickup for when I needed to deliver a pizza to Susan.

As I waited, I scrolled through a few booking photos of Cokey McMichael on my phone. His real name was Lawrence, but Cokey seemed to fit. He had a broad, pockmarked face, piggy blue eyes, and a receding head of gray curly hair. He looked like the kind of guy that made mothers gasp and clutch their children to their bosom.

Cokey had been arrested on charges of theft, assault, vagrancy, public intoxication, dealing in stolen goods, and a hit-and-run. He was fifty-three years old, five-foot-seven, and weighed nearly three hundred pounds. If things got down to a footrace, I was pretty sure I could ace him.

I sat on the warehouse for a good hour and a half. I left for twenty minutes to use the bathroom and grab some coffee, but soon returned.

Hawk and I had worked out a schedule when Carolina got back that afternoon to make sure she had round-the-clock protection. If needed, we could bring on Vinnie and I might be able to enlist the services of some new friends at Cambridge PD to keep watch on the condo. *Spenser. Loyal as a Labradoodle.*

At about three o'clock, just as I'd started to scroll through my phone for a nearby sandwich shop, I spotted a familiar vehicle roll past me on the access road, drive under the elevated walkway, and park right in front of Cokey McMichael's off-the-grid dealership.

It was a black Chevy Tahoe with plates I recognized. Lou Pasquale crawled out, still dressed in his black suit, and pulled out a cigarette pack from his coat pocket. He cupped his hand around the cigarette and set fire to it.

A second later, a side door opened and a man who resembled a human turtle wandered out. His face was flat and broad, with a complexion like he washed his face with gravel. He had on a ball cap and a black tank top with sweatpants. He clasped Lou's shoulder and they both began to laugh.

Cokey McMichael and Lou appeared to be familiar with each other.

I considered racing up to where they stood and yelling "Gotcha."

Maybe it was just better to know Cokey was working with Frankie Farrell and that Lou was working with Cokey. It didn't take much to connect the key to the headquarters to the Tommy Flaherty International Fan Club.

I reached into the passenger seat and pulled out a Nikon with a lens the size of an elephant trunk. Through the viewfinder, I viewed the jovial interaction between the men. I snapped several shots of the two in action, making sure to find angles where both their faces were in full display. I was nearly certain none of them would grace the pages of *GQ* or *Esquire*, but they might have a chance for the cover of *Livestock Weekly*.

I wondered how much they were paying Lou to keep

tabs on Carolina, or if he was truly hanging on to the tailgate of the Flaherty bandwagon.

By the time Lou had spent the second cigarette, I'd had enough. I watched them go inside the warehouse as it started to rain. I cranked the ignition and turned toward the Back Bay and my office.

When I reemerged from the Sumner Tunnel, I called Rosen.

25

Shit," Rosen said.

"Well," I said. "Yes."

"Shit, shit, shit," he said. "Son of a bitch."

"That, too."

"I mean Lou," he said. "Fucking Lou throwing in with Flaherty's people. I didn't see it coming. I thought he was all in with us."

"I had my doubts."

"And you're sure?"

"Yep."

"Really sure?"

"Lou's meeting up with some unsavory folks who do business with Frankie Farrell," I said. "I even have photos suitable for framing."

"That doesn't necessarily mean he's the one who facilitated the break-in."

"True," I said. "But do you really want to keep Lou around?"

Rosen shook his head. He seemed to deflate in the passenger seat of my car sitting outside campaign headquarters, staring glumly out the window. The rain tapped off the front hood as the windshield wipers intermittently cleared the glass.

"Have you told the police?" he said.

"Nope."

"Good," Rosen said. "The last thing we need is a goddamn scandal two weeks from the primary. Now, that is something that would make Carolina look weak and disorganized. If voters knew her driver was a spy for Flaherty . . . Well, you know how people talk."

"Yep," I said. "Loose lips sink congressional campaigns."

Rosen closed his eyes and dropped his head into his hands. He squeezed his temples with his thumb and forefinger and breathed deeply in and out of his nose. His hair looked to have been styled by an electrician.

"When Lou comes in, I want you to be there."

I nodded.

"You know," he said. "In case he makes trouble. Or denies it."

"He can't deny it."

"I'm sure he'll try."

I reached into the backseat for the camera with the extra-long lens. I turned it on and scrolled through several high-res digital images of Lou having a meet-and-greet with Cokey McMichael in Chelsea. I then proceeded to show Rosen a mug shot of McMichael I'd downloaded on my phone. He was even uglier on screen than he was in person. I didn't think that was possible. But somehow Cokey pulled it off.

"Is that the right thing to do?" Rosen said. "Not charge him?"

"If you could connect him with the break-in, I'd charge him," I said. "But the chances of that happening are about as good as Cokey McMichael beating Usain Bolt in the hundred-meter."

"Quick and easy," he said. "Sure. But I'm so damn mad. I'm just furious we let him in. We talked about really private stuff in that car. He knows everything. Not just pickups and drop-offs but our whole damn game plan. So much of our campaign has been hammered out between stops."

I watched two volunteers walk from the front door of the headquarters—a stylish young black woman in a tight-fitting yellow tee with flared blue jeans stood tall over Monique the scheduler. Monique explained her points with a lot of finger pointing and head shaking. Whatever it was, she wasn't pleased. The young woman laughed, hands on her hips. When she turned, I saw that her T-shirt read WHAT WOULD CGR DO?

"I'm sorry," I said.

"Well, you didn't hire him," he said. "Our polling numbers have been slipping. It felt like Flaherty had been anticipating everything Carolina wanted to highlight."

"At least you know."

"I wish you'd take Lou out back and beat the crap out of him."

"That might not look good for the congresswoman, either."

"True," Rosen said. "But it sure would make me feel a lot better."

The attractive young woman walked back into the office. Monique wandered over to the Honduran restaurant. I guess she couldn't stand it anymore, either. We all had to know about the *pollo frito.*

Rosen appeared deep in thought. He scrolled through his cell phone and then glanced at me again.

"You still having dinner with Carolina tonight?"

I nodded. "I guess she'll be upset when she gets the news about Lou."

"*Upset* isn't the right word," he said. "She'll be both apoplectic and incandescent."

"That means mad, right?"

"Extremely."

Kyle reached out his hand and I shook it. The rain had slackened and the wipers began to make annoying squeaking sounds. I turned them off as Kyle crawled out of the Mustang and hustled back toward campaign headquarters. Just as he ran inside, thunder rumbled and shook the car.

I started the engine and turned back toward Charlestown and my condo. After a long day's stakeout, I looked a little like Leon Ray Livingston's less fortunate little brother. A sitting U.S. congresswoman and a Harvard-educated shrink deserved better.

I would shower, shave, and put on my best sport coat. God forbid, I even entertained the idea of wearing socks.

26

I picked up Carolina and her significant other that evening for dinner at Harvest.

Her boyfriend's name was Trey Shaw. He was white, late twenties, with a casual, unkempt style that went with his zip code. Despite it being in the eighties all day, Shaw chose to wear a plaid flannel shirt and lumberjack boots. He was tall, lean, and scruffy-jawed. Something about him was both goofy and immediately affable.

I held the door open for Carolina and Shaw, and we met Susan at the bar. She set down her vodka gimlet as I introduced them.

"If you're half as good as he says," Carolina said, "you must be wonderful."

"That's nice," Susan said. "But he's only trying to get lucky."

I intertwined my index and middle finger and held them up. Susan looked to Carolina and rolled her eyes.

We gathered together at the end of the Harvest bar.

The congresswoman ordered the house sangria. Shaw and I drank a German-style beer made in Framingham. Susan had on a new seersucker shirtdress she'd bought on Newbury Street. The dress had a neckline with a deep V, and her shiny black hair was pinned up high off her neck. I wanted to reach out, pull her close, and kiss her, but PDAs in such distinguished company might be frowned upon.

It was dark and cool inside, and the polished wood of the bar gleamed in the soft track lighting above. Outside the window, students back from summer vacation milled about Brattle Street. I always looked forward to their return; they gave a good energy, a needed rhythm to Harvard Square that always felt like optimism and hope. The beer wasn't bad, either.

"I was particularly interested in your ideas on police officers in schools," Susan said.

"In another life Susan was a guidance counselor," I said.

"Is that how you two met?" Carolina said.

"Yes," I said. "I was only a junior and knew it was wrong. But Susan couldn't help herself."

Susan shook her head. She elbowed me softly in the ribs.

"Millions are being spent sending cops into schools," Carolina said. "That money could be diverted to much better places. Tutors. Counseling services."

Susan nodded. "All schools could use more counseling services," she said. "Mental health providers for kids are at an all-time low."

I'd been to a few schools in Dorchester where little Johnny might knock your teeth out if you gave him any lip. I also recalled what those damn kids had done to poor Glenn Ford and Sidney Poitier, but didn't comment. Trey Shaw continued to check his phone before feeling the gaze of Carolina and slipping the phone into his back pocket.

"You're a graphic artist?" I said.

Shaw nodded. "I also do some woodworking," he said. "Woodcuts. Some furniture and wall hangings. Right now I'm working with a new boutique hotel in the Seaport."

"I used to fiddle around some," I said. "I once whittled a replica of the statue out front of the MFA. The Indian and the horse."

"There's been a lot of discussion about that statue."

"It's a good-looking statue."

"*The Appeal to the Great Spirit?*" he said. Shaw made an unpleasant face.

"You seem dubious."

"I just think some things should be put out to pasture," he said. "Unless contextualized."

"I better be careful, too," I said. "Or someone might hang a placard around my neck."

Shaw wasn't sure if I was joking before lifting the beer to his lips. He downed nearly half while I tried to pace myself. Susan often remarked I consumed all beverages at the same rate of speed, be it Pappy Van Winkle or low-ethanol gasoline.

We were all early, but I never minded a wait when a

bar was involved. I drank more beer as Susan asked Carolina more about growing up, her childhood, and her parents. It wasn't shrink talk—Susan actually cared about getting to know people. She was a curious person with a deep empathy. Her entire person was turned to Carolina, listening with everything she had, not just waiting for another moment to speak.

"I became my mother's translator," she said. "By the time I was ten, I helped her book jobs and did a fair amount of negotiations."

"Housecleaning?" Susan said.

"Housecleaning, but also work at a lot of downtown offices," Carolina said. "Lots of times at night we'd ride into the city on the T to some tall building to empty trash cans and clean windows. I'd go with her."

"That must've been hard," Susan said.

"Not really," Carolina said. "My mother paid me an hourly rate. I learned a lot about how much time it took to make a decent living. I had my own bank account. As a teenager, I bought my own clothes. Worked some with my father. He says he always wished I'd gone into an honest profession like a mechanic."

"Honest mechanics are few and far between," I said.

"Perhaps you need to quit buying cars old enough to vote," Susan said.

"Classics," I said. "I appreciate the classics."

Susan and Shaw sat on the barstools. Carolina and I remained standing. As we talked, I watched the doorways, glanced at the people flitting past the plateglass window. Mostly students and a gathering of much older women. Not that older women couldn't be threats. I remembered what Rosa Klebb kept in the pointed toe of her shoe.

"Kyle says you might be driving me for a while?" Carolina said.

I nodded. I was surprised they'd spoken.

"He said we need to discuss Lou," Carolina said.

"More on that later," I said. "In private."

Carolina kept eye contact and nodded. She knew everything.

"Loyalty is rare," she said.

"Very."

"People who do what they say," she said. "Word is your bond and all that."

"There's still a few people like that."

"I learned that from my parents," Carolina said. "They never asked for more than they'd agreed upon. I've seen my father fix an engine for free if someone couldn't pay. He knew they'd pay him when they could. I saw my mother take on jobs that were ten times harder than she expected, but never argued about what she promised to charge."

"They sound like admirable people," Susan said.

"My father still works," she said. "Same shop. Same hours. He never went to school beyond the ninth grade but can take apart and put together an engine with his eyes closed. They both taught me to never take on a job that I can't finish."

I nodded. Carolina nodded back.

"Kyle warned me you have a reputation for being difficult," Carolina said. "But I don't find that true at all."

"I'm only difficult to difficult people," I said. "Or those who don't have any honor."

"I think you and my father would get along."

"Does he watch baseball?" Susan said.

Carolina cocked her head and lifted her eyebrows. "He's Dominican," she said. "It's almost a religion."

"Hallelujah," I said.

One of the waiters had recognized Susan and stopped by to say hello. Dining out with Susan Silverman in Cambridge was like taking a tour of the Vatican with the pope.

"Her father is still skeptical of me," Trey Shaw said. He stood up and then finished his beer. "I don't think he believes I have a real job. He thinks I just play around with posters and wood blocks."

"It's hard for a man like my father to wrap his head around making a living being an artist," Carolina said.

"I think it has more to do with us living together," Shaw said.

Carolina shrugged. "Maybe a little."

Susan turned to us. Our table was ready. As we followed the waiter to the table, I glanced about the room, to the front door and then back to the kitchen. I didn't see any danger lurking about but did notice a few of the menu highlights. Oysters and a lovely seared tuna.

I took a seat opposite Carolina. Susan sat across from Kyle. Specials were announced. Menus were handed out. Drinks ordered, although I abstained from another.

Susan looked shocked. Carolina looked up at me.

"I think you're safe to have another beer," Carolina said. "Especially now."

"Lou's not the end of it," I said. "Besides, what would your parents say about me drinking on the job?"

"They wouldn't ever consider it," Carolina said. "But tonight isn't about business."

"It's all business," I said. "Until the primary."

"Excellent point," she said. "Then they won't be able to stop me."

27

Susan drove my Mustang back to her house, where we'd trade cars later. I drove Susan's new car, a dark green Subaru Forester with an actual backseat, to take Carolina and Trey to and from Harvard Square. I'd stick around until three a.m., when Hawk and I would trade duties.

I was wide awake after having two cups of coffee with pistachio white-chocolate cake.

"Susan's lovely," Carolina said.

"None lovelier."

"And you both seemed to get along well," Carolina said.

I looked into the rearview mirror. She was seated with ample space between her and Trey Shaw. Shaw was checking his cell phone, something he did constantly at dinner.

"Not at all like a bickering older couple," she said.

"We bicker," I said. "But artfully."

"And you don't think you'll ever get married?" she said.

Trey looked up from his phone. He looked over to Carolina and then up into the rearview mirror. I felt a little like Max on *Hart to Hart.* I just prayed that my new duties wouldn't require me to wear a cap.

"No," I said. "It's been discussed. But just as quickly dismissed."

I drove slow and easy down Mount Auburn, turning down onto Putnam toward the river.

"Never?"

"Never say never," I said. "But never."

Trey leaned forward. "You don't believe in dated societal expectations, either."

"No," I said. "Susan and I both like being together. But we also like to be alone."

"Absence makes the heart grow fonder?" Carolina said.

"We spend a lot of time together," I said. "But I have my living space and she has hers. We live our own lives. We do our own things. We shop, or choose not to shop, for our own groceries. We do our own chores, work our personal schedules. The messiness of life doesn't bleed into how we feel about each other."

"Wow," Shaw said.

"That sounds exhausting," Carolina said.

"Sometimes," I said. "Especially during rush hour from Charlestown to Cambridge."

"And will you stay there tonight?"

"Later," I said. "When Hawk comes."

"You know," Carolina said. "I've never seen Hawk. I'm not even sure if he's real."

"That's the way he prefers it," I said.

"Why not just leave us for now," she said. "And go back to Susan's?"

"Nope."

I passed the Whole Foods and turned down Prospect Street. We'd had a long dinner and it was past eleven o'clock. I drove slow and easy, the streetlights strobing through the windshield. Carolina rested her head on Trey's shoulder, a pleasant quietness spreading through the car. When I stopped, she reached up with her hand to stifle a yawn. I got out and waited for them to follow.

I'd walk them to the door and then I'd find a new parking spot down the road. Somewhere a dog started to bark. I could smell the river a few blocks away.

It was dim along the frontage to the condos. We had to walk through a parking space for four cars and into a small common area for Trey's second-floor unit. Carolina had just reached into her bag for the keys when I spotted a dark car traveling at a high rate of speed with the headlights off.

I pushed Carolina forward between two of the parked cars as Trey rolled up onto one of the trunks. I barely made it through when the car sideswiped the rear of the two parked cars, bucking the cars forward and taking off a lot of chrome and plastic in a screeching crash.

I reached for my gun and popped up to take aim. The dark car was already twenty feet away and I didn't think firing a weapon in a family neighborhood was a good idea. It was a navy sedan, an Acura, Honda, or Toyota. They all looked the same at night from the rear.

Carolina and Trey made a run for their condo. I told them to call the police while I jumped back into Susan's car and followed.

At Pleasant, the driver made a hard left turn onto Memorial and raced toward MIT. Susan's new ride had a lot of pickup and I closed the gap, moving up around several cars, speeding through two stoplights, the skyline of Boston flickering on the other side of the Charles. I checked in my mirrors to see if we'd drawn the attention of the police, but we were nearly alone, moving in and out of cars on Memorial. A midnight race along the curves of the river.

I saw the Harvard Bridge coming up fast and big, and the sedan launched forward around two cars and disappeared up onto the bridge. I followed, careening hard on the turn, the city of Boston growing closer, bigger, and brighter, office lights flickering in the distance. Pru Center and the Hancock Tower lit up in irregular checkered patterns. The sedan showed itself again in front of another car and zipped ahead on Mass Avenue into the city. If they got any farther ahead, I'd lose them. I'd hoped to either force them off the road or get a better description of the car or the plate. The plate would be stolen, probably the car, too. But losing the car that tried to take out my client would be poor form for a working investigator. Having to explain to Carolina how I lost them wouldn't be any fun. Of course, explaining to Quirk that I was involved in a high-speed chase from Cambridge into the city wouldn't be much fun, either.

As we crossed into Boston and over Storrow, any thoughts of a high-speed chase ended. There had been a ballgame that night and traffic was jammed up into the Back Bay. I was at least four cars back. I almost hopped out to make a run at the car before the light changed and traffic began to flow over Beacon and Marlborough. I made it past two more cars. The driver made it past three. There was a red light ahead on Comm Ave that the driver ignored, nearly getting T-boned by a public works truck in the process, and leaving behind a few cars sliding into a halting, screeching standstill. Horns were blown, Comm Avenue partially blocked. By the time I made it up and around the mess, I couldn't find the sedan. I drove past Newbury Street and spotted a blue Toyota just on the other side of the pike, parked up on a curb by the protective chain-link fencing with the doors wide open.

I stopped and got out, pulling my gun, keeping it out of sight and down by my leg. The Toyota's two front doors were wide open and it was empty. I looked across the street at a bustling after-game crowd along the sports bars and pubs. Lots of folks milling about. I tucked the gun back into my jacket pocket and walked up and down the block. Anyone could get lost in the crowd, especially someone I didn't recognize.

I walked back up the street and crossed over the road to where I'd left Susan's car behind the blue sedan. The flashing hazard lights pulsed on and off.

I had just speed-dialed Quirk when two BPD patrol cars converged on where I was standing. The officers jumped out of their cars, hands on their weapons, and asked that I step back and raise my hands.

I did as I was told.

From the phone in my hand, I heard Quirk pick up.

"What the holy fuck?" he said. "Spenser? Christ."

28

You want to go back and repeat that story?" Belson said. "Maybe leaving out the parts where you committed several speeding violations and broke one or two city ordinances."

"I pursued the assailants with great caution."

"Bullshit," Belson said. "You were playing Steve McQueen across the Harvard Bridge and were lucky no one got killed."

Belson was behind the wheel of his unmarked unit parked on Boylston right behind one of those city bike-rental racks. His boss, Lieutenant Lorraine Glass, sat in the passenger seat, looking less than pleased to see me so early. We wouldn't see the sun for another three hours.

"Cambridge PD says this was attempted murder," Glass said.

"They tried to take all three of us out."

"Maybe it was just a drunk driver clipping a few cars," Belson said.

"Not the way they drove," I said. "If they hadn't gotten jammed up here, we wouldn't have found the car."

Glass had a notebook and a pen in her hand. She pointed out the locations of three different city cameras. She was efficient and precise but shockingly had never been a big fan of mine.

"Got any suspects?" she said.

"Only a few hundred," I said. "But I'm trying to narrow it down."

"Cops found you at twelve-twenty-five," she said. "How long had you been here?"

"Maybe two minutes," I said. "They abandoned the car and ran into the crowd."

"How do you know it was more than one?" Belson said.

"Driver and passenger doors were open," I said. "I also could make out two figures as they drove."

"And Quirk says there have been some death threats?" Glass said.

"Someone has been leaking the congresswoman's schedule," I said.

"And there was a break-in?" she said.

"At her headquarters in Roxbury."

"Yeah," Belson said. "I heard about it. Someone took a crap in her office."

I leaned back into the cool darkness of the patrol car. The nighttime crowd had thinned, most of the bars closed now. I could hear the muffled zoom of cars passing through the Pike underpass where Mass Ave crossed over Boylston.

"Better tell Susan you're gonna be a little late for nooky-nooky time," Belson said.

"Is that what you and Lisa call it?" I said.

"And you and Susan don't?" he said.

"No," I said. "We've never called it that."

Glass ignored us as she took notes, eyeing the position of the cameras. Without a word, she got out of the car and walked over to speak to a plainclothes officer.

"I'm getting the feeling the lieutenant is never going to warm up to me," I said.

"No shit," Belson said.

Glass returned a few minutes later. She made a few notations and then turned back toward me.

"Okay," she said. "How about we cut the horseshit and you tell us everything you know. Who the fuck are these guys?"

"I don't know," I said. "But I do think I know their employer."

"Are you gonna share with the class?" Glass said. "Or just sit in the back of the patrol car stringing us along at three a.m. A goddamn attempted hit-and-run is a little below my paygrade."

"But you'll be glad to take the credit if I find these guys," I said.

"Fuck you, Spenser," Glass said.

"See?" I said, looking up into the rearview mirror at Frank. "I don't think she's ever gonna accept me as part of the crime-fighting team."

"You got that straight," Glass said. "Now, who the hell is behind this?"

"I found out the congresswoman's driver is working for the other camp," I said. "I think he's the one who gave the vandals a key to the back door."

"I heard they busted in the front window," Belson said.

"You heard wrong," I said. "They broke out the front window on the way out. They opened the back door and took their time making a mess of things."

Glass rested her chin on the back of the passenger seat. She stared at me, the crime lights overhead illuminating half her face. She wasn't smiling and made no attempt to fill the silence.

"They work for some nitwits hired by Tommy Flaherty's campaign manager," I said. "Frankie Farrell."

"Fucking Frankie Farrell?" Belson said. "As in the guy who used to polish Joe Broz's pistachios?"

"One and the same."

"Christ, Frank," Glass said. "You got a real way with words."

Belson chuckled and reached into his coat pocket for a half-finished cigar. He let down the window, but before he could light up, Glass snatched the cigar from his hand, opened the passenger window, and chucked it from the car.

"Hey."

"May I remind you I'm your superior officer," she said. "And please remind me how it's okay for a Boston police officer to smoke while on duty."

"Cops smoke," Belson said.

"Not in city property," she said. "Come on. Nothing

else we can do here. I talked to some people at the bar. No one noticed a damn thing. We can pull the feed from those cameras back at headquarters."

I nodded. "Meet you there?"

"Ha," Glass said. "In case you hadn't noticed, hotshot, your little car has been impounded. How the hell do you fit in that car, anyway?"

"It's Susan's car."

"Haha," Belson said. "That's rich."

I didn't answer. Glass rolled up her window as Belson started the car, pulled out, and U-turned to get back on Mass Ave.

"I guess no nooky-nooky for you," Glass said.

"You've been hanging around Frank too long," I said.

"You really think Frankie Farrell would try to kill Flaherty's opponent?" Glass said. "Sounds a little extreme. Farrell's no prize, but I worked with him when he was on the city council. There are bigger assholes in the Cracker Jack box."

"Desperate times call for desperate assholes," I said.

"Like who?" Belson said. "Speaking theoretically."

"Cokey McMichael," I said.

"I used to bust Cokey's ass when he worked with the Burkes down in Southie," Belson said. "Trying to clip someone from behind? No style or planning. Yeah. I could see that on Cokey. Want to bring him in, Lieutenant?"

"Let's see the video first," Glass said. "Maybe Spenser can actually be useful to us for once and ID these dipshits."

29

One man on surveillance video was heavyset, but not heavyset enough to be Cokey McMichael. The other was of average size and build, so average, in fact, that he could be practically anyone. Both men had on hoodies and ball caps.

Glass ran the footage of them crossing Boylston again and again and then tried to connect the pair to more security cameras in the area. I began to have flashbacks to watching game film in college.

"This is why I need one of those wall-sized computer screens," Belson said. "I could pull up secret satellite photos and pictures from every drunk with a cell phone on that street. We can get pinpoint accuracy within ninety-nine percent. Would you believe it?"

"Sure," I said. "Can't wait to see the advances here at BPD."

"Give me a second," Belson said. "And I'll shoot a laser out of my ass."

I leaned back in my chair and Glass stood up to hit the lights. The computer monitors glowed on the laptop computers.

"Can I have my car back?" I said.

"I don't know," Glass said. "Promise to be a good boy?"

I dangled my two front paws in front of my chest and pretended to be panting.

Glass made a call, and by daybreak I had Susan's car back and was crossing the Charles.

On the drive back to Susan's, I decided to call up a sergeant I knew at Cambridge PD and inquire about any Toyotas stolen in the last twenty-four hours. I knew BPD would be doing the same thing, but didn't think there was any harm beating them to the punch.

It didn't take long before I found out a blue 2015 Corolla had been reported stolen at the Porter Square Shopping Center a little past seven o'clock last night. The stolen plates connected to a Kia Sorento boosted more than a year ago in Dorchester.

I bypassed Susan's and a warm bed and headed north to the shopping center just as the sky began to lighten. I wasn't sure what I expected to find. Probably more security cameras, and those security cameras might take the cops to pull the footage.

I parked and checked in with Rosen and Hawk. Carolina was still safe and well and being watched. After I hung up, I got out of the car to walk back to a Dunkin' that had just opened up in the mall. I figured after a long night of work, I deserved two corn muffins and a hot coffee.

Across the nearly empty lot, a lone silver Nissan pickup in the far corner caught my eye. Perhaps someone had car trouble or had left the truck to head out with some friends. Or perhaps the thieves had left their car in the same lot where they stole the blue Toyota I chased last night. In my experience, criminals weren't always clever. Or very bright.

I got back in my car and drove to the truck.

The rear window was filled with antigovernment, antiestablishment stickers. Punisher symbols with crossed AR-15s daring anyone to *Come and Take It.* Another bragged to be an *All-American Infidel.* Not a single *Honk If You Love Jesus* on the entire truck.

I circled back to the Dunkin', properly fortified myself, and then parked close enough to the truck to watch yet far enough away to appear aloof.

I called Susan and updated her on my night.

"I can't believe Belson called it nooky-nooky," Susan said.

"Glass said it, too."

"Is she being any nicer to you?"

"So nice it's started to embarrass me," I said. "My cheeks still hurt from all the smiling."

"She still hates you."

"*Hate* is a very strong word."

"But she finds you intrusive to her work?"

"Quirk did, too," I said. "Once upon a time."

"Might be harder for Glass," Susan said. "You, Belson, and Quirk and all your male bonding."

"She's welcome to join the club."

"Perhaps she doesn't want to become a member."

"'I refuse to join any club that would have me as a member.'"

"Your Groucho is almost as bad as your Bogart," she said, sounding sleepy. "Call me when you're done surveilling. I know you haven't slept since I left you."

I listened to *Morning Edition* as I drank coffee and ate the muffins. At ten, I walked the entire perimeter of the shopping plaza parking lot and returned to my car. At eleven, I did the same thing. By noon, the sun was high and hot above me and the lot was nearly full. I was having fantasies about falling asleep on Susan's couch, Pearl nestled beside me and gently snoring.

I nearly nodded off when I spotted another pickup truck, a maroon Ford with very large tires, wheel into the parking lot and drive to the far end. A thick-necked man hopped out of the Ford and went right for the silver Nissan.

"Aha," I said.

I almost said that the game was afoot out loud. But Susan had warned me against talking to myself. Apparently psychologists frowned upon that kind of behavior.

I watched the Ford wheel away and drive past my windshield before I started the engine. The Nissan truck backed up and drove toward the exit opposite Mass Ave.

Very slowly, I counted to ten. And then followed.

I whispered as I turned the wheel. "The game is afoot."

30

I trailed the Nissan truck up and over the Mystic River, and deep into Malden. Thirty minutes after leaving Porter Square, the truck parked beside a ramshackle two-story house in a ramshackle neighborhood filled with liquor stores, greasy spoons, and corner groceries.

I passed the house, doubled back, and parked at a gas station across Highland Avenue.

I filled up with gas and coffee before moving Susan's car to a lot beside a nearby garage where I could do my job without being seen. The coffee tasted as if it had been made fresh in the last week or two. But I drank it anyway.

I waited only ten or fifteen minutes before another truck pulled up and parked behind the Nissan. It was a brand-new Chevrolet with a camper top over the bed and big mag wheels. Two men dressed in jeans and dark T-shirts crawled out and hopped to the ground. From the distance, they looked nearly identical. A little under six feet, white, with dark hair. One had a beard. The other was scruffy-faced. Both wore sunglasses and walked with a bulge against their right hip.

Five minutes later, a dirty white Ford Explorer drove up and parked along the street. A white man in his fifties or sixties with a white mustache/goatee combo walked up the front steps and headed inside. He had on a khaki-colored sport coat with a bulky object under his right arm. He had the walk and demeanor of a cop.

I'd stumbled upon either a suspicious gathering or a well-armed surprise party.

Out of habit, I speed-dialed Mattie Sullivan.

"I thought we agreed not to talk until I finished studying for the police exam?" Mattie said.

"Are you studying?"

"I'm watching some stupid shit on TV."

"Can you do me a favor?"

I'd noted the address and all three license plates.

"You know you can do that from your phone?"

"True," I said. "But the text is really small. And you're much faster."

"You forgot your glasses?" she said. "Didn't you?"

Out of pride, not dishonesty, I did not reply.

"Okay," she said. "Whaddya got?"

I told her. Twenty seconds later, she gave me the name of the property owner, Cole H. Buckley. He was thirty-eight, with a possible criminal record.

"I'm shocked."

"You know this police test isn't as easy as when you took it."

"When I took it, you had to work by firelight on the cave walls," I said.

"For fuck's sake," she said. "Hold on."

I held on. Mattie inhaled a long breath and let out a low whistle.

"Is that the equivalent to me shouting 'Eureka'?"

"Cole Buckley is a real creep," she said. "Ag assault. Ag assault. Attempted murder. Felon in possession of a weapon. Silver Nissan Frontier registered to him. Give me the other plate numbers."

I gave her the plate numbers for the other three cars. She wrote them down and promised to get right back to me. Being a dogged and curious sleuth, I looked up Cole Buckley from Malden on the Massachusetts Department of Correction site.

He'd served five years for manslaughter. But I'd have to pull his whole court file to get details.

I searched online for any news stories. Coming up empty, I turned to the deep, dark social media accounts. I found Buckley on Facebook with what appeared to be a dead account. He hadn't posted anything for three years.

But his social media feed wasn't altogether unproductive. It appeared he was a member and proponent of a group that called themselves the Minutemen. I was pretty sure this wasn't simply a patriotic society dedicated to preserving the deep and rich history of the Commonwealth.

I jumped from Buckley's page to the Minutemen page. It had been removed from Facebook. I dialed

Wayne Cosgrove and was sent straight to voicemail. I left him a detailed message about Cole Buckley and the Minutemen Society.

The rain set in while I settled into Susan's car with half a cup of bad coffee and the vague memory of the corn muffins. I should've bought an extra when I had a chance.

No one had come out of the two-story house. No one peeked through curtains with a set of binoculars. No one tapped on my window to ask why I was just sitting there. I just sat and waited. If a car pulled out, I could follow, but there wasn't much use. I'd soon know who they were and hopefully what brought them all together in Malden hours after Carolina had nearly been killed.

After about fifteen minutes, Cosgrove called me back.

"Damn if you don't know the finest people."

"You southerners always sugarcoat your news?"

"Always."

"The Minutemen?"

"Never heard of 'em," Cosgrove said. "But I have a friend who works for the Southern Poverty Law Center. They keep tabs on all these nuts. You'd be surprised how many of them we have near us."

"Not at the moment."

"I know the type," Cosgrove said. "These assholes are against a lot more than they're for."

"For instance?"

"They don't like Muslims, Jews, gays, blacks, Hispanics."

"Do they like dogs?"

"Even Hitler liked dogs."

"Big following?" I said.

"Hard to say," Cosgrove said. "Not a lot is known about them. I have some people you can talk to. What's the connection to Carolina?"

"Working on it."

"You're more than working on it," Wayne said. "You have something. What exactly is going on, Spenser?"

"You might want to check with Cambridge PD."

"I don't want to check with Cambridge PD," Cosgrove said. "I want you to tell me."

"Someone took a run at Carolina and her boyfriend last night," I said. "They tried to run her over outside her condo."

"Anyone else know about this?"

"Besides Cambridge and Boston PD?" I said. "I don't believe so."

"And one of these assholes is tied to the Minutemen?"

"Stay tuned," I said. "Sleuthing in progress."

"If you do make the connection," Cosgrove said, "you won't forget about your favorite reporter?"

"Stephen Kurkjian?"

"Screw you."

"Need I remind you, great works are performed not by strength, but perseverance."

"But if there's an arrest imminent," Cosgrove said. "You better let me know."

I agreed and hung up the phone. I stayed on the house another thirty minutes and called Belson as I headed back to Susan's.

31

It was late afternoon and now raining. I opened an umbrella Susan had given me for Christmas and decided it would've looked better in a mai tai than it did in my hand. At least it kept the rain off my head as I crossed through the Northeastern campus and headed into a sleek modern building to meet with Marianne Whitlock, a noted sociologist and the author of several books on the modern rise of white nationalism.

Whitlock ran the largest think tank in the Northeast on the subject, collecting names, locations, and websites often found on the darkest corners of the Web. Wayne Cosgrove called her a virtual *Who's Who* of bigots.

Whitlock's office was bright and airy, with windows facing out to Renaissance Park. Scholarly journals and books, neatly cataloged and arranged in six gray metal cases, lined one wall. Her slim laptop computer sat on an orderly desk with an Aeron chair behind it. I took a seat on a small black leather couch on the right-hand wall.

"Pardon me if I say you look a bit rumpled," she said.

"It's been a very long thirty-six hours."

"May I offer you something to drink?"

"If I have any more coffee, I might just start tap-dancing across your desk."

"I agree," Whitlock said. "It's too late for coffee."

She turned her back, walked to a shelf, and returned with a bottle of whiskey and two square-cut glasses. She pulled the cork from the bottle.

"I thought department heads frown on professors who drink during office hours?"

"They do," Whitlock said, pouring out two neat fingers in each glass. "That's why I do it. Also, Wayne told me you sounded as if you might need one."

"Wayne and I have been friends for many years."

Whitlock was a small woman with hawklike features and brownish hair cut in a blunt bob. She wore a loose and flowy green silk top and black trousers. Not a trace of makeup or jewelry. Both probably reflected the burdens of living in a modern patriarchy.

The front of my shirt and pants were soaked and I'd felt a slight chill walking into the air-conditioning. I took a long pull of the whiskey for the medicinal effect.

"I heard you've crossed paths with the Minutemen?"

I nodded. I tilted the whiskey in the glass, feeling a warm glow in my cheeks, and explained my recent work with Congresswoman Garcia-Ramirez.

"And there was some kind of trouble last night?"

I nodded. "Some men tried to run over Carolina and her boyfriend," I said. "I followed them to their white nationalist clubhouse out in Malden."

Whitlock took in some whiskey. Rain tapped pleasantly against the glass. I could see people rushing in and out of the rain down on the brick mall. Many with umbrellas much more impressive than my own.

"That's Bishop Graves's group," she said.

I nodded. "I was hoping you might be able to tell me more about them."

"The press often doesn't know about these people until it's too late," she said. "No one wants to cover their rallies or hate speeches. They'd like nothing better than to get quoted in the news or have their faces on TV. But Graves is quite the Internet sensation. He wraps up his white nationalism with toxic masculinity and a modern hipster style to recruit restless and angry young men."

"Is he dangerous?"

Whitlock shrugged. "He's arrogant and obnoxious," she said. "He has some schooling. Went to Duke for a master's degree in European history. More than anything, he wants to facilitate the idea that America is a white nation of Western Europeans, and those with that background must do all they can to fight for it."

"What about *E pluribus unum*?"

"You're kidding," she said, "right? They believe that white men should run everything."

"What about white women?"

"Oh," she said, swallowing most of the whiskey.

"They have certain roles in housekeeping and making more white babies. Just not in leadership roles."

"Sounds like something Margaret Atwood would create."

"How do you know the Minutemen are behind what happened last night?" she said.

"I did a little detective work," I said. "That detective work led me to Malden and their clubhouse."

"Did you see Graves?"

"I don't know," I said. "I've never had the displeasure. I followed a man named Cole Buckley. Have you heard of him?"

She shook her head before picking up the bottle and tilting the top toward me. "There's so many of them. We try to keep tabs. I hate to say, their membership continues to grow."

Whitlock poured a little more for us both. "Not bad on a rainy afternoon."

"'The vine still clings to the mouldering wall.'"

"And where did you go to school, Mr. Spenser?" she said.

"Two years at Holy Cross," I said. "And then the Army."

"A literate detective," she said. "How novel."

"I try and keep up with my significant other," I said. "She often reminds me she has a Ph.D. from Harvard."

Whitlock rolled the whiskey around in her glass, smelling its essence or whatever it is you're supposed to do, and took a long pull. Most people I knew just drank the stuff straight from the bottle.

"What almost all these groups have in common is that they all feel like they've been maligned in some way," she said. "That as a straight white man in America they're the victim and are standing up to reclaim what they believe to have always been theirs. It's homophobic, antisemitic, racist, and ultranationalistic. They believe America is a white country and should remain a white country by any means possible."

"Sounds like *Birth of a Nation*."

"Oh, they're not the Klan," she said. "They don't hide who they are or what they do with robes and hoods. This group, and others like them, flaunt who they are and what they do—white supremacy is like a full-time job for some of them. They sometimes wear white shirts to their rallies or protests. They often have fancy facial hair. Beards. Mustaches. Several come from an upper-class background and have money. This isn't just a group of rednecks out burning crosses. Graves brings in young professionals, many he's recruited while in college or straight out of college."

"What's their goal?" I said.

"Chaos," Whitlock said. "I think they just want to see this country crumble and burn and maybe from the ashes they'll be able to build their version of America. They despise seeing whites and blacks together. They use derogatory terms for men they consider weak or soft for not embracing their white male heritage. Again, it's all about persecution. Or a sense of persecution. Graves has a way of finding disassociated young men and giving them a sense of identity."

"With the polo shirts and chinos."

"And the beards and the Minutemen T-shirts," she said.

"Trendy," I said.

Whitlock gave a wry smile. She leaned back in her seat. The rain tapped at her window and sluiced across the glass in diagonal patterns. "Don't fool yourself," she said. "These people have always been here. They've just been more empowered in the last few years to come out to act and speak in ways that wouldn't have been as socially acceptable five years ago. Often these groups ebb and flow with the rise of populism. It often takes a horrendous event to scatter them back into hiding. Like the Oklahoma City bombing in the nineties did to the militia movement."

"How many are there?"

"The Minutemen?" she said. "Oh, I don't know. I only know what we track online. Their numbers, as their egos, are often inflated by Graves himself."

"Have you ever met him?" I said.

She nodded and finished off the whiskey. "I caught him at one of his white-power shows on the South Shore. He was very taken with himself. He's arrogant and pugnacious. He has an obvious hatred of any woman who might challenge him."

"All in all, he sounds like a lovely person."

"To the point, he embodies nothing but hate and division."

Whitlock rolled her chair closer to her desk and flipped open her laptop. She tip-tapped at the keys until she found what she wanted and turned the screen around to face me. "This is him," she said. "Bishop Graves. I think his beard is even longer now. But those eyes. Something in him is seriously disturbed."

I studied the picture and nodded. I knew the beard, the crazy eyes, and the odd haircut. Shaved on the sides and slicked back on the top.

Graves was the man at Carolina's speech at Harvard.

32

I drove back to Charlestown, where I found Susan and Pearl waiting for me.

"You look like crap," Susan said.

"So I've been told."

"Clean yourself up and I'll make dinner."

"Haven't I suffered enough today?" I said.

Susan tossed a red pepper at me, which I caught neatly in my left hand. She had a cutting board out, along with too many of my knives. The rain had intensified on my way back over the bridge. There were flashes of lightning over the darkened skyline of Boston, followed by the brief rumble of thunder.

"The next object I throw is much sharper," she said.

I complied and showered and changed into a pair of fresh blue jeans and a navy T-shirt given to me by a friend at Boston Fire. Susan handed me a bourbon over ice and I sat down on the couch, where Pearl instantly lumbered up and jumped in my lap.

"She still thinks she's a puppy," I said.

"And don't ever tell her any different."

"Carolina has police protection," I said. "For now."

"Then what exactly have you been doing?"

I explained the chase along the Charles in greater detail and shared how my sustaining on corn muffins and coffee led to a Minuteman named Cole Buckley returning to the scene of his crime to retrieve his truck.

"You'd think he'd have someone drop him off if he intended to steal a car," Susan said.

"Might have been an impulse boosting," I said. "Along with the idea of trying to sideswipe the congresswoman."

"And where is Mr. Buckley now?" Susan said.

"Cambridge PD picked him up about an hour ago," I said. "I'm sure he's been highly cooperative."

"Highly," Susan said.

From the couch, I watched her chop peppers, onions, and mushrooms while I rubbed Pearl's ears. Sometimes when we were all together it was as if time had not passed, and we were the same people with the same dog as we'd been many years before. But I knew Pearl wasn't her predecessor or the Pearl before that. Even though they shared the same name, I knew each was a sentient being with their own love and loyalty. Every dog was missed, but having a new one made the pain a little more bearable.

"I don't think they'll stop," I said.

"Of course they won't," Susan said. "Their hatred of her offers these young men purpose."

I told her about Bishop Graves and all I'd learned at Marianne Whitlock's office.

"And you're sure it was him at Harvard?"

"Need I remind you I am a trained investigator?"

"You remind me quite enough," Susan said.

Susan removed a large stainless-steel pot from my cupboard and began to fill it with water.

"Pasta?"

"Just like you used to make for me and Paul," she said.

"Don't forget the raspberry vinegar."

Susan raised a knife by the blade and aimed it in my direction. Pearl looked up from my lap and tilted her head.

"Pearl," I said, pointing toward Susan. "Attack."

"Please."

Pearl lay her head back in my lap. Susan boiled the water and sautéed the vegetables, adding a little olive oil and raspberry vinegar. I had a bottle of Barolo in the cabinet along with some cold beer in the refrigerator. Susan heated up a loaf of ciabatta and she allowed me to grate some Parmesan over the spread.

We both set the table with old china and new linen and some silverware that had belonged to my mother. I opened a beer and the Barolo.

"Double-fisting tonight?"

"Might be my last night off," I said. "For a while."

"I assume she won't alter her campaign stops," Susan said.

I shook my head. I drank a little beer. And then drank a little wine.

"People like this Graves often have nothing to lose," she said. "Being arrested or the threat of being arrested won't mean anything."

"I read the Minutemen don't acknowledge local law enforcement," I said. "They only selectively follow what's in the Constitution."

"And how many of them are there?"

"I don't know."

"Six," she said, "or six hundred?"

I shrugged. "They don't exactly issue an annual report," I said. "But they also don't look that tough, either. This guy Bishop Graves looks like he should be leading a barbershop quartet."

"Need I remind you what they say about cowards?"

"That they die a thousand times before their death?"

"That you almost never see them coming," she said. She spooled up some pasta and took a bite.

"Hawk and I have faced much bigger and much badder."

"But perhaps not so many."

"I might argue that point," I said. "After we eat."

"Can you at least step back?" she said. "And let the police handle it? Resume your work as a bodyguard."

"I prefer the term *security consultant*," I said.

I ate some pasta and then ate a little more. We drank the wine and I poured another glass for us both. The rain intensified and hammered the plateglass window overlooking the Navy Yard. I turned my head to see the lights atop the ships' masts rocking in the harbor.

"You did what you said," Susan said. "You found both a mole in her office and the men issuing death threats."

"Since you encouraged me to take the job, do I get some kind of bonus?"

"And just what were you thinking?"

I thought about it and offered Susan several options for activities on a rainy evening.

"You have quite an imagination."

"Often on stakeouts my imagination runs wild."

"It always does," she said. She set down her fork and looked up at me with her very large and very dark eyes. "What about the baby?"

"I'll put on the end of the game for her."

"What if it goes into extra innings?"

"Even better," I said.

33

I left my car in a garage along Boylston and walked the block over to my office. That morning, the rain was gone and the sky was blue, and it almost felt like being in love.

I cracked open my windows, turned on my table fan, and set about to make more coffee when Lieutenant Lorraine Glass walked into my office.

"Of all the gin joints in all the world," I said.

"Do you ever stop?" she said.

"Christmas," I said. "And occasionally on the Fourth of July."

"Well, it's a long time until both," Glass said. "Put on some for me, too?"

I nodded and did so. A wind came off Berkeley Street scented with that oddly pleasant smell of the city. Diesel fumes and fried foods from the restaurant down across the alley. A trace of cigarette smoke that came from an open door somewhere in the building, although smoking hadn't been allowed for a decade or two.

"Where's Belson?" I said.

"Do you feel better when Frank is around?" she said. "Don't tell me you're one of those namby-pamby men who are afraid to do business with a woman."

"Actually, I prefer doing business with women," I said. "Although from the looks of it, I don't think I'm going to like the kind of business you bring with you today."

"Why do you say that?"

"You have a particular kind of scowl today," I said. "One that reflects immense dissatisfaction."

Lieutenant Glass nodded as she watched me measure out extra scoops of coffee and turn on the machine. I'd tried to use one of those single-serving mechanisms for a while. But there was nothing like a full pot of coffee all to yourself when working a particularly hard case.

"Good work yesterday," she said. "We would have never found those assholes if you hadn't staked out that truck."

"Cambridge would've gotten them," I said. "There were security cameras all over the strip mall."

"Not that reached to that back corner," Glass said. "That's why the assholes got sloppy."

I sat down at my desk, propped up my feet, and placed both hands behind my head. I moved my butt a little to the left and right for a nice swiveling motion.

"No other way to say this," she said. "But Cambridge had to let those two go."

"The assholes?"

"Yep."

I dropped my hands to my lap and my feet to the floor. I leaned into my desk. The coffeepot now making pornographic slurping sounds as it brewed.

"No prints in the vehicle they stole," she said. "No evidence they'd switched cars in that lot. Lawyer got them out in less than twenty-four hours."

"But they're still charging them?"

"They're gonna try," she said. "But we figured you needed to know that guy Cole Buckley is out. Also the owner of the truck that dropped him off, Josh Dillon. Did you know he has a twin brother named Noah?"

"Must come from a solid biblical family."

"Sure," Glass said. "Holy hell, Spenser. Does the coffeemaker always make that noise?"

"Only when it's happy," I said.

"The brothers are both Army vets," she said. "Twenty-five years old. Buckley is another story. Did you see his record?"

"Yep."

"Professional fuckup," she said. "He's been stacking up aggravated assaults most of his life. Charged with manslaughter, but DA couldn't make the case. A B&E. Some minor possession shit. Looks like a head case to me."

"What now?"

"Officially, this is still Cambridge's case," she said. "But BPD kind of frowns on guys who attack our duly elected officials."

"What about Bishop Graves?"

Glass bit the inside of her cheek and nodded. Her hair had been recently cut stylishly, and even shorter than mine. The look suited her. She took a long breath and crossed her legs, the Glock on her hip not appearing to be a distraction.

"Quite a guy," she said.

"He was at the congresswoman's talk at the Kennedy School," I said. "I thought he had an interesting look. Like a Hitler Youth but all grown up."

"If he was at that house in Malden, he was long gone by the time the locals showed up," Glass said. "The only connection we can see between Cole Buckley and the Dillons is through social media. And you might be aware, guilt by association doesn't exactly stand up in court."

"At least we know where the threats are coming from," I said.

"And does that make you feel any better?"

"Nope."

"Or Hawk?"

"Hawk doesn't discriminate," I said. "He looks to everyone as a potential foe."

"Must be a tough way to live."

I shrugged. "Are we any different?"

I stood up and poured out two mugs of coffee. Glass asked for cream and I made sure she got some. I wanted sugar and I made sure I got sugar. I set her mug down on the desk and felt good enough to rest my shoes on the edge and lean back in my chair to sip mine without feeling the danger of spilling. Spilling coffee down my shirt in front of a BPD lieutenant might prove embarrassing.

"Have you spoken to the Feds?" she said.

"Hawk mistook one of their agents for a threat."

"And I hear you know Agent Nguyen."

"We ran across each other down in Georgia," I said. "A few years ago, when he was with ATF. My feelings were hurt a bit when he didn't let me know about his promotion."

"He's kind of a prick," Glass said.

I sipped the coffee. A little wind rushed into my office, flipping up the pages of a yellow legal pad. I set down the mug on top of the pages.

"What do you think they have cooking?"

"The Feds?" I said. "No idea."

"Me, either," she said. "But I'll bet you dollars to donuts that those bastards got something big against this asshole Bishop Graves."

"My thought, too."

"And you're tracking mud and bullshit right through the whole operation."

"But if they're so close to something," I said. "Why didn't they tip the congresswoman off to an imminent threat?"

Glass hadn't taken a sip of coffee. Her eyes were almost sleepy as she stared at my face and tilted her head. "Something bigger," she said. "Something much bigger. What happened the other night must've only been a warning."

"Sure didn't feel like a warning," I said. "They got any closer and I'd have had to go home and sew up the back of my pants."

"If I were you, I'd stick close to the congresswoman," she said. "Everything is theoretical and tactical with the Feds. They probably have known what they're going to do and when they're going to do it for months. Never trusted them. Never will."

"Brothers in arms."

"Do you trust 'em?"

I drank some more coffee. I shook my head.

Glass stood up. She hadn't taken a single sip of her coffee, and steam rose from the mug where I'd set it.

"You're putting in a lot of work for a major crime that's yet to happen."

"You call attempted murder something minor?"

I shrugged. She turned to the door and opened it halfway.

"Oh," she said. "By the way. Noah Dillon is dead. We pulled his body out of a dumpster behind a fucking Papa John's in Eastie. Go figure."

34

After I found Bishop Graves's address online, I drove out to Newton to offer my condolences.

Graves lived in a large, two-story brick house with a steep gabled roof and tall sashed windows set in concrete turrets like an English country estate. As far as I could tell, Graves wasn't employed and hadn't been since leaving college. As I walked up the driveway, the sprinklers ticking across the lawn, I wondered how he made ends meet.

I knocked on the door and was soon greeted by an old woman who said she was Graves's mother.

"Mitzie," she said.

"Hello, Mitzie," I said. "I'm Chuck Lindbergh. Call me Lindy."

She invited me in and offered me a seat across from her on the sofa.

Mitzie was in her early sixties, with well-coiffed blondish hair and very large blue eyes. She wore a turquoise

Nehru jacket with black pants, substantial diamonds on her hand and in her ears, and a gold necklace with intricate designs that looked as if it had been swiped from Tutankhamun. Now I understood who paid the bills.

"And how long have you known my son?" she said.

The room was large, with immaculate white carpet, long flowered draperies, and a grouping of chairs upholstered in a light pink. Everything was clean and airless and didn't seem to have been touched by a decorator since the mid-1990s.

"I've known men like your son most of my professional life," I said. "We were in the Ayn Rand appreciation society."

"You seem a bit older than my son."

"I bloom faster than most," I said. "Thank you for inviting me in."

She nodded and offered me tea and cookies. I accepted the cookies and inquired when Bishop might be home. The trim in the house was all dark wood, with four long steps up to the entryway. The entire house smelled like a museum. After a few moments, she appeared with a tray of fancy little cookies coated in powdered sugar.

"You know, we still call him Jimmy," she said.

"Good ole Jimmy Graves," I said. "What a scamp. What is he up to these days?"

"Oh, I don't know," she said. "He's so secretive about everything he does. He's been that way since his father died."

"And when was this?" I said.

"When Jimmy was a teenager," she said. "Still a little boy. He hasn't told you about the accident? He hates to talk about his father. That's why he doesn't drink. Won't touch a cigarette and won't touch a drop of liquor. I'm very proud of him. He doesn't want to be anything like his father. He wants to be clear of mind."

"I never touch the stuff myself," I said. "Is this Jimmy's full-time residence?"

"Oh, yes," she said. "He moved in after he left Duke for his master's and hasn't had the time to find a place of his own. I don't blame him. He has his own apartment downstairs and still has a mother to care for him. I make sure he eats and that he has clean clothes. He's still a little boy at heart."

"That's so sweet," I said. "When do you expect him back?"

"Back?" she said. "I didn't know he was gone."

She turned to look at the landing at the top of the short staircase.

Graves stood at the top.

I smiled and winked but he didn't seem happy to see me. He had on a white shirt with the sleeves rolled up, a tweedy-looking vest, and dark blue jeans. He stroked his long beard as he stood there, and in the harsh overhead light, I saw his face was fatter than I realized. He was more pale and softer up close and in person.

"This is Mr. Lindbergh," Mitzie Graves said. "He said you two are old friends."

Graves stared down at me. He removed his right hand from his beard and placed it in his right pocket. He had a very expensive-looking gold wristwatch but was dressed as if he needed an old-timey one on a chain.

"Jimmy?" she said. "Are you okay?"

I stood up and walked up close to him. He looked down at me from the staircase.

"I came to talk to you about Noah Dillon," I said. "You must be heartbroken. What a tragedy."

Graves didn't answer. Something very dark and angry simmered beneath the surface.

"You head up some kind of club he was in?" I said. "Arts and crafts. Birdfeeders. Maybe a few resounding renditions of '*Die Hitlerleute.*'"

"Ha," he said. "You have me confused with someone else. I'm no Nazi."

"But you know the song," I said.

It seemed odd to finally hear his voice. The words hanging there in the wide open space of the Graves family foyer in Newton. Mitzie Graves gave a polite little laugh, looking to me and then back up to her son. She seemed confused by the situation, left hand shaking in midair, almost unable to speak.

"What happened to Noah?" I said.

"I don't know what you're talking about."

"Noah Dillon," I said. "His brother dropped off Cole Buckley to pick up his truck after they tried to run over Carolina Garcia-Ramirez."

He tried not to show anything, but he couldn't help smirking a little.

"The congresswoman?" Graves said. "Oh, no. What a shame."

I moved my right foot up and down against my knee while I waited.

"I don't like that woman," he said. "So arrogant."

"But you do know Cole Buckley?" I said. "He has a lovely place in Malden across from a gas station and a liquor store."

Mitzie stood up and walked over to the banister. She looked up at her son.

"Jimmy?" she said. "Jimmy? What is this all about?"

"Leave us, Mother."

"Jimmy," she said.

"Goddamn it, I said 'Leave us,'" he said. "This is between me and Mr. Spenser. Go off and talk to your silly friends."

The words were loud and sharp and left the room with the electric ping like after a gun was fired. Mitzie Bishop lowered her head, rushed up the steps, and disappeared into the big house. She'd left the cookies. I turned back and picked one up.

"You know who I am," I said.

Graves didn't speak.

"I want you to leave the congresswoman alone," I said. "You don't and I'll drive back here to Newton and make sure you'll be whispering sweet nothings into your own asshole."

"I didn't take you to be such a crude man."

"You don't appear to be someone who deals in subtlety."

"The Minutemen is a very large organization," Graves said. "We have hundreds, if not thousands, of members.

I can't be expected to know every person or be responsible for all their actions. We are a fraternal organization with many branches throughout New England."

"White Power Rotarians."

"Is it wrong to be proud of your race?" he said. His doughy face scrunched up and snorted. "Is that so wrong? Spenser. That's a nice Anglo-Saxon name. Are you not proud to be a white man with a white European heritage? Blacks have black pride. Hispanics have their thing. Whatever it is. Why not us?"

"I think the proper term is *Latinx*."

"Spare me all the PC bullshit," he said. "And please don't ever come to my house and harass me over something I know nothing about."

"It appears this is your mother's house," I said. "Jimmy."

"Don't call me that," he said. "And don't come back here ever again. You're not a policeman. I looked you up. You're a nobody."

I took the steps and walked up close to him. "Perhaps you need to look harder."

"Everything I do is pro-America," he said. "Everything I do is to respect our founding fathers. White men discovered this world. We made this country. Our organization wants to see that it remains pure and not diluted with the criminals flowing in from every crack and every border."

I smiled. "Hold on," I said. "There's a little spittle on your lip."

His black eyes grew smaller. Veins bulged in his neck.

I was pretty sure he hadn't enjoyed our talk. From deep within the house, I heard sobbing. Ma was crying upstairs. If I had a son like Jimmy Graves, I'd probably cry all the damn time.

"Goddamn it," Bishop Graves said. "Shut up. All of you just shut the hell up."

I stepped closer. Nearly nose to nose. "Leave the congresswoman alone."

"You better go now," he said. "Or you'll get hurt."

I made sure my lower lip didn't quiver. Beyond my shoulder, something had caught his eye out on the street. I turned to see two men I'd never seen before leaning on my car. I was pretty sure they weren't the welcome wagon, as they had on matching white polos and khakis.

Bishop Graves grinned.

His confidence made me smile.

I nodded at him and let myself out. I could still hear his mother crying upstairs.

I walked down the short drive out to the street and my Mustang. The men were still there, luxuriating on the hood. Each looked as if they weighed half of what I weighed and wouldn't leave any dents.

One man had a similar hairstyle to Graves's, but instead of a full beard, he wore just the Rollie Fingers mustache. I hadn't felt so bad for Rollie since he did those Miller Lite ads. The other guy was older, with greased-back hair and an unkempt beard trained into a point. His eyes were so wide-set that he reminded me of a Boston terrier. The eyes were light and colorless and his face was flushed red. They reposed on my car but didn't look relaxed in the least.

"Don't come back here no more."

"Don't come back here," I said. "*Any*more."

"Yeah," Rollie said. "Fuck off, Snowflake."

I clutched my heart as if it had been penetrated by an arrow and then snatched up the front of Rollie's polo and tossed him about five yards onto Bishop Graves's lawn. If I hadn't been in such a good mood, I would've tossed him onto the street. The Boston terrier came at me swinging and I caught his fist in my right hand and then punched his face three times with my left. His nose leaked out a lot of blood as he dropped to his knees. He grabbed hold of my side mirror as he tried to stand and I kicked him hard in the groin. It was difficult to find replacement parts for classics.

I wiped off my hands on my pants, got in my car, and started the engine. The engine made a reassuring, punctual growl.

I could see Bishop Graves standing in the windows of his mother's house. I honked my horn twice merrily as I left.

No reason to be rude.

35

I didn't notice the tail until I crossed over the canal by the Museum of Science.

The car was black and government-issued and seemed so obvious, they might as well have painted FBI on the hood. I kept the sedan in my rearview as I wound my way over the train yards and under the interstate and back into Charlestown. I made my way in, out, and around the monument to lose them, although I knew they knew where I lived.

It was more of a professional courtesy to try to shake them.

Soon I headed south on Bunker Hill Street and drove back into the Navy Yard. Although one of Spenser's cardinal rules was to never grow complacent, I figured I was home free. I'd darted through a collection of old maritime warehouses back to my condo off First Avenue when I saw two cars blocking the entrance to the street where I lived.

Car doors opened and men in suits and sunglasses got out. I spotted Nguyen in the second car, looking particularly unhappy to visit me. I nodded as he made his way slowly to my driver's-side window.

"Sorry, Officer," I said. "This new car sure has a lot of get-up."

"Why were you in Newton?" he said.

"Hitting the links."

"You play golf?"

"Not if I can help it."

Nguyen shook his head and told me to park the car. He wanted to discuss something with me in private.

"We can't discuss it here?" I said.

"Please move your vehicle," he said. "Me and you are about to take a walk."

"Yippee."

I parked my car and met Nguyen and another agent on a vacant stretch of mall separating two of the large brick warehouses turned into condos. A brisk wind came off the bay while I slid on a pair of sunglasses and walked out to meet them. The other agent was white, a little taller than his boss, and not much younger than me. His hair was silver and looked to have been cut with a laser.

"How do you guys all have great hair?" I said. "Is there a federally funded barbershop I don't know about?"

The agent smiled. A little.

Nguyen did not. Maybe Glass's assessment had been correct.

"Come on," he said. "Smart guy."

We headed onto a brick walkway into the park. It was

cooler under the trees, the air smelling strongly of the harbor and the sea beyond. A young man in a backpack holding a map passed us with a young woman walking beside him with a phone, pointing out he was going in the right direction. I could see the block of buildings facing the shipyards through the trees. Nguyen walked toward the sun, dressed in a full dark suit, a black tie, and spit-polished shoes.

"You're taking exception that I've been proactive on this investigation."

Nguyen didn't look at me. But walked by my side.

"We need you to leave Bishop Graves alone."

"But I enjoy him so much."

"He's a goofball," he said. "But don't underestimate him. He's dangerous. He's a sociopath with nothing to lose."

"I know," I said. "My hands haven't quit shaking since I left the house."

"You're lucky his boys didn't file charges against you."

"For what?" I said. "I was merely helping them up off the street."

"You broke that one guy's nose."

"My hand slipped," I said.

"Of course it did."

We moved into the circle around the Korean War monument. There was a big handsome bronze statue of an American soldier with names of the dead written nearby in marble. The soldier clutched a rifle with a parka over his head, looking bold and determined and very cold.

"They're planning something," he said.

"They already tried something," I said.

"That was nothing," he said. "That was just a run-through for what they had in mind. They were never supposed to get that close to the congresswoman."

I nodded. We both took a seat on a marble bench. It was early afternoon and a group of schoolkids, maybe nine or ten, walked through the western path. Their guide pointed out the monument and the importance of the Navy Yard during World War II. She said women played a big role in the war effort at the docks.

"Take a knee, Spenser," he said. "Okay? I don't have time to jump in my car at Government Center every time you try to screw up one of our investigations."

"You have someone on the inside," I said. "Don't you?"

Nguyen ran a hand over his lean, hard face. He looked into the sun and then back at me. He'd crossed his legs at the knee and his arms across his body. "We did."

"Noah Dillon?" I said.

He didn't answer.

"Just what do they have planned?"

Nguyen shrugged. "Leave Graves alone," he said. "But stay tight with the congresswoman. When all this goes down, you'll be the second to know."

"Who's the first?

"Carolina," he said. "We briefed her this morning. By the way, why aren't you guarding her instead of being a pain in my ass?"

"Hawk's on duty."

"God help us," he said. "A felon on protective detail."

"That was a long time ago," I said.

"You mean the last time he was caught."

I shrugged. Nguyen had me there.

"Want to give me a hint on what they're planning?" I said. "The suspense is killing me."

Nguyen shook his head and stood up. He offered his hand.

"Do I have your word you'll stay away from the Minutemen?"

I shook my head. "For me to do that I need more assurances."

"Will you be at her debate with Flaherty?"

"Wouldn't dream of missing it."

"Okay, then," he said. "You're officially on a need-to-know."

With that, the agent turned and left, disappearing down the brick path.

36

Having much fun?" I said.

"Oh, yeah," Hawk said. "Pancake breakfast for JumpStart. Groundbreaking down in Southie. Watched Carolina shake hands with a thousand folks in the Common. I was on her so tight she forgot I was even there."

"Forget you?"

"Hard to believe," he said. "Fine specimen like myself."

We stood outside the Cambridge City Hall on Central Square, watching Carolina speak to the local news about a plan to bring affordable and safe housing to her constituents. Along the City Hall steps, a dozen or more cops kept watch on Carolina and her team.

"Anything?" I said.

"Nope," he said. "You?"

"I introduced myself to Bishop Graves."

"Do tell."

"I would've invited you to come along, but you might've frightened his mother."

"Man lives with his mother?"

"You know us white boys," I said. "Kind of a Norman Bates bed-and-breakfast over in Newton."

"Damn," Hawk said.

Carolina patiently stood and answered questions. Adam Swift stood at her side, slyly reaching into his oversized bag and passing her a bottled water while she was peppered with questions. The day was blue and bright, lots of Cambridge-type bicyclists passing by, including an old guy towing a short trailer filled with recyclable plastics.

"You convince Graves to forsake his racist ways?"

"I did my best," I said. "I did leave an impression on a couple of his Minutemen. They are surprisingly light. And fly through the air with the greatest of ease."

"Haw," he said. "Those boys try and brace you?"

I nodded.

"Almost don't seem fair."

I shook my head. Across Mass Ave, a used-book seller had set up some folding tables with boxes of old books, magazines, and records. He was white-haired and wore a pair of headphones, flipping through an old magazine while waiting for customers. Down the path by the bus stop, three homeless men had gathered, sharing a bottle wrapped in a brown paper bag.

"These guys aren't tough," I said. "But they are inscrutable."

"No honor," Hawk said.

"Nope."

"No code."

I shook my head. "Not a bit."

"So what do they want?" Hawk said.

"Chaos," I said. "Dissension. They want to tear it all down and watch it burn. They want to turn the white folks on the black folks. Especially those with common goals."

"Damn," Hawk said. "And me and you just got to be friends."

Hawk had on a black linen sport coat. The outline of his .44 Magnum barely noticeable under the perfect cut and drape of the jacket. But it was there. Accessible and handy and ready to restore order at any moment.

"What these folks got?"

I told him about my second meeting with the Feds, the dead Minuteman's twin named Noah Dillon, and Nguyen's reluctance to fight crime cooperatively.

"Those boys gonna make a run against Carolina," Hawk said.

"Certainly appears that way."

"But that little Fed won't tell us where or when."

"He says they got it all in hand."

"Shit," Hawk said. He drew out the *I* for emphasis.

"Do I sense apprehension?"

"Those boys in suits wouldn't say shit if their mouth was full of it."

"Nguyen says we're on a 'need-to-know.'"

He said "Shit" again. Again with the same emphasis.

Hawk handed me the keys to the SUV parked nearby and disappeared down the street toward a Middle

Eastern café he frequented. He said they had the best hummus and tabouli in Boston. I wasn't sure where he was going after or how he'd get there and didn't ask.

I followed the walkway into the shadow of City Hall, a big handsome Victorian made of granite and brownstone with an impressive belltower. I moved closer to Carolina as she spoke about upgrading the Boston transit system and helping undocumented immigrants gain access to healthcare and legal aid.

Adam Swift caught my eye and I met him by the driver's-side door.

"Second team has arrived," Swift said.

"Second team?"

"Hawk's words," Swift said. "Not mine."

"That's okay," I said. "That's his insecurity talking."

"Hawk says he taught you everything you know."

"Lucky that didn't take too long."

Swift had on a seersucker suit with pink stripes with a white button-down, a bluish tie, and a matching show hankie. In the bright midday sun, his hair seemed even more blond. He looked up at Carolina and then glanced back down at his phone.

"Won't be much longer," Swift said.

I held up the keys in my hand. He nodded. "I know Lou was a spy for Flaherty," Swift said. "But I kind of miss having him around."

"Even after your offices were broken into and ransacked?"

"He brought me coffee in the morning," he said. "Two creams. Two sugars. And all the local papers."

"Hawk didn't bring you coffee?"

"Hawk barely spoke," he said. "Except for letting us know when the second team was on the way."

We continued to watch Carolina as she shook hands with two city council members and thanked the local media for coming. It was all reporters and cameramen. A few onlookers stood close by on the steps, watching. A young woman in yoga pants carrying a straw purse, a middle-aged black woman with cornrows and a dashiki top. She clapped as Carolina walked back toward the car. There was a youngish white man standing off to himself on the lawn, wearing jeans and a T-shirt and carrying a red backpack.

Swift and I joined up with Carolina and walked down to the SUV parked along Mass Ave. The white man with the red backpack continued on toward us. I watched him out of the corner of my eye as we got close to the SUV, my right hand loose and ready at my side.

The man was thin, with receding blond hair. His T-shirt advertised a place called TRINA'S STARLIGHT LOUNGE. He seemed nervous and fidgety.

He dropped the backpack off his shoulder and reached into it. My hand went into my coat.

I felt for my gun as the man smiled and asked if he might get a picture. Swift looked to me and closed his eyes for a moment, letting out a long breath. She posed for the picture and then followed us to the SUV.

"Okay?" Swift said.

I nodded and opened the back door for Carolina and then settled myself in the front seat. Swift was still chatting with the fan of the congresswoman and two of the cops.

"I just had a call from the local office of the FBI," she said.

"I heard."

"The special agent in charge urged me to fire you and work directly with his people." I watched her in the rearview mirror and saw she was no longer smiling as she had for the cameras. She just looked right at me, her face tight and jaw clenched. "I was told you would only make things worse for my campaign."

"The new Boston SAC isn't a fan," I said. "He and I had a run-in down in Georgia a few years ago."

Carolina nodded and tilted her head to look up into my eyes in the rearview.

"What the hell is going on, Spenser?"

"Someone is going to make a run at you," I said. "The Feds know it. And they don't want me to get in the way."

"God."

Swift opened the passenger door and crawled in beside Carolina. He looked to Carolina and then back to me. He pulled the show hankie from his seersucker jacket and dotted his forehead. "Oh, no," he said. "Did I miss something?"

"I need you to get Special Agent Nguyen back on the phone," Carolina said.

"And?" Swift said.

"Tell him that my personal security is my business," she said. "And if he can't work with Spenser, that's his own damn problem."

37

Noah and Josh Dillon's father, Max, lived in Salem in a run-down yellow two-story across the street from a cemetery. The house was surrounded by a six-foot fence made of split landscaping posts with a tall gate warning that the occupant was both armed and dangerous. There was a replica of a ship bell that I reached up and tinkled. The tinkling wasn't loud or very tough-sounding. But being a tenacious bastard, I tinkled again.

I heard a door open behind a fence and steps down a rickety staircase. "What the fuck do you want?"

"Peace, love, understanding," I said. "Why do you ask?"

"You're the one ringing the fucking bell."

Without seeing him, I told the man who I was and what I wanted. There was a long silence before I heard more creaking steps and the back gate open. He looked through a narrow slot. His breath smelled like a Jim Beam truck had jackknifed down his mouth.

"Kid's dead," he said.

"I know."

"It's his mother's fault," he said. "His goddamn mother."

"Can I come in?"

"I ain't got nothing to say," he said. "Nothing to tell you. A bunch of reporters called me up, too. Wanted to ask all kinds of stupid questions. How the fuck I'm supposed to know about those boys? We don't even talk that much. Their mother. *Jesus.* Their goddamn mother."

"Are you curious as to what happened?"

There was a long silence. His face disappeared behind the door. I waited for the gate to close again, but then I heard the rattling of a chain and it swung open. I was glad I didn't have to tinkle the bell again. It might have bruised my fragile male ego.

"This can't take too long," Max Dillon said, moving on ahead of me. He was stoop-shouldered and skeletal, with a bald head and lots of white scruff on his face. He had on well-worn chinos, a black sleeveless Bon Jovi T-shirt, and unlaced work boots. "I gotta go to work."

"Where do you work?"

"Quarry," he said. "Is this gonna take long or what?"

By the back windows there was a dinette table like everyone's favorite mother had back in the sixties. A white wicker lamp stained with age and nicotine hung on a gold chain. A couple of prints advertising Rome and Paris hung on the wall.

Dillon lit up a cigarette and leaned against the back of

a stove that had been pulled from the slot in the kitchen. "Well?"

"When's the last time you spoke to Noah?"

"Shit," he said. "I dunno. He came by around Christmas and brought me a six-pack and a carton of Benson and Hedges. We drank some beer and watched some TV and he left. Don't ask me about his brother. Something fucked-up happened to that kid in the Army. He's got the shell shock or something."

"I don't think they've called it that since the Great War," I said.

"PTSD or whatever," he said. "Ever since he got home he'd been on meds that either make him nutso or leave him crying in the goddamn closest. What were you saying about Noah? You think you know what happened to him?"

"I have some idea," I said. "Noah ever talk to you about the Minutemen?"

"Ha," Max Dillon said. He scratched at the white whiskers on his chin. Even though the man was a decade or so younger than me, he looked thirty years older. "He was into all that shit. They wouldn't take jobs I got 'em because they told me that the great race war was about to begin. I said to them, 'Okay, then. Think you can give me a heads-up so I can quit at the fuckin' quarry? Might need some time to stock up on beer and ciggies before the bullets start to fly.'"

I leaned against the window frame. The light was soft and weak coming through the glass. Behind the house a rusted jungle gym and a rotten picnic table stood among yellowed grass. A white Plymouth Neon without wheels sat up on blocks.

"You don't share their views?"

Dillon shrugged and blew cigarette smoke out his nose. "That there's about to be a big war?" he said. "I got too much shit to do to get pulled into that crazy mess. I try to talk sense. But they're kids. Or act like kids. I don't know."

Dillon shook his head. He pulled out a fresh cigarette. He looked at his watch and then back at me.

"You think this Minutemen shit has something to do with what happened to Noah?" he said. "The cops told me they thought it was about drugs. If it had been Josh, I would've believed it. But Noah was clean. He drank some beer. Maybe smoked some weed. But he wasn't into all that shit. He hated drugs. And hated the goddamn zombie his brother had become."

"You ever meet a man named Bishop Graves?"

"No," he said. "But I seen him on the Internet. My boys think he really fucked the moon. They buy his T-shirts and go to his rallies. They think I'm the one who's stupid and not paying attention. Who's got time for that crap? I don't know. Their mother met this guy and he had a real hard-on for blacks and spics. You know. I think that's where they come into all this."

"Know a guy named Cole Buckley?"

He shook his head. "Another Minutemen fuckwad?"

I nodded.

"Noah trusted people," Dillon said. "He always

trusted people. I thought if he came to work with me after he got out of the Army, that might toughen him up. The kid didn't even make it a week. Took some job spraying for fucking bugs. He spent every free moment on the Internet, chatting with people he's never met in his life. When his mom and her boyfriend kicked him out, he came over here. When I couldn't stand him sleeping all day and staying up all night, I kicked him out, too. I guess that's how he met up with these assholes."

"Have you talked to Josh since Noah's death?"

He nodded. "Just funeral shit."

"You think you can get him to talk to me?"

Max Dillon scratched at his chin some more. He eyed me through the smoke. "You really think you can find who killed my boy?" he said. "Or are you just fucking with me, too?"

"I want to get the guy who killed your son."

"Fucking A."

"Words, if not wise, at least well learned."

38

"Do you think the brother will talk to you?" Susan said.

"Josh Dillon would have good reason to turn his back on the Minutemen."

"Brothers have been known to kill one another before."

"Don't I know it," I said. "I worked the Cain and Abel case."

Susan didn't smile. She often resisted my humor in her search for greater psychological meaning. I couldn't blame her. We were in her office, between patients, and I'd decided to lie across her settee. I wasn't sure if the piece strictly met the definition of a settee, but I knew it was much fancier than a plain couch.

"Do you have to do that every time you're in my office?"

"I've been having fantasies," I said. "Very dirty ones, in fact."

"This is a professional office."

"I think I'm in love with my therapist," I said. "Would you please join me on the settee to discuss."

"It's just a couch."

Susan got up from behind her desk and walked over to the sliding doors that closed off the private office. She rolled them open and whistled for Pearl, who bounded in and took a flying leap onto my crotch.

"Was that strategic?" I asked.

"Very."

"Good thing you don't want kids."

Pearl lapped at my face. I rubbed her neck. She ran off into the other room for a tennis ball and promptly returned with a slobbery yellow Wilson.

"Did you get a feeling for why these men were drawn to this organization?" Susan said, returning to the subject at hand.

"I think calling it an organization might be a bit of an overstatement," I said. "It's more like a club."

"A club with very specific requirements."

"Yeah," I said. "I had to break it to Hawk that he couldn't join."

"And you still don't have an idea of the membership?"

"It could be fifteen," I said. "It could be five hundred. It appears most of their communications are in secret chatrooms. Encrypted messaging systems."

"That's part of the allure," she said. "Most cults, or fringe groups, cultivate those who don't have a family and then give them a family structure."

"Max Dillon didn't seem like a great parent," I said. "But not awful, either. He said his ex-wife's new boyfriend had some pretty extreme views on people of color."

"And if you meet Josh Dillon what can you say to combat those views?"

"I'll let him know I'm under the influence of a comely Jewish shrink."

Susan again didn't smile, but it looked like a true struggle. She swung around in her swivel chair and placed her heels on top of her desk. Pulling a pencil out of the drawer, she began to tap at her lower lip with the eraser.

"What about my dreams, Doc?" I said.

"I spoke to a former teacher at Harvard," she said. "She has some experience in studies on those with extremist views. She said the ones who are most successful at getting out are those who can find bonds with other groups. Some might start a new job or get into a new relationship. Something that pulls them away from the family patter of the club."

"Are you suggesting I take Noah Dillon's brother out for ice cream?"

"No," she said. "But try and build trust with him. Bring up something to anchor him back to when he was a boy. Maybe the father could help you recall some better times before the kids joined the Army."

"Max Dillon said Josh suffers from PTSD," I said. "Although he called it 'shell shock.'"

"No one's called it shell shock since—"

"I know," I said. I held up the flat of my hand. "Trust

me, Max Dillon has much deeper problems than his terminology."

"You think by getting closer in with the members, you can make these threats stop?"

I shook my head. "Nope," I said. "But I am pretty sure that Josh Dillon won't like me annoying his dear old dad and will most definitely agree to meet with me."

"To scare you off."

"Maybe."

"Or kill you."

"They'll try."

"But not succeed."

"If these guys succeed," I said, "Hawk would never let me rest in peace."

"That's the best reason for staying alive?"

"That," I said. "And some other things."

Susan stopped tapping with her pencil. She stood up and walked over to her window facing Linnean and closed the blinds. The room was very cold and very quiet. I tossed the ball into the next room.

Susan smiled. She closed the door behind Pearl.

Pearl scratched at the door and then stopped. Susan moved over to the desk and sat at the edge. She had on a cream silk blouse with a knee-length black skirt. Her hair had been pulled into a ponytail and her eyes were very brown and luminous.

"How exactly are you and Hawk going to reason with this group while also protecting Carolina?"

"Well," I said. "I'm working on a short list of additional resources."

"Anyone I might know?"

"Most definitely," I said. "I'll explain later. Can we continue on with the therapy?"

"I have a client due within the hour."

"I can work with that."

"What about the baby?"

"She and I both know what you were doing when you closed the blinds," I said.

"Maybe the sun was getting in my eyes."

"Maybe," I said. I patted the leather cushion next to me. "Come join me on the settee and let me tell you all about my dreams."

39

Josh Dillon called me early the next morning.

"This Spenser?"

Since I'd answered the phone that way, I presumed the answer was obvious. But I gave him the affirmative anyway as I leaned back in my office chair.

"My old man said you wanted to talk to me."

"This is true."

"Says you think maybe I know something about who killed by brother."

"Also true."

"Well, I don't," he said. "And why don't you leave my old man alone. He's a drunk and a fuckup."

"Tell me about it in person."

"What difference would that make?"

"I'd like to assist your family in finding out what happened to Noah," I said. "I know you and every one of the Minutemen are just heartbroken."

"Noah's dead," he said. "And I didn't have nothing to do with it."

"Didn't say you did," I said. "I hoped you might answer a few questions."

"Shit."

"I promise it will be quick and painless," I said, lying through my teeth on one and possibly both counts.

"If I meet with you will you leave my father alone?" he said. "And quit bugging me. My mother said you called fifteen times."

"My word is my bond."

We agreed to meet in Concord on the walking trail at the battleground park. I figured it was open and full of enough people to dissuade an ambush by a wannabe militia. Hawk was too busy guarding Carolina to be taken off his duties. Although I'd never call them "duties" to Hawk. Hawk was dutiful to no one but himself.

I parked in the narrow lot fronted by a low stone fence. I had Pearl with me that day and figured she could get a little exercise and provide emotional support for a grieving brother.

It didn't take long to find Josh Dillon. He was the only one on the walking trail wearing a bright yellow Minutemen T-shirt emblazoned with the DON'T TREAD ON ME snake from the Gadsden flag. Subtle. He nodded at me from behind a pair of narrow black sunglasses.

He looked very much like the picture of his brother, but not identical. He had a long black beard and wore a ball cap over a shaved head. I'd often thought white men looked terrible with shaved heads, and Josh Dillon was no exception.

"Nice dog," he said.

"The best."

"I like dogs."

I nodded. "'Louis, I think this is the start of a beautiful friendship.'"

"Josh," he said. "My name is Josh."

Josh and I followed the trail populated by schoolkids and walkers, both young and middle-aged, old and older. We headed into the open green spaces of the original battlefield where the North Bridge spans the Concord River. Sometimes I thought I could hear the sounds of fife and drums.

"Josh," I said. "I think Bishop Graves had your brother killed."

"That's a lie," he said. "Bishop wouldn't ever do that."

"Nope," I said. "It's a fact. Did you know your brother was working as an informant?"

Josh didn't answer. He just kept on walking beside me as he headed toward the bridge. Pearl trotted beside me, pleased to be out of the house and out for a little exercise.

"Graves is the only person who'd want it done," I said.

"No fucking way," he said. "Noah was like his family. He would've told me. He would've let me know what was going on."

"You mean Bishop would've done it himself?"

"I didn't say that."

"But you knew that your brother was turning on your fellow Minutemen?"

Dillon didn't answer. Silence may be complicity. But it also seemed to be an affirmation in Josh Dillon's case.

"You're just trying to make trouble," he said. "You work for that dumb bitch congresswoman. She hates men like Bishop. She wants to turn America into a godless communist nation. She hates what we stand for."

"And what exactly do you all stand for?"

"The right to be a proud white American male," he said. "Don't lie and tell me that you're ashamed of your race."

"You know," I said. "I never gave it much thought. Other than the fact I know I've been afforded many opportunities some don't have."

Dillon snickered. The sound rousted Pearl and she turned back to look over her shoulder. Besides having an incredibly sensitive nose, she could also detect bigots at under five feet. The trail was crushed rock and smooth. Up ahead, two men in period dress read pronouncements to schoolkids by the bridge. It was too hot a day for powdered wigs.

"May I ask what makes you place your confidence in a guy like Graves while turning your back on your own brother?"

"Bishop is a great man," he said. "He sees things that you can't. He's not persuaded by so-called journalists or people who brag about their degrees. He can't be manipulated or controlled."

"Good for him," I said. "Did you go to college?"

"What the fuck does that have to do with anything?" Josh said. "But yeah. I went to UMass in Lowell for a while. That's where I heard Bishop speak for the first time. He was talking at the student union, saying things that I never heard anyone say out loud. He made me feel proud of my race and proud to be a white man. Just in case you haven't noticed, things are going to hell in this country. The blacks and wetbacks want to turn the U.S. into a socialist shithole. Why would I stand for that? Why would you stand for it? Think about it. We're standing right here. Isn't this where the first blood was spilled in the Revolution?"

"I was hoping you'd notice the irony."

"I'm not some dumb hick," he said. "I am alive and aware of taking a stand for what makes this country great."

"Hooray."

"I won't be replaced," he said. "Bishop Graves is making sure we keep America run by actual Americans. That's the blood that was spilled where we're standing. And it might be spilled again."

"Lot of people died on both sides here," I said. "For a very different reason."

Pearl had taken that moment to perform her daily constitutional. Although sometimes she performed her duties more than once. "What if Bishop did have your brother killed?"

"Noah had problems."

I'd walked a little off the main path, but Pearl's morning miracle was still close to pedestrians. I bent over and picked it up with a plastic baggie. *Spenser. Professional pooper scooper.*

"We all have problems," I said.

We walked a little farther. I liked the battlefield and the excited energy of the schoolkids out to learn about American history. I knew our nation's history wasn't perfect, but there were many moments to be proud of. Especially when it came to standing up to blowhards and bullies.

"Noah got himself into something he couldn't get out of," Josh said. "He should have never turned his back on the brotherhood."

"You're his brother," he said. "Not Bishop Graves. Bishop Graves is a thirty-six-year-old weirdo who's unemployed and lives with his mother in Newton. Not to mention, he makes her cry."

"What's done is done."

I tossed the baggie into a small metal trash can close to the bridge. Pearl tugged at me to cross over the river. Josh Dillon folded his arms across his chest and turned his head to spit.

"Only reason I came was to give you a warning," he said. "Back off that bitch or something bad is going to happen to you."

"Eek."

"She chose her side, and if you want to get caught in the middle, that's on you."

"Are you going to try to run her over again?" I said. "That was pretty cowardly."

"A war is coming," he said. "Think about it."

Josh Dillon squatted down and patted Pearl on the head. If he hadn't been so kind to her, I might have drop-kicked him off the bridge. "Sorry your dad's been a disappointment," I said. "But joining up with a guy like Graves won't end well. You're either going to get free one day, if you're lucky, or end up like your brother."

"My brother was a traitor."

"Your brother found a way out."

Dillon took his sunglasses off and tucked them into the neck of his Minutemen T-shirt. I wondered what other kind of swag the group sold. Coffee mugs. Panties. Athletic socks and do-it-yourself anarchist kits.

I reached into my pocket and took out my card. He looked at it in my hand and then turned his head to spit again. I was beginning to think he didn't like or trust me. At least he liked Pearl. But then again, Hitler would've, too.

"Get the fuck out of our way," Josh said.

I watched as he strutted off, cocky and arrogant and flying high on Bishop Graves's homemade Kool-Aid.

I didn't think he'd turn. But I had to try.

40

When I returned to Roxbury to switch up with Hawk, I found three suspicious-looking government vehicles parked at the strip mall. Hawk was inside campaign headquarters, seated in a chair beside Monique, saying something that made her laugh.

"How come you don't laugh at my jokes?" I said to the receptionist.

"Because you ain't funny," Hawk said.

"Is that true?" I said, clutching my heart.

Monique shrugged and went back to something more interesting on the screen. Hawk stood and motioned his head back toward the conference room.

"Nguyen and two suits just showed up," he said. "They in there with Carolina and Rosen. No one else invited."

"Don't you find that offensive?"

Hawk grunted. We walked back to the conference room and I opened the door and walked inside.

"Knock, knock," Hawk said.

"Do you mind?" Nguyen said.

The man was seated at the head of the oval table. His hands were steepled and he was leaning toward Rosen and Carolina. He seemed to be making a very pressing and urgent statement that he didn't wish for me to hear.

"Not at all," I said.

I sat down at the opposite side of the table. Hawk leaned against the wall in a menacing fashion. He had on a very tight black T-shirt and his arms looked capable of tossing all three of the Feds through the front window with very little effort.

"This is confidential," Nguyen said. "Need I remind you I am the special agent in charge of Boston."

"The cheap shoes were a dead giveaway," I said. "Carolina?"

She met my eye and nodded. "Spenser and Hawk stay," she said. "They need to hear everything you're saying in case they have questions."

I looked to Nguyen and winked. His jaw tightened and he swallowed, still keeping the steepled fingers across the desk. He glanced up at the two men over his shoulder and then back to me.

"They're going to make a run at the congresswoman," he said. "After the debate."

"Then we call off the debate," I said.

"No way," Carolina said. "Nothing changes."

"They don't want to hurt her," Nguyen said. "Not now, anyway. They want to kidnap her and take her up to some place where they do their training. A place up in

Maine. They want her to be able to answer for her crimes."

"I hope you have detailed plans to thwart this effort?" I said.

Hawk looked over at the two Feds. One of the men shuffled in his suit to show off the butt of his gun. Hawk nodded and flexed his biceps in syncopation.

"They plan to hold a trial for her," Rosen said. "They want to convict her of treason."

"And if she's guilty," I said, "I guess that doesn't mean a trip to Disney World."

"No," Nguyen said. "It does not. But we'll be there. We will have the entire banquet room at UMass loaded with agents. If one of Graves's people so much as scratches their behind, we'll have them. Their plan is to take her as she's leaving."

"And how would they get away?"

"They have a boat," he said. "They think they can get her out that way."

"Do you have a boat?" I said.

"We have three," Nguyen said. "Trust me. We have every angle covered."

"Last time I heard that was from Freddy the Fence in Quincy," Hawk said. "Never could trust that motherfucker."

Carolina's face tightened with the talk of plans for her. She chewed her lower lip as she contemplated. Not once did she ask Rosen a question or look to him for guidance.

"Can you get all of them?" she said.

Nguyen didn't answer. His hair was parted slick and

neat across his forehead. His suit was black and funereal, but his tie and show hankie were a festive red.

"Do you have someone else in the organization?" I said.

Nguyen didn't answer. I was worried that his action would be as forceful as his talk.

"Or is this old intel," Hawk said. "From the dead kid?"

Nguyen didn't answer. "This abduction has been planned for a long while," he said. "A lot of things had to be set in motion. We don't think they'll deviate from it."

"And Graves?" I said. "Will you get him there, too?"

Nguyen leaned back in his chair and let out a long breath. He looked to Carolina and then Rosen and then fixed his stare somewhere beyond me in the windowless room.

"He's very well insulated."

"And without your star informant," I said. "You're just hoping this all comes together."

"It's a little more complicated than that, Spenser," he said. "I know you come from a limited experience in law enforcement."

"Deeply colored by my run-ins with bureaucrats," I said. "I don't think using the congresswoman for bait is much of a plan."

Hawk pushed off the wall and walked out the door. I stood up and planned to do the same. Solidarity.

Carolina stared down at her hands as Rosen looked up at me with wide eyes, shaking his head.

"We'll get Graves," Nguyen said. "We'll get all of them. Our intel is solid."

"And what if it's not?" Carolina said.

"Then we keep trying."

"Someone slipped up," I said. "That's why Noah Dillon is dead."

"Noah Dillon is dead because he tried to deprogram his stupid brother," Nguyen said. "We all have to keep our mouths shut and stick with the plan."

The Feds left with few other words. I stayed behind with Carolina and Rosen. Rosen took to pacing the room, running his hands through his frizzy hair and muttering all the reasons Carolina should just cancel. Or at least try to reschedule. I decided it wasn't the time to ask about the overtime I'd accumulated.

"I'm not afraid of them," she said. "You and I know that once these assholes are gone, more will replace them. I trust Agent Nguyen. I'll be fine."

My stomach felt a bit uneasy. I knew what Rosen was thinking and he knew what I was thinking. But both of us knew there wasn't a damn thing we could do to change her mind.

"The debate," Rosen said. "We have to focus on the debate."

"Sure," Carolina said. "But at the moment, it's kind of hard to memorize talking points."

41

That night, while the Feds kept watch on Carolina and Trey's condo, Hawk and I drove to the airport.

"Little man thinks he got the whole thing wrapped up."

"I hope he can get to Graves," I said. "It's hard to defend your plan when your star witness is dead."

"Maybe if we stand back, these motherfucker Minutemen just kill off each other."

"Where's the sport in that?"

"Give me a reason," Hawk said. "I'd be pleased to thin the herd."

"You don't think they're entitled to their First Amendment rights?"

"To marginalize and vilify people of color?" Hawk said.

"I withdraw the question."

Hawk drove in silence along the Mass Pike and into the Ted Williams Tunnel. The fluorescent lights created a strobing pattern in his Jag. Hawk played a CD while he drove. *The Best of Charley Pride.* I was beginning to detect a theme. It was only a matter of time before Hawk purchased a Stetson.

"Nguyen tell you to quit doing your thing?" Hawk said.

"Yep."

"What we supposed to do when the bogeymen try and disrupt the debate?"

"Whistle Dixie."

"I ain't never whistled Dixie in my life."

"How about 'Don't Take Your Guns to Town'?"

"Haw," Hawk said.

"You ever going to tell me why you want me to find this woman, Dominique?"

"Yeah," he said. "When you find her."

"Must be some woman," I said. "After all this time."

"Mm-hm."

"You've had dozens."

"Hundreds."

"You and Wilt the Stilt."

"Some you remember more than others."

"And some women you can never leave."

"I didn't leave."

"Oh."

"Wasn't like that," Hawk said. "Was nothing like that. Another time. Another place."

Hawk's voice had some edge to it. I didn't push. We headed down into the lower level at Logan and slowed in front of the baggage pickup. I checked my phone and directed him toward the next doorway. Hawk wheeled around three cars and pulled into the arrivals lane.

"Tomorrow we stick on Graves."

"Oh, boy," Hawk said. "Those white boys gonna love me."

"They bother Carolina," I said. "And we reciprocate."

"You trying to throw Graves off his game."

"That's the idea," I said. "He's holding a rally in the Common tomorrow to appeal to all able-bodied white men to stand up against the tyranny of all you darker people."

"Too afraid to march in the 'Bury."

"Wouldn't you be?"

Hawk slowly drove up to the entrance of the airport. I watched the sliding doors. A middle-aged white guy wheeled out a suitcase. He looked like he'd passed through Dallas/Fort Worth twice. A couple in their twenties followed, looking up and down the pickup lane. She pointed one way. He pointed another.

"Good to have backup," he said.

"He's almost as good as us," I said.

"Nah, man," Hawk said. "Now he's as good as us."

I glanced back at the doors while Hawk stayed silent behind the wheel. After a few moments, a very large muscular man walked out. He had on a navy V-neck T-shirt busting at the seams, with blue jeans and cowboy boots. His black hair, pulled into a low ponytail, had grown even longer.

The man stood out. There weren't a lot of Cree Indians at Logan this time of night.

"Sixkill has landed," Hawk said.

I nodded and stepped out of the Jag. I greeted him with a handshake and then a hug. Zebulon Sixkill was a little taller than me but just as thick. A long time ago, Hawk, Henry, and I had made a good investment by training a young man with unlimited and untapped potential.

I grabbed his Nike bag and placed it in Hawk's trunk. Sixkill piled all two hundred and forty pounds into the backseat.

"You said two weeks?" Sixkill said.

"Maybe less," Hawk said. "Got some local boys who gonna just die when they meet you."

42

The next morning, we parked in Beacon Hill and walked down Charles Street and into the Common. The day was cool and cloudless and I wore a navy Nike workout jacket over a gray Northeastern T-shirt. The jacket was loose, an XXL, and nicely hid the Browning under my arm while a camera swung over my shoulder. Hawk had on a black linen jacket, a black T-shirt, black jeans, and a pair of snakeskin cowboy boots.

"What kind of snakes were those?" I said.

"Mean ones," Hawk said.

"Don't you feel bad they had to die for fashion?"

"A duty," Hawk said. "And a privilege."

We followed the winding footpaths past the ball fields and the Frog Pond. It wouldn't be long until the leaves would fall and the Common would be blanketed over like a frozen tundra. We passed the memorial to the Massachusetts 54th Regiment in the Civil War and moved toward the bandstand and the T station. We were early, but a crowd had already started to gather at the bandstand. Police barriers corralled off the area where Bishop Graves was scheduled to speak.

Counterprotesters stood nearby holding signs and yelling through megaphones. Someone had an airhorn.

"Toto," Hawk said. "Look like we in Kansas again."

"You ever been to Kansas?" I said.

"Once," Hawk said. "Had an uncle incarcerated at Leavenworth."

"There's a lot more to Kansas."

"Died there, too," he said. "Naw. I never want to go to Kansas again."

We veered off the path north of the bandstand, over toward the old fountain facing Tremont. I wanted to get close enough for Bishop Graves to see me before he spoke. I wanted him to know we were here and he was being followed. Although I was sure Josh Dillon had already told him everything I'd said.

"Lots of people against these fine folks," I said.

"And a lot of people with him, too," Hawk said. "Boston wants to believe it's progressive. But we ain't. They just hiding. Waiting for their time."

Bishop Graves stood in a throng of Minutemen wearing their prerequisite white polo shirts and khakis. They looked like servers at a beach wedding. Josh Dillon was among them, as well as Cole Buckley and an old Malden cop I'd identified by the name of Finley. Altogether, I counted two dozen men in white.

I pulled the camera off my shoulder and adjusted the long lens. I began to capture as many faces of the Minutemen as possible. If there was a run at Carolina tonight or at any time, we could have evidence of their membership in the Minutemen.

An assortment of Boston cops stood along the barricade. Cops of all colors, shapes, and sizes. They looked about as pleased to be there as Hawk and I were. Protecting free speech and a democracy was hell. I was pretty sure if people like Graves ever won, there would be much less interest in protecting the rights of all.

"Have pride, white people," Graves said. The PA system weak and tinny. "Have pride in your race and your culture. Boston was founded by white Christians and should continue to be run by white Christians. This is the birthplace of our proud nation. Stand up and be counted."

I looked to Hawk. "You taking notes?"

Hawk didn't answer. A single drop of perspiration ran down his forehead and under his sunglasses. He didn't speak. He didn't move.

Graves held his right palm in the air, his long brown beard jutting from his chin. His hair slicked tight against his skull. "White blood has been shed," he said. "And perhaps it's time for it to be shed again."

"I guess he never heard of Crispus Attucks," I said.

"Crispus Attucks would think this guy's a motherfucker."

The counterprotesters began a chant that sounded a lot like "Fuck the Nazis." As it grew louder, I was sure of it. Hawk and I scanned the crowd. I took several more close-up photos of the men standing nearest to Graves.

He seemed to delight in the attention and the chanting. He smiled, facing the crowd and walking from corner to corner of the bandstand as if he were the captain of a ship. He pulled at his beard as he reveled in the hate.

"I say we kidnap Graves," Hawk said. "I know this old warehouse in Quincy where we can beat on his ass like an African drum."

"Why not a Celtic drum?"

"Be any drum you want," Hawk said. "Bring Sixkill. Let him get some of that Indian drumming on his ass."

"Native American."

"Native American, African American, Irish American," Hawk said. "Still an old-fashioned beatdown."

I slung my camera back over my shoulder. It bumped against the Browning while I watched Graves try to continue with the speech, but he was now drowned out by the protesters. "Fuck the Nazis" soon became "Fuck the Fascists." "Go Home Little Hitler" was another favorite.

"If we get down and dirty," I said. "Aren't we the same as them?"

"Nope."

"Let me rephrase the question," I said. "Isn't it up to us to find a better and smarter way?"

"Can't reason with man with a brain size of a lizard."

"That's insulting to lizards."

"Me and you been around Boston too long," Hawk said. "You know how this all gonna go. And how the song got to end."

"They hardly seem like worthy opponents."

"Same as cockroaches," he said. "If you don't get rid of one soon as you see it, they multiply."

Hawk watched Graves leave the bandstand surrounded by the white-shirted boys as they walked down to their waiting vehicles along Park Street.

"They made the play," Hawk said. "Actions have consequences."

Hawk looked as if he was about to say more. But he stopped speaking. Something had caught his eye. Three men had moved into the rush of the white-shirted crowd, keeping a tight perimeter on the flow of the Minutemen. One looked like a Bulgarian weight lifter. The other smaller but thicker, with a bald head and a Sox hoodie. I could see the outline of a gun under his right arm up under the hoodie.

"Well, well, well," Hawk said.

"See someone you know?"

"Hired muscle," he said. "Big man's name is Guzman."

"Guzman?"

Hawk repeated the last name.

"Smaller guy is goddamn Bamm Bamm Bonzini."

"Guzman and Bamm Bamm," I said. "Sounds like a Hanna-Barbera production."

"Used to run with your boy Jumpin' Jack Flynn," he said. "I don't think they walk behind any crew now. Muscle for hire."

"Cokey McMichael?"

"If you say so."

"Can you make some calls?"

"Me being a disreputable thug and you being an upstanding investigator?"

"Yep," I said. "Exactly like that."

"Or maybe we just follow their ass."

"In this traffic?"

Hawk pulled out his phone and dialed a number. He asked a few very direct questions. When he got the answers, he slipped the phone back into his pocket.

We followed the police barricades to Tremont and got within fifteen feet of Bishop Graves. Protesters were screaming at him. One young woman holding a baby offered her middle finger as he passed. He looked absolutely thrilled with all the attention. He was feeding off it. Graves waved to the crowd like a conquering hero.

Guzman and Bonzini held the door to a red Ford Expedition open. Graves gave a Nazi salute as he crawled inside. Guzman got behind the wheel and they were gone just as fast as they'd arrived. The small crowd started to disperse.

Police shouted directions and began to dismantle the barricades.

"Bring around the car, James," Hawk said. "Susan ain't gonna like where I'm taking your ass."

43

Shenanigans Tap Room was in a stand-alone brick building in Chelsea with a lovely view of the Route 1 overpass. The sign outside boasted the holy trinity of food, cocktails, and entertainment. I was disappointed to learn that meant soggy chicken wings, shots of cheap liquor, and two women in bikinis trying not to fall off the stage.

I walked in first and found a spot at the bar. Christmas lights twinkled overhead. A DJ played some music I couldn't recognize and hoped to never hear again. It sounded as if it had been arranged and performed by a computer. Hawk followed a few moments later and took a seat two stools down from mine.

Greenish light pulsed from LED rope lights wrapping the poles framing the bar. A bony and lethargic woman onstage bent over and flapped her nonexistent butt up and down. It was about as sexy as watching ice cream melt.

A white woman in a bikini top and a Russian fur hat

worked the bar. I ordered a Sam Adams. Hawk asked for ice water.

There were two men playing pool in an open back room, an old man in brown coveralls holding a wad of cash by the stage, and two women in bikinis smoking cigarettes by the bathrooms. No sight of Guzman or Bamm Bamm. Maybe they were all hanging out at the Minutemen clubhouse in Medford.

The woman brought me the beer. It was lukewarm.

"Spasibuh," I said.

She rolled her eyes and walked off.

I hoped Guzman would show soon. Not a bad place to hang out if you were fully up on your rabies shots.

"Are you sure this is Guzman's place?" I said, glancing at Hawk. "Or did you just come for the chicken wings?"

"You think all brothers like chicken wings?"

"Everyone likes chicken wings."

"I wouldn't feed that shit to a rat."

Hawk watched the performances onstage without a gesture or a comment. The woman in the Russian hat asked if I'd like another beer. I still had half left of the first. Restraint. I placed a five on the bar and, satisfied, she walked away.

"Don't thugs ever hang out in nice places?" I said. "Like the MFA or the Four Seasons?"

"You and I hang out at the Four Seasons."

"You and I are a different breed of thug."

Hawk nodded and walked up to a tired dancer hanging upside down from a brass pole and tucked some cash into her garter. He did it with as much enthusiasm as someone stuffing the Salvation Army bucket.

He sat back down. "Momma working hard."

Twenty minutes later, light spilled into the bar and a large man darkened the doorway. We watched as Guzman strolled into Shenanigans with Bamm Bamm Bonzini and a small, mean-looking guy with a shaved head. Bamm Bamm had on workout pants and one of those oversized cut-off sweatshirts they sell in bodybuilding magazines. His light brown hair had been sculpted in what appeared to be a shark's fin on top of his head.

"Mm-hm," Hawk said. "Showtime."

It was dark inside and the music was deafening. I'm pretty sure the song had changed since we'd walked in but couldn't really tell any difference.

Guzman hopped onstage with one of the dancers, bent her over, and then made a roping motion like a cowboy. Bonzini and the little mean guy laughed and then headed to the back poolroom, talking to the guys around the table.

Hawk intercepted Guzman when he hopped offstage. Guzman was dark-complected, with a round face and ham-sized arms. He had on a white tank top and a camo-colored flat-billed ball cap. His head looked like something Pete Weber could use to knock down a dozen pins.

Hawk whispered something in Guzman's ear.

Guzman looked taken aback.

Hawk smiled. He looked to me and tilted his head.

The girl in the fuzzy hat walked back up my way. She

leaned in to the bar, placing her chin into the palm of her hand.

"Is Guzman a good boss?" I said.

The woman looked at me as if I were crazy. "He's an asshole."

"Good," I said. "Don't be too quick to dial nine-one-one."

She started to ask more, but I pushed myself off the bar just as Hawk punched Guzman once in the right ear and then two times fast in the stomach. Guzman rushed Hawk and drove him hard and fast back past me and into the bar, toppling the rest of my beer.

Hawk picked up the beer and broke the bottle over Guzman's head.

The action got the attention of Bamm Bamm and his pal Pebbles, and they came running out of the poolroom. Pebbles had a pool cue in his hand, holding it like a guy who was about to perform an overhead press. His face was pinched like a small feral animal looking up from his hole.

Bamm Bamm rushed toward Hawk, and I body-checked him hard into the stage, knocking the legs out from under a dancer. They fell into a tangled mess as the music continued to play, a song that kept repeating "I Feel Just Like a Rock Star."

Pebbles rushed me, swinging the cue like Toshiro Mifune. I dipped my shoulder and took a hard blow across my back. I reached up and snatched the cue from his hands, getting a good grip and taking aim at his head.

There was a sharp crack against his skull before I took

out his left knee with a swift kick. Pebbles was down and writhing on the floor, blood across his ear and chin.

The music stopped as Bamm Bamm leapt offstage and onto my back. I spun him off and he crashed into two tables. He toppled onto the floor but was back on his feet fast and raised his fists.

The stripper behind me yelled encouragement. "Kick his ass, Bamm Bamm."

I looked back at her and placed a finger to my lips.

Hawk had Guzman down on his knees, his thick arm across Guzman's throat. Guzman's ball cap lay on the ground as he attempted to break free. Hawk seemed to be giving little effort as he leaned down and whispered something in Guzman's ear.

Bamm Bamm was back on me, his hair still gelled up into a perfect fin on top of his head.

I led with a quick left, catching him in the arm, and followed with a cross to his ribs with my right. I hammered him twice in the ribs as he pushed off at me and swung with an overhead that connected with my ear. I heard the ocean and rocked back on my feet before rolling forward with a quick combo that finished with a right cross against his jaw. The fin on top of his head sunk. He wobbled. And then fell down.

One of the dancers came around and helped him into a chair. She called me a few unpleasant names while she clutched Bamm Bamm tight to her bosom. His pal Pebbles had pushed himself against a far wall, holding a hand to his bleeding ear.

I looked around the bar, which glowed with red and

green light. Shenanigans was no worse a mess than it was when we'd entered.

I turned to Hawk. He'd let Guzman go. Guzman was on all fours now, struggling for breath but answering Hawk's questions. Hawk patted his head. "Nice doggie."

I walked up to Hawk.

"They with Cokey McMichael?" I said.

Hawk nodded and walked back up to the stage and showered the girls with a fistful of cash.

"Make it rain, Daddy," I said. We both walked toward the entrance and the outdoor light and fresh air.

"Hard work," he said. "Keeping time in a joint like this."

44

I had Lou Pasquale meet me at the Wheelhouse Diner in Quincy.

The building looked like a large breadbox and had traditional counter service and a single open griddle inside. It smelled like coffee and bacon and I hadn't eaten all day. I ordered a club sandwich, fries, and a Coke. I didn't think Lou would mind. I wasn't sure how long it would take him to get here or if he'd get cold feet and not show up.

Hawk was back at the campaign offices with Sixkill. I'd promised to give Sixkill a proper welcome to Boston later at the Russell House Tavern with Susan.

I sat in a back booth facing one of two exits. There was a chalkboard over the grill listing the specials and assorted homey bric-a-brac on the walls. A captain's wheel clock. A large wooden fork. The diner was empty except for the cook and the waitress. A middle-aged guy in a hoodie and a ball cap worked on a cheeseburger while he flipped through his cell phone.

I'd finished three-quarters of my club and half my fries when Lou entered the opposite end of the diner. His face and head were clean-shaven and he wore a blue Pats T-shirt over his large stomach and a pair of khaki pants. He looked clean, fresh, and possibly sober as he slid into the booth.

"How's King?"

"Kidneys acting up," he said. "On some new medication. Won't be long. I just don't want to do it too soon. Or too late."

"I've been there."

"It's the worst," Lou said.

I nodded. I glanced up at the chalkboard. "Hungry?"

"Nah," he said. "I'd just ate when you called. This place wasn't far."

I drank a little Coke and smiled at him. I let the silence hang between us. He looked at my face and pointed at me. "What the hell happened to you?"

"I had a disagreement with Bamm Bamm Bonzini."

"Never heard of him," Lou said. "But he clipped your ear good. Better put some ice on it."

I nodded.

"Jeez," he said. "And there's blood on your shirt, too."

"Don't worry," I said. "It's not mine."

The waitress reappeared. She was a middle-aged woman who looked as if she had never had any other job than waitress. Bleached blond curly hair, smoker's lines around her mouth, and an affable way of making you feel welcome at the Wheelhouse.

Lou ordered some coffee with cream and sugar.

"These guys," I said. "The ones I got into a disagreement with. They work for your pal Cokey McMichael."

Lou leveled his eyes at me. He swallowed. The waitress brought some coffee along with some creamer in a little dish with ice. Lou added a lot of creamer and a lot of sugar. I used to like coffee like that, too, but then learned I could live without it.

"Bamm Bamm Bonzini?"

"Get the fuck out of here."

"Nope," I said. "Worked with another guy named Guzman. They pull tight security jobs. Off-the-books bodyguard work."

"Don't know 'em."

"But you know Cokey."

"I only know Cokey to pay Cokey," Lou said. "Farrell and people didn't want any shit tracked to their back door. Cokey broke into Carolina's office to scare her and make her drop out."

"What about the hard drives and computers?"

"I guess it didn't hurt nothing to learn a thing or two," Lou said. "It was all fucked-up. That's why I quit."

"I thought you quit because I was checking up on you?"

"I quit because I thought you were checking up on me because you knew I worked for Farrell and Flaherty. Christ. I've known Frankie Farrell forever. We went to high school together. There wasn't much to it. To start with."

"Did you start working for Carolina because of Farrell?"

Pasquale slurped at his coffee while simultaneously holding up the flat of his hand and shaking his head. "No," he said. "No way. It was an honest job and honest work. Frankie came to me. He wanted to know some things about Carolina. And her schedule. They just wanted some inside information to start with."

"Were you paid?"

"Yeah," he said. Pasquale dropped his head. "I was paid. I gotta be honest. I don't give two shits about politics. Flaherty or Carolina may talk different and act different, but there's not much space between them. If I can make a little money on the side . . . Oh, well. Arrest me."

"You really could get arrested for that."

Pasquale nodded. He craned his head behind him to look at the guy at the counter and then back at me. He leaned in to the table between us to make sure that no one was listening.

"What happened to Carolina the other night," he said. "Someone trying to run her over. That wasn't Flaherty or Frankie. They'd never want to see something like that."

"But Frankie hired Cokey and now Cokey is working with two goons working security for a guy named Bishop Graves."

"Never heard of those guys," he said. "Bamm Bamm whosis."

I explained what I'd learned about Bishop Graves and

the Minutemen. I left out the part about Noah Dillon and his brother and Noah getting killed. No reason to scare Lou off from helping.

"I swear to you, Flaherty and Frankie would cheat their own mothers, but they're not into some nutso movement like that," he said. "They just want Flaherty back on the payroll and sending money back home to Boston. You know, a little cream on top. They had a real nice system going until Carolina beat him and knocked him to the sidelines."

I nodded. I decided to spare the last wedge of the club sandwich. Although I did eat a few fries. Lou stared at it; for a moment I thought he might lick his lips.

"You never heard of the Minutemen before just now?"

"Only Paul Fuckin' Revere."

"Or Bishop Graves?"

He held up his right hand. "I swear on my dog's life," he said. "Is that good enough for you?"

"What was it exactly that Flaherty and Farrell hoped to accomplish with Cokey McMichael?"

"Disruption," he said. "They wanted to rattle Carolina's cage is all. Get her to maybe drop out. Jesus. They didn't want to fucking kill her."

"Then why is Cokey working with Graves?"

"I got no fucking idea," Lou said. "Seriously. Ever think those assholes were pulling your chain? Cokey is a crook, but he'd never work with fuckups like that."

Lou kept eyeing my sandwich. I looked right back at him and pushed the plate in his direction. "Think you can find out?"

"You want me to spy on Frankie for you?"

"You know what they say about turnabout?"

"That it can get your ass in the sling with the wrong people?"

"Maybe," I said. "But it would make us even."

45

On the way back downtown, Hawk called.

"The congresswoman's safe," he said. "But her man Swift ain't looking so good."

"What happened?"

"We took her to the Hilton for that charity luncheon," Hawk said. "I stayed on Carolina. Sixkill brought the car around. Her team got separated. Two men jumped Swift in the elevator. By the time the elevator got to the ground floor, those boys were gone."

"Minutemen?"

"Doesn't all shit smell the same?"

Hawk said he'd left Sixkill with Carolina and Kyle Rosen at Mass General. I changed up my route and headed that way. Thirty minutes later, I found Carolina and Kyle in the ER waiting room. Sixkill stood nearby, keeping watch. He nodded in my direction as I sat down.

"Three busted ribs," Rosen said. "And a broken nose."

"Been there," I said.

"Not like this," Carolina said. "Not under these circumstances. Where the hell was this new guy when Adam was attacked?"

"He was bringing around the car," I said. "Hawk was on you. We're paid to keep you safe. If the team strays, there isn't much we can do."

"Then why did you bring on this new guy?" Rosen said. "Is his name really Zebulon?"

"Call him Z," I said. "Zebulon takes a while to pronounce."

Carolina exhaled a long breath. She was dressed in a black pantsuit with her hair worn loose around her shoulders. She clenched her jaw as she looked to Rosen and then back to me.

"What are we supposed to do?" she said.

"You want to cancel the debate?" I said.

"Hell, no," she said. "I want all these people in jail."

"Cops are pulling security cameras at the hotel," I said. "I have some photos I took of Bishop Graves's personal fan club earlier today. I believe we'll get a match."

Rosen had his elbows on his thighs and his hands in his frizzy hair. His phone sat in an empty seat next to him, buzzing and buzzing. His knee popped up and down like a piston.

"Press?" I said.

"We don't need this," Rosen said. "Jesus, Spenser. Your people were supposed to watch our backs."

I was quiet. There wasn't much else I could say. I looked to the front desk and asked if I could see Adam before the cops arrived. Rosen nodded and walked with me to the desk, vouching for me being a part of Carolina's team. As he said it, he didn't look like he believed it much.

A nurse brought me through double security doors and into a room. Adam Swift was in a bed with cotton up his nose and tape across his face. He looked like he'd gone a few rounds with Marvin Hagler.

"How you doing, kid?" I said.

Another man sat by his bed. He had sandy hair, a neatly trimmed mustache, and was impeccably dressed. He wore a light green button-down with a tailor-fitted blue blazer. I wondered if it was wrong to chalk up his impeccable clothes to his sexual orientation.

Swift tried to raise up as I entered. The man stood quickly and told him to lay back.

"I'm Brandon," he said. "Adam's husband."

We shook hands. Brandon sat back down while I continued to stand. I offered Adam my apologies for what had happened at the Hilton. He closed his eyes for a moment and shook his head. When he tried to speak, he winced with pain.

"Not much can be done about busted ribs," I said. "Except to rest."

"There were two."

"Think you can ID them?"

The room was dark and quiet and windowless. Swift had an IV going and wore a hospital gown. Brandon stood up and held out the flat of his hand to me.

"I think he can deal with that later," Brandon said.

"Weren't you supposed to look out for them? Someone tried to kill Carolina. How could these people get so close?"

"Could have been much worse," I said.

"Thanks so much for that," Brandon said. "Look at him. Does he look like it could've been much worse?"

"They wanted me," Swift said. He spoke very softly. His vocal cords sounded brittle. "They knew who I was. They called me 'faggot.' An abomination that needed to learn his lesson."

I could feel my trapezius muscles tighten.

"They told me if I showed up tomorrow night, I'd be dead, too."

"Those guys can't stop running their mouths," I said.

"One of them wouldn't stop kicking me," Swift said. "Even when I was down. They tore clothes and tried to strangle me with my tie."

"They wanted to humiliate you."

Blood dotted Swift's right eye. His eyes moistened, but he didn't cry. His husband sat back down and turned his head from me.

"Please don't let Carolina get hurt," Swift said. "My ribs may be broken. But I'll come after you with everything I have."

I nodded.

"He means it, too," Brandon said. "Even after all this, Adam still believes in you. That has to mean something."

I bent down and lightly touched Adam's shoulder. "I'm sorry," I said. "What do I need to know about watching Carolina's back?"

"To keep her running and on track?"

"Yep."

Swift turned to Brandon and told him to grab his bag. "You look strong enough to carry it around."

"Sure," I said. "But I have someone else in mind for the job."

46

You want me to carry a what?" Sixkill said.

"A bag," I said. "If it's any consolation, it's a very heavy bag. More like something you'd hang off a horse."

"Terrific."

"And a good place to stash an extra gun or two."

Sixkill, seated in the cafeteria at Mass General, didn't seem opposed to the plan. I'd gotten a cup of coffee while Sixkill finally got to eat. The daily special was jambalaya, and surprisingly enough, it didn't look horrible for hospital food.

"I don't get it," Sixkill said. "If the Feds know where and when the Minutemen are planning to attack, why not just round up these assholes now?"

"I asked precisely the same question," I said. "It seems much of their evidence and case was destroyed when their informant was murdered."

Sixkill shook his head. He had on pretty much the same clothes as when we'd picked him up at the airport last night. He kept the standard uniform of black T-shirt, faded jeans, and cowboy boots. Since he hit Boston, he had a collarless biker jacket to cover the gun I'd given him last night.

"I told Swift he needed to stick with us," Sixkill said.

"I know."

"I told him we shouldn't separate," Sixkill said. "But he insisted on meeting us back at the campaign headquarters."

I nodded and told him he'd done his job properly. I drank some coffee and checked the time. No one was getting to have a meal at Russell House Tavern tonight. I'd already called Susan and told her the latest. I would sleep at Susan's while I passed the keys to my place in the Navy Yard to Sixkill.

"Are they sure they're going to try something tomorrow?"

"Feds are sure about everything," I said. "Even after they're proved wrong."

"And we're just supposed to get out of their way?" Sixkill's face was flat, with wide-set black eyes. His black hair pulled into a ponytail.

"Nope," I said. "We do our job as we see fit. Someone makes a rush at the congresswoman, we won't have time to form a committee."

"Why won't she just cancel?" Sixkill said. "That guy Rosen says her numbers are pretty good. He said the debate was more of a formality."

"The congresswoman is like us," I said. "She doesn't run from a challenge."

"This doesn't sound like a challenge," he said. "Sounds like a trap."

Sixkill ate some more of the jambalaya and a roll that went with it. I drank some coffee and checked my phone for messages from Susan. The Feds had agents on the hospital and BPD had two cars out front. I absently stirred at my coffee, although I'd given up sugar.

"How's business?"

"It's L.A.," Sixkill said. "Jem and I've been busy. Just worked a big case for Mr. Del Rio."

"Be careful," I said. "Mr. Del Rio will try to add you to his stable of men."

"Already has," Sixkill said. He smiled and pushed away the plastic plate. "I said no. Too much like you and Hawk. I only work for myself."

"And Jem?"

Sixkill smiled. There was a lot more, but I didn't pry. Jem Yoon was a talented and beautiful woman I'd met on my last trip to Los Angeles. She'd helped out me and Z, and I figured them for a great team. Like a Native American and Korean American Bogie and Bacall.

"I better get back to Carolina," Sixkill said.

I shook my head. "I got the overnight," I said. "Go to the Navy Yard and get some rest. Susan and Pearl send their love."

"I'm sorry about the last Pearl," Sixkill said.

I smiled and drank some coffee. Sixkill had come a long way from when we'd first met. There had always been strength and potential, but he used to lack confidence and contentment in who he was beyond a college football player or a kid who'd grown up hard on the rez in Montana. Along with Paul Giacomin and Mattie Sullivan, Sixkill was family.

"Hawk said I look skinny."

"Hawk would say that."

"Says maybe we can stop by the gym tomorrow," Sixkill said. "See Henry."

"Henry would be hurt if you didn't."

"Don't tell me he's changed."

"If anything, he's only grown saltier and shorter."

"Good."

We shook hands. I took the elevator back up to check in with Kyle Rosen about tomorrow.

47

The next morning, Hawk and Sixkill stayed on Carolina. I drove back to my condo for a shower, a shave, and breakfast before returning to my office. When I walked toward my door a little after nine, Cokey McMichael and a stout little guy who resembled a Boston terrier were waiting for me.

"To what do I owe this dishonor?" I said.

"You know you have a reputation for being a smart-ass?" McMichael said. His voice sounded like someone gargling with marbles.

"It's on my website."

I unlocked the door and waved them inside. I figured they could shoot me just as easily in the hallway as in the street. I moved from the anteroom and into the office, setting my ball cap and jacket on the hat tree. I took a seat behind my desk, waved them to my client chairs, and smiled as I slid open the right-hand drawer.

"Ennie Guzman is a fucking liar," McMichael said. He shuffled his large backside in my client chair. I could hear the protest of the wooden legs.

"I'm shocked."

The Boston terrier–looking guy hadn't sat down. He'd turned his back to us and was studying the framed artwork on the wall.

"You a Vermeer fan?" I said.

"I guess," he said. "This broad in the painting looks like my kid sister."

"*Study of a Young Woman.*"

"Yeah," he said. "But I still can't tell who the fuck it is."

Cokey McMichael coughed to alert us back to his presence. I turned. My right hand rested on my knee near the right-hand drawer. The noise would be harsh and might burst my eardrums, but I could take them both out quick. Cokey was much too large to toss out the window.

"Sure, Guzman used to do some work for me," he said. "But that's ancient history. This shit you was telling Lou Pasquale about yesterday? The goddamn Nazi creeps. That's not on me. That ain't got nothing to do with me or Lou or the deal with fucking Frankie Farrell. Unnerstand?"

"Unnerstood."

The little terrier guy kept on sniffing around, bending down to look at more photos and framed prints. He seemed particularly interested in one I'd bought at the Musée d'Orsay in Paris. A true art connoisseur.

"Heard you rammed Guzman's head into the wall," Cokey said.

"That was my associate."

"Yeah, yeah," he said. "I know who Hawk is. And I know who you are. I swear to Christ, you do someone a favor and you get bit in the ass every time."

"Working for Farrell."

"Yeah," he said. "Hawk didn't ask Guzman any questions. He tried to rip his head off while making Ennie admit he was working with me. You're a detective. That ain't no way to do business."

"So you guys broke into Carolina Garcia-Ramirez's headquarters?"

Cokey grinned. He shrugged. In the language of a guy like Cokey McMichael, that was better than a signed affidavit.

"Which one of you isn't house-trained?" I said.

The terrier turned from my wall and snickered. I wanted to whack his nose with a rolled-up newspaper but waited for Cokey to get on with whatever it was he came here to say.

"Just for the hell of it, how'd you figure me for working for Frankie Farrell?"

"I heard you ran errands for him," I said. "Even picked up his laundry. And cut his grass."

"So fucking what?" McMichael said. "You go from me working for Farrell to me joining up with the fucking Nazis? Sure, sure, maybe Frankie and Tommy might cheat a little, but that don't make them criminals."

"Farrell never had a problem carrying water for Joe Broz."

"Ha," McMichael said. "Funny you bringing up the late, great Joe Broz. I came to set you straight. You come to me for this shit and you should be going to Joe's fucking son. You know anything about him?"

"Gerry?" I said. "Sure. We've met on a few previous occasions."

"And?"

"And," I said. "He's no Joe Broz."

"Ain't that the truth," he said. "Jeez. Last time I worked with Gerry, he screwed me over big-time. I did all the work and he made most of the profit. I can't believe someone hasn't put a bullet in his head already. That's no way to do business in this city."

"So you're saying Guzman and Bonzini work for Gerry Broz?"

"Maybe."

I leaned forward in my chair. The Boston terrier had exhausted my office tour and sat down in a client's chair. He slumped and chewed gum. He had the kind of a face that demanded a spiked collar around his neck.

"Yes or no," I said. "Is Broz working with the Minutemen?"

Cokey McMichael scratched at his cheek. He looked to his associate and then back to me. He tilted his head forward and lifted his eyes at me. "I don't want no trouble with you and no trouble with Hawk," he said. "I don't have time for it."

"Yes or no?"

Cokey swallowed. He nodded lightly.

"You're saying Bonzini and Guzman pulled guard duty for neo-Nazis in the Common yesterday on orders of Gerry Broz?" I said.

"Yep," he said.

"To get to Carolina."

"Jesus," he said. "This is Gerry Fucking Broz. It has nothing to do with politics. The kid doesn't have the patience and the temperament for it. He's doing business with these creeps."

"With what?"

"I don't know," McMichael said. "But a friendly warning. Ennie and Bamm Bamm ain't like me. They don't have an understanding soul. They're gonna try and level things with you and Hawk."

I stifled a yawn with the flat of my hand. I swiveled my chair back and forth.

"You think you can't be hit," Cokey said. "Please. You and Hawk getting too old for this game. Shit. Why don't you just knock it off and go for a nice cruise somewhere?"

"I get seasick."

"South Florida," he said. "South Florida is where it's at."

"I'll have to take your word for it," I said. "What exactly do you know about the Minutemen and Gerry?"

"Nothin'," he said. "Never heard of these assholes till you put the squeeze on poor Lou. Never want to. I may be a crook, but I'm a goddamn honest crook. I ain't supporting some young douchebags who want to overthrow the government. Christ. I love this country. Equal opportunity for all. My grandfather came here off the boat. Didn't have two potatoes to rub together."

I turned slightly to my right and looked out the turret and onto Berkeley Street. Carolina's debate would start at seven. With Hawk and Sixkill on her, I might just have time to pay a visit to an old friend.

"Where's Gerry these days?"

"I dunno."

"Oh, come on, Cokey," I said. "You've come this far. How about come all the way?"

"I don't want no trouble."

"And no trouble you will get."

"Shit."

"Come on," I said. "I won't even hold it against you for ripping apart my client's campaign headquarters. Forgive and forget."

"Okay," he said. "Maybe you heard Gerry Broz has gone into the seafood business. Done real good for himself."

Cokey did the whole air quotes thing around "seafood business."

"Why'd you do that?"

"Do what?"

"The air quotes," I said. "That makes me think that Gerry isn't actually in the seafood business. Is he or isn't he?"

McMichael looked to the terrier and then back to me. He shrugged.

"Maybe a little," McMichael said. "But he ain't making the kind of money he's pulling down selling lobsters and clams. It's called Neptune's Delight. Right there hanging its ass off on Pier 44. Christ, open your windows. You can probably smell it from here."

48

I have to admit I miss fried clams and haddock," Sixkill said.

Hawk had replaced Sixkill on CGR duty and we decided to make a quick stop before heading back to the Navy Yard.

"After this is over, I'll drive you up to Woodman's," I said. "All the fried clams you want."

"Is that how I'm getting paid?"

"I'd throw in a bucket of beer," I said. "But you don't drink."

I found an open lot in the Seaport and we walked toward the old Boston Fishing Piers, twin brick buildings that ran a couple football-field lengths into the harbor. Neptune's Delight Inc. was on the far end of the first pier on the north side. Fishing boats lined the docks, the access street choked with delivery trucks, empty plastic ice bins, wooden pallets, and the strong smell of fish. A wiry guy with leathery skin in rubber waders hosed off the concrete platform below the NEPTUNE sign.

He had in ear pods and made time with the music as he hummed. Sixkill and I walked right past him, into the loading dock, and through a side metal door. In all the years I'd come into contact with Gerry Broz, he'd worked as a pornographer, blackmailer, fence, sports bar owner, tropical fish breeder, and now fresh seafood salesman. A true Renaissance man.

We moved into a narrow reception area without a receptionist leading into an industrial stairwell up to the second floor. We followed the stairs and found a large, open warehouse space filled with row after row of floor-to-ceiling metal racks stacked with what looked like televisions, computers, and power tools. There wasn't a fresh haddock or scallop to be seen.

Gerry Broz sat on top of a metal desk by the windows while he yelled at someone on his cell phone. There was an open sack from Burger King next to a laptop computer, a half-eaten Whopper, and an empty carton of fries.

Broz looked at me. And then looked at Sixkill.

"Sure, sure, sure," Broz said. "Okay. Yeah. Whatever. Go fuck your mother."

He clicked off and slammed down the cell.

It had been a while and I wasn't sure that Gerry recognized me. He reached for a supersized drink and started to slurp from the straw. Gerry had been a doughy kid, but now he was a middle-aged fat man. He tried to hide it in a blue Under Armour shirt worn loose over a pair of skinny jeans.

"You're too old for skinny jeans, Gerry," I said. "They make you look like a stuffed sausage."

"Spenser?" he said. He squinted at me and Sixkill.

"Congrats on the new business," I said. "We'd like six dozen extra-large scallops to go."

"Sorry," Broz said, slurping his soda. "We're fresh out of scallops."

"How about two dozen live lobsters," I said. "Surely you have those."

"Nope," he said. "Been a slow day on the water. What the fuck do you want?"

"Come on," I said. I looked over at Sixkill and then back to Broz. "Is that any way to greet an old friend of the family?"

"My father hated you till his dying day," he said. "You've been a pain in my ass since I was in college."

I jacked my thumb in the direction of Broz. "Once upon a time, Gerry liked to have sex with horny old women and make videos. Then he'd blackmail them or their husbands."

"Wow," Sixkill said. "A real entrepreneur."

Broz snickered, reached onto his desk for a pack of cigarettes, and tucked one into the corner of his mouth. He still had all his hair, gelled back and off his doughy face. His belly as neat and round as a basketball hidden up under his spandex shirt. A gold earring glinted from his left ear. "That was something, wasn't it?" he said. "I really gave those old broads the business."

"You've come a long way, baby," I said.

"Yeah," he said, looking around his warehouse. He

cupped his hand around the cigarette and snapped open a Zippo. "I sure have. Now tell me what the hell you want. I got work to do."

"I can see," I said. "That Whopper won't just eat itself."

"That's why he has on the workout shirt," Sixkill said. "He's curling the Whopper in one hand and the soda in the other. If you really squint, you can see the definition."

"Who's he?" Broz said. "Your fucking warm-up act?"

"This is Z."

"He looks like a fucking Indian."

"You know," Sixkill said, "there's a good reason for that."

"You really an Indian?" Broz said. "No shit. Most of the Indians I meet around here look just like white people. All in the casino business. You look like one of those guys in the movies."

"Shucks," Sixkill said.

Broz picked up his phone and started to text. I asked him to stop and pay attention.

"I'm listening," he said. "I'm listening."

"Who'd you text?" I said.

"My exterminator," Broz said. "Got some rat problems around the docks."

I glanced at Sixkill. He moved back to the far wall by the staircase door. A few moments later, I heard footsteps as the door opened. Bamm Bamm Bonzini walked out holding a scoped AR-15.

"Hands up, dickhead," Bamm Bamm said. His jaw still looked swollen from yesterday.

Sixkill stepped up behind him and placed my .357 to the back of his skull. Sixkill whispered something in Bamm Bamm's ear and he dropped the gun. It just wasn't Bamm Bamm's week.

"Shit," Broz said.

"Did you know Bamm Bamm and Ennie Guzman joined the Minutemen?" I said. "They're walking behind a guy named Bishop Graves, who's hoping to ignite a national race war right here in Boston."

Broz shrugged. He blew smoke out his nose.

"You into that stuff now?" I said. "I knew you were dumb. But I never knew you to follow any kind of ideology."

"I don't know what my guys do in their off time," Broz said. "What the fuck? You come in here threatening me, pulling guns on my people?"

"I didn't threaten you," I said. "Not yet. And we didn't pull a gun until you summoned Bamm Bamm."

"I don't know a goddamn word about what you're saying," Broz said. "How about you, Bamm Bamm?"

"Nope," he said. "This old guy comes into the club yesterday with some big nigger and starts some shit. I think he's nuts."

Sixkill increased the pressure on the back of Bamm Bamm's head. He closed his eyes in pain. He made a yelping sound.

"This can't be ideological," I said. "You have no code.

Good or bad. Or any belief system. So that means this is all business. Just what are you selling the Minutemen, Ger?"

"Go fuck yourself."

I glanced around the warehouse, spotting mainly TVs, heavy-duty tools, and restaurant equipment. I didn't see what I was looking for, but knew exactly what Gerry was into.

"You must keep the guns somewhere else," I said.

"That's a goddamn leap," Broz said. "My dad always said you were nuts."

"Only thing that makes sense," I said. "Guns for the big race war. And maybe a little protection for their traveling medicine show."

"Bullshit."

"You like the idea of some nutcases with money to spend," I said. "I just don't think you understand what these people want to do."

Broz sucked on the cigarette. He let the smoke spew from the corner of his mouth. "What the fuck do I care?" he said. "If some assholes want to ride around and play war in the sticks, that's none of my concern. I'm just a simple fishmonger."

"Joe wouldn't trade with these people," I said.

"What the fuck do you know about my father?" Broz said. "Don't come in here with that bullshit."

"You've never had any honor, Gerry," I said. "But this is different. I promised your old man I wouldn't kill you. But if you're working with these people, that's all gone."

"My father's been dead ten years," he said. "Go piss up a rope."

Sixkill told Bamm Bamm to get on his knees and lace his hands behind his head. Bamm Bamm did as he was told. Sixkill picked up the rifle and tossed it to me as we walked out. I checked the magazine and found it loaded.

Down the steps and outside, I chucked it into the water. It landed with a splash and scattered a bunch of gulls picking at fish parts.

"He gets in the way with Carolina," Sixkill said, "you're gonna have to kill him."

"I won't have to," I said. "Gerry Broz always trips over himself."

49

I'd never met Tommy Flaherty, only seen him on TV. In person, his head looked even larger and more potato-like. His hair was silver and curly, and the skin around his neck was loose and soft. He wore a navy suit, a blue dress shirt with a red paisley tie, and glasses so oblong and narrow they made him appear to be constantly squinting.

At the moment, Flaherty was holding his own with Carolina. Her go-to strategy of making him seem old and out of touch wasn't working. He'd memorized locals with issues on a first-name basis and rattled off clear and detailed talking points about the district. He was particularly fixated on her lack of effort to improve on public transportation and the Silver Line. Carolina countered that there was more to Boston than just two bus stops, letting everyone know Flaherty meant the older mainly white districts.

"That asshole hasn't taken public transportation his

whole life," Kyle Rosen said, whispering to me. "His wife grew up on Beacon Hill. She raises fucking Pekingese dogs."

The candidates had garnered a nice crowd at the UMass Campus Center that night. I'd spent the last two hours working out details with the campus cops and Boston police. I knew the Feds were out there in force, but as they'd not seen fit to include me in their plans, I wasn't counting on them.

I kept on scanning the crowd for any of the Minutemen or Bishop Graves himself. I saw a few who might've fit the description, but none I recognized. Hawk did the same. Sixkill stood right off the stage in case someone made a run at Carolina or if she needed a Tic Tac. To the untrained eye, it did appear Sixkill was carrying a large, overstuffed purse, but I doubted anyone would make fun of him.

"You don't think this is about race?" Carolina said. "Mr. Flaherty, need I remind you, everything is about race."

The moderators included a well-known male columnist from the *Globe* and a female commentator from WBUR. They did their best to keep Flaherty and Carolina on track. But both politicians liked taking wide interpretations of the questions. A question about gun control ended up with Carolina accusing Flaherty of accusing her of playing identity politics.

The argument that followed nearly took a wrestling referee to stop the squabbling.

The woman from WBUR had to stand up from her

seat and ask both candidates to let the other answer. I looked across the room and stopped on Frankie Farrell. He wasn't even listening, scrolling through his phone and smiling at something he'd read.

When he stopped scrolling, Farrell looked over at me and pointed his index finger and raised his thumb. He dropped the hammer and grinned.

"What a dick," Rosen said.

I'd picked six Feds in the crowd of a hundred people or so. Most of the crowd were either local press or UMass students and faculty. There were four doors leading back into the Campus Center building and two rear exits behind the stage. The crowd was gathered in folding chairs, with the two moderators on a raised dais to the left of the candidates. A plastic sign had been unfurled advertising both the *Globe* and WBUR. A campus cop kept watch at each exit. Two patrol cars were parked at the drive running along the waterfront.

If the Minutemen decided to act, they wouldn't get very far.

"See anything?" Rosen said.

"Lots of Feds."

"How do you know they're Feds?"

"Cheap shoes and expensive haircuts."

"Always?" Rosen said.

"Always."

As the moderators gave the candidates the cue for closing remarks, Hawk and I met by the outer doors to the conference room. I would join Sixkill and walk Carolina and Kyle Rosen down to the main entrance. Hawk would pull around the SUV, and we'd all head back to headquarters and split up. That was the plan, anyway.

I'd drive Carolina to the Eliot Hotel, where she was now staying. And Sixkill would keep watch in the lobby until the morning.

"They ain't here," Hawk said.

"Maybe they've disguised themselves as students?"

"This ain't the place," Hawk said. "This ain't the time. I know these boys are motherfuckers, but no one's that dumb."

"Nguyen is sure of it."

"Nguyen been wrong before."

I walked back into the conference room as the candidates were wrapping up. There were thank-yous from the moderators and applause from the crowd. I nodded to Sixkill and he nodded back. He flanked Carolina as she reached out to press the flesh.

I was less than ten feet away, watching the room. The campus cops stayed on the doors. The Feds I'd noticed did their best to look inconspicuous among the fan base. There were hugs and handshakes, pictures and autographs, and a few minutes later we were walking down the open staircase to the big glass front entrance.

The sun had started to set along the shore. *A gold fringe on the purpling hem.* I searched for the ursine legend prowling the banks alone. But didn't see one lurking about.

The two cop cars had blocked the curving entrance to

the student union. Hawk and I flanked Carolina and Rosen and watched as the black SUV started to move forward for the pickup.

The campus cops cleared the walkway. Three Feds did their best to be part of the crowd in sport shirts and dress slacks. To me, they all looked like Pat Boone at a Metallica concert. As Hawk drove toward the patrol cars blocking the entrance, a white cargo van sped in front of him and drove right toward the Campus Center building.

I held up the flat of my hand to stop the congresswoman. I didn't look back but knew Sixkill had walked Carolina back into the building.

I ran toward the two BPD cars, blue lights flashing, as they pulled a scruffy man out from behind the wheel of the van. He came out grudgingly, hands raised as the two campus cops joined two BPD officers and hammered on the back of the van. The casually dressed Feds surrounded the van with guns drawn.

I waited for the van door to open and for a crew of Minutemen to jump out.

But nothing happened.

I looked behind the glass front of the Campus Center. I saw Sixkill and shook my head.

Hawk jogged up beside me.

"Catering van," Hawk said. "Running real late for a reception."

"Empty?"

"Besides some of those little quiches you like."

"Who told you?"

"Susan," Hawk said. "We laugh about it sometimes. She said she once saw you eat a dozen."

"Lies," I said. "All lies."

Hawk shook his head. I let out a long breath. The shoreline at UMass quiet and golden. A warm breeze buffeted the rocks along the shore. Gulls circled and surveyed the beach and flew north from the point.

The cargo van started to beep and backed up to clear the way for Hawk and the SUV.

"I thought that was it," I said.

"Yeah," Hawk said. "So did the Feds. That caterer's gonna have to change his drawers."

50

The next morning, Boston police responded to a call of a body floating in the river near the Museum of Science. A group of tourists on a Duck Boat had first spotted it, and by the time I arrived, it had been retrieved and brought onto shore. There were a lot of cops and flashing lights and crime scene tape.

I spotted Lieutenant Glass and Frank Belson standing with the coroner and three uniformed officers. Glass saw me first and pretended she didn't. I waved to Belson. He didn't wave back but met me at the edge of the yellow tape.

"Ready to take a look-see?" Belson said.

"Sure," I said. "I haven't had breakfast yet."

"After this," Belson said, "even you won't want to eat. You won't believe who it is."

"Any hints?"

"And spoil the surprise?" he said. "No way."

Belson raised the tape and I slipped under. I joined

Glass and the coroner, a stoop-shouldered graying man named Eddie Vincente. Vincente greeted me and then looked to Glass. Glass shrugged and Vicente pulled back the plastic sheet along the sloped entrance to the water.

He didn't look his best. But it was Gerry Broz.

Gerry appeared to be naked from the waist up and was full of a lot of holes. Most of the blood was gone, but his skin was a pale, purplish color. His eyes were open and his mouth hung wide, showing a lot of silver dental work.

"Sorry to break it to you," Belson said. "I know you must be real busted up."

I was never a fan of Gerry Broz. But this wasn't what I expected when Belson called me. I expected another Minuteman. It was odd to see the life taken out of him, just an empty, bloated shell. The end of a criminal era in Boston.

"Pulled out a 45-millimeter bullet," Glass said. "One of many. Looks like someone took him for target practice."

"Like Noah Dillon," I said.

"Just like Noah Dillon," Belson said.

I shook my head. I'd warned Gerry not to work with Bishop Graves. Over the years, I'd warned Gerry off a lot of things. He never seemed to listen.

"Gerry would've sold out his own mother for a nickel," Belson said. "But jeez. I almost hate to see him go. The Broz family been around a long time."

"Since I got started," I said.

Glass stepped back and looked at me. She cocked her

head. "Pretty convenient," she said. "Maybe someone else killed him, someone who hated his guts, and made it look like the same people who killed Noah Dillon?"

"Trust me," I said. "If I'd killed Gerry, I would've stopped off at Mike's and brought pastries and coffee for all you guys."

"Didn't you want to get even for all the times he wanted you dead?" Glass said. "Even a little?"

"Maybe a little," I said. "But not like this. Something big was supposed to happen last night with the Minutemen. Broz must've gotten in the middle of it."

Two unmarked black cars pulled up behind my Mustang. Nguyen and three Feds finally decided to show up. It was always a point of pride for me to beat the Feds to a crime scene. They must've been having their daily haircut and shoulder rub.

Nguyen flashed his badge. The uniformed officers opened up the yellow tape.

"He lives to flash that badge," Belson said. "Must give him a real hard-on."

Nguyen wore a crisp blue suit, perfect hair glistening in the morning light. He stepped up, flanked by the three Feds. All wore sunglasses except for Nguyen. He placed both hands in his pockets and rocked up on his toes. The effort increased his height by an inch or two.

"A fucking Duck Boat?" Nguyen said. "With old people and kids?"

"Got to love Boston," Belson said. "Happens all the time."

"At least they got their money's worth," I said. "The

old burying ground can't compete with a fresh dead body."

The agent turned on me, eyed me hard, and pointed his finger at my chest. "What the hell is he doing here?" he said. "He can't be walking all through my crime scene. Is that the way things are done around here?"

Belson shrugged. Glass's mouth twitched.

"This is my crime scene," Glass said. "And Spenser has a special relationship with the deceased. We're hoping he might be able to explain a few things."

"Gerry Broz and I go way back," I said.

"How far back?" Nguyen said.

"Spenser used to annoy the shit out of his father," Belson said. "Ole Man Broz tried to clip Spenser a few times."

"And Gerry?" Nguyen said.

"Oh," I said. "He tried to clip me, too. But at that point, his old man and I had an understanding."

"Joe Broz protected you?" Nguyen said.

"No," I said. "He was protecting his son. Joe knew his son was out of his league and didn't want to see him get hurt."

Nguyen looked down at where Gerry Broz lay and asked to see the body. Eddie pulled back the tarp and Nguyen studied the holes. Gerry still looked ugly and bloated, although death seldom looked good on anybody. His face and chest were smooth and hairless, reminding me of the cocky kid I'd met working for Meade Alexander.

"Why would Broz join up with these creeps?" Glass said.

"He didn't," Nguyen said. "It was all business. We raided the Minutemen clubhouse in Malden last night. You should've seen all the guns. It looked like they were planning to invade fucking Grenada. Something went wrong."

"Like maybe Bishop Graves needed to resupply?" I said.

"And wanted a steep discount," Belson said.

"If you know what they're planning, Agent Nguyen," Glass said, "Boston Police would appreciate you letting us in on the details."

I looked to Nguyen and nodded. It wasn't often Glass and I were in complete and total agreement.

"We got this," Nguyen said. "We had a warrant on Graves's house in Newton."

"To be specific," I said, "the deed is in his dear ole mother's name."

Nguyen shot an unpleasant look in my direction. I waited for him to elaborate on the conversation with Mrs. Graves.

"So you got him?" I said.

"Not exactly," Nguyen said. "But it won't be long. It's not the case we wanted. But it's enough. And it was time. Bishop Graves is done. The congresswoman can rest assured."

"So much for Gerry," Belson said.

"His play," I said, shrugging. "Who else don't you have?"

"Ex–Malden cop named Finley."

"I saw him at Cole Buckley's house," I said. "Older guy with a white goatee."

"We got the clubhouse," Nguyen said. "We have their weapons. We've impounded several of their vehicles. They have nothing."

"They got something from Gerry last night," I said. "And he tried to stop them."

"Now these assholes have nothin' to lose," Belson said.

"Lots of time went into building this case," Nguyen said. "We can't help what happened here. Gerry Broz was a crook, maybe a weapons dealer to terrorists, and now he's gone. How often do you tie everything up so neatly at the end?"

Belson shrugged and reached into his jacket pocket for a small and cheap-looking cigar. He lit up and blew his smoke downwind and into Nguyen's face.

"Only cost two bucks," he said. "Can you believe it?"

51

On the fourth floor of the Eliot Hotel, Sixkill let me into Carolina's suite. I had made it past two doormen, three Feds in the lobby, and a BPD officer before I got into the room. Carolina had on jeans and a T-shirt and no shoes. Trey Shaw was with her, watching television in the sitting area, switching between the local news coverage of the Minutemen roundup and a competitive baking competition.

Shaw didn't get up, and greeted me with a loose wave. Carolina brought me into the sitting area with a nice view of Comm Avenue and the Charles River beyond. A room-service cart had been pushed against the far wall, filled with empty plates and two carafes of coffee. I tested each and found one half-full. I poured a cup, sat down, and relayed the latest.

"Agent Nguyen assures me that I'm safe to resume my schedule," Carolina said.

I made a meso-meso gesture.

"The threats are minimal," I said. "But there are still threats."

"Because they haven't found Bishop Graves?"

"They only rounded up a half dozen of his people," I said. "We have no idea how many are out there. I saw at least two dozen at the rally at the Common."

"They're cowards," she said. "They're probably long gone. Scurried back under their rocks."

"*Probably* doesn't work for me," I said.

I told her where I'd been and what I'd seen. I gave her the CliffsNotes version of me and Gerry Broz.

"So?" she said. "I don't see what that has to do with me or my schedule. I have three events this afternoon. And two appearances tomorrow morning. I think you've done what you needed to do. These people have been identified and the FBI is looking for them. I've got more than ample protection."

"A few days probably won't make or break your campaign."

"*Probably* doesn't work for me, either," she said. "Flaherty did a lot better in the debate than we'd hoped. He was prepared this time and seemed to actually convey some knowledge of the district. He didn't take the race for granted like he did last time."

"Just a few days."

Carolina stood up and crossed her arms over her chest. She walked to where her boyfriend sat on the couch watching the news coverage. The weatherman promised some cool evenings ahead with a slight chance of rain. Back on the baking competition, the front-runner's cake had fallen flat, the icing was runny. Trey Shaw flicked off the television and scratched at his beard. He had on one of the Eliot's complimentary white terry-cloth robes and disposable slippers.

He walked over past me, patted my shoulder, and rifled through what was left of room service.

"Can I get you anything?" Shaw said.

I shook my head.

"You know she's not going to change her mind?" he said.

I nodded. I heard the door open and close and Sixkill walked back into the room. I watched as he placed several bottled waters into Carolina's oversized bag.

"How's Adam?" I said to Carolina.

"Much better," she said. "He's being released tomorrow. But I don't expect him back anytime soon. I wish I could hire Sixkill to be my interim body man."

"That's up to Sixkill," I said.

"He's very handy," Carolina said. "And can carry twice as much as Adam."

"Strong like bull," Sixkill said. He pretended to curl the oversized bag with great effort.

"The last person I heard say that was Uncle Tonoose," I said.

Shaw and Carolina both walked back to the little grouping and sat on a sofa across from me. Shaw wrapped his arm around her and pulled her close while she rested her head on his shoulder. Shaw was scruffy, goofy, and lumbering, but Carolina seemed very fond of him. It was the first time I'd ever seen her relax or show an ounce of vulnerability.

"Can I at least talk you out of greeting commuters before the Sox game tonight?" I said.

I'd memorized her schedule for the rest of the week. She thought about it, looked up to Shaw and then back to me.

"That's a tough crowd," I said. "Kenmore station is a less-than-ideal place to make secure. Even on a slow day, it's a constant flow of people. Besides, I don't hold out much hope for the game. As much as it pains me, the Yankees look unbeatable this year."

"Maybe I can rally the fans," Carolina said.

"You'd need to rally the team," I said. "We've lost the last six straight."

"Okay," she said. "But no complaints on the One Boston rally tomorrow. No one is going to make trouble in Government Center. That's about as secure as it gets. And Agent Nguyen says he'll have me completely covered. That place will be thick in cops and Feds."

"Okay," I said. "But we cancel the dedication at Copley Plaza later in the day."

"What do you have against Copley Plaza?" she said.

"Too accessible," I said. "Too many ways in and out. It's a terrible place to put you in front of a crowd."

Carolina agreed. I stood up and walked to the window and called Rosen, running down the plans for the next forty-eight hours. I watched traffic along Comm Avenue and could see the doorman had left my car where I'd parked it behind a patrol car.

On the way out, I told Sixkill that either Hawk or I would replace him in a few hours. Not that he showed it, but he had to be exhausted. He walked with me past the cops and to the elevators.

"Are you sure the Minutemen killed Broz?" Sixkill said. "From what you told me, Gerry had a lengthy list of enemies."

"He was killed and dumped pretty much the same as Noah Dillon."

"Lots of people shot up and dumped in the river," Sixkill said.

"The Feds took away the Minutemen's cache," I said. "They had to be desperate. And lacking in funding."

"Now what?" Sixkill said. "We stand back and protect Carolina while the Feds round up the rest?"

"No fun in that," I said.

"You've never been about the fun," Sixkill said. "You gave your word to Carolina that you'd stop the threats. You can't walk away until these people are dead or caught."

"That's going to be completely up to them," I said. "With Gerry Broz dead, we're not the only ones looking for them."

"Gerry's crew?"

"Sure," I said. "And Vinnie as well."

"Vinnie cares?"

"Yeah," I said. "A lot more than you'd think. Vinnie always thought he could help Gerry. And Gerry always failed him."

"Like a father."

"Something like that."

52

I'm sorry, Vinnie," I said. "You knew Gerry most of his life."

"He wasn't any good," Vinnie said. "Couldn't help it. He was born that way. Sometimes I wondered if he was even Joe's kid."

I stood with Hawk and Vinnie in the parking lot of Vinnie's bowling alley. He was smoking and leaning against his red Cadillac. Hawk's Jaguar parked across from him, diagonal in the open lot. Traffic zooming past on Route 2.

"He shoulda never done business with these people," Vinnie said. "Anyone with half a brain would've known better."

I nodded. Hawk had his arms crossed over his chest. We didn't like Gerry, had never liked Gerry, but knew Vinnie had a different experience with him. Gerry never tried to kill Vinnie, as he'd tried with me on more than one occasion.

"There was a time when Gerry was sixteen, maybe

seventeen," Vinnie said. "Wrote some bad checks on Joe's business account and was afraid to tell Joe. When Joe found out, he went apeshit. He tossed the kid out of his office and onto the street. Busted Gerry up pretty good. If I hadn't been there, I think Joe would've killed him with his bare hands."

"Can you find out about his dealings with this guy Bishop Graves?"

"I dunno," Vinnie said. "I wasn't tight with Gerry lately. He was into things that I wouldn't ever touch."

"Like what?" I said.

"Women," Vinnie said. "Working with Fast Eddie Lee in some nail salon action up in Blackburn. You know all that. Drugs. Always the drugs. I heard something about guns. But I can't be so sure. I don't know why anyone would want to touch guns and drugs; that brings the Feds crashing down on your head."

"The Minutemen were apparently well armed," I said. "The Feds found a pretty hefty cache at their clubhouse in Malden."

"Malden?" he said. "What the fuck are they doing up there?"

"Plotting."

"Plotting what?" Vinnie said. "What the fuck can you plot in Malden?"

"Ah," I said. "Therein lies the rub."

"What the fuck does that mean?"

"Means," Hawk said, "these white boys planning something big. We just don't know what."

"Big and bad?" Vinnie said.

"So they say," I said.

"Got any idea on where they scattered after they got raided?" Vinnie said.

"Maybe," I said. "I think I can draw out one of their members. Bishop Graves killed this guy's brother."

"Killed his brother?" Vinnie said. "Christ. And this asshole still follows him? That's some kind of nuts. No offense. But there's professional relationships and then there is blood. You kill someone in my family, even someone I don't like, and you can kiss your ass goodbye."

"Think maybe you can reach out to some of Gerry's associates?" I said. "I would call up Ennie Guzman and his pal Bamm Bamm. But they may hold a grudge against me and Hawk."

"I heard," Vinnie said. "Those two want you dead."

"Get in line," Hawk said. "And take a number."

Vinnie blew out some smoke. He watched the traffic along Route 2. He scrolled through his phone and then looked back at us, cigarette bobbing between his lips.

"Stupid," he said. "Joe set his son up for freakin' life. He didn't have to do a thing but get fat and spend his old man's money."

"Always had something to prove," I said.

"But didn't have the talent or the sense to do it," Vinnie said. "What can you tell me about these assholes?"

I told him everything I knew.

"Jesus Christ," Vinnie said. "Makes me want to puke we got people like that here. The shit my grandfather had to endure for just coming to this country and working until he dropped."

"Try being black," Hawk said.

I raised my hand. "What about 'Neither dogs or Irishmen should apply'?"

"Ha," Hawk said. "Y'all really want to argue on this? Ain't no competition."

Vinnie nodded. He dropped the cigarette, ground it under his dress heel, and dialed up someone on his cell.

"I'll see what I can do with Gerry's guys," Vinnie said. "I'll ask that they don't shoot you in the back until everything is over. Cool?"

"Mighty white of you, Vinnie," Hawk said.

"Hey." Vinnie winked at him. "What are friends for?"

53

Hawk and I drove up to Salem and waited in front of Max Dillon's house, hoping the prodigal son would return. Three hours later, I wasn't even sure Max would return. Maybe he was at work. Maybe he was at the end of the bar calling for another shot of Jim Beam. I checked a database I subscribed to for his phone number. I got two. No answer for either, but one had a voicemail. I left a message just as it started to rain.

Hawk began to hum "Into Each Life Some Rain Must Fall."

"'*But too much is falling in mine*,'" I said.

"That white boy better pray we the ones who find him."

"A similar thought had crossed my mind."

"Vinnie is half Italian," Hawk said. "That half gonna tear that boy's ass up."

"He promised to let us talk to him first."

"Sure," Hawk said. "Right before he put a bullet in

his head. We both know Vinnie. We both like Vinnie. But neither of us would want to run up against Vinnie."

"I have before."

"Before y'all become friends," Hawk said. "Joined our association of the disreputable."

"That's what you call it?"

"Sure," Hawk said. "Sounds about right."

There were few places more lonely than the end of a road in Salem bordered by a cemetery. Although, come Halloween, this would be the place to be. I wondered if Mr. Dillon got into the spirit, hobbling up to the front door and handling out candy bars. It wasn't that long ago that both his boys would've been of the right age. Before they joined the Army, traveled halfway across the world, and came back to meet up with a swell guy like Bishop Graves.

"You ever going to tell me about Dominique?" I said.

"Ain't much to tell," Hawk said. "We met. Liked each other. Then she split."

"Went back to France."

"Nothing new?"

"Been a little busy," I said. "But my friend of a friend promises to come through. His name is Philippe Maurizi. He's Corsican. If he can't find her, no one can."

"You ever know a woman you can't keep thinking about?" he said. "Even though it's been years?"

"Susan."

"Oh, hell."

"You asked."

"Nobody else?" he said.

"There was a woman named Brenda Loring," I said. "I don't know what happened to her. Sometimes I wonder about her."

"But you don't bring it up, because it would be disrespectful to Susan."

"In case you haven't noticed, Susan is fairly confident in our relationship," I said. "It's more that I feel it's another life. I was different then. She was different then. I wouldn't seek someone out unless I had a good reason."

The statement and my subtle question just kind of hung there. The rain fell. I turned on the wipers and they tick-tocked across the glass. Hawk hummed some more of the song.

"Before she left, she told me she was pregnant," Hawk said.

"What did you say?"

"The wrong thing," Hawk said. "Wasn't ready to accept it."

"And she left?"

"Not long after," he said. "Don't know if she kept the baby. Don't know if she didn't. Don't know if she alive. Don't know if she dead."

"And the not knowing is the problem."

"Been some time," Hawk said. "Got me some perspective on things."

I nodded. I glanced into my rearview mirror and then up at the fence line along the Dillon house. Few cars had passed. None had moved. All was quiet across the tombstones beyond the stone fence. *The graveyard draws the living still, but never any more the dead.*

"The picture you have of her was beautiful," I said.

"Man, you got no idea."

"I got some idea," I said. "You've known many beautiful women."

"Beautiful, smart," Hawk said. "She was an artist. Called me her Nubian warrior."

"Maybe she's alive."

"Long ago," Hawk said. "Not sure she ever wants to hear from me."

"Because you hurt her."

Hawk didn't say anything. The rain slowed. The end of the street in Salem was quiet and empty. I turned on the radio and found an afternoon jazz show. Blossom Dearie singing about the "Surrey with the Fringe on Top." The music matched the melancholy mood, Dearie's voice sounding innocent and childlike and reminding me of times long ago. Susan in deep blue eye shadow.

"I didn't hurt her," Hawk said. "I wanted her to stay."

"It's not too late."

"I don't know if you've noticed," Hawk said. "But we getting a little long in the tooth. That kid be about same age as Mattie."

I was about to argue the point about me getting long in the tooth when my cell rang. I hoped it was Max Dillon calling me back. It was a number I didn't recognize, but I took the call anyway.

"Josh Dillon says you and him are real tight," Vinnie said.

"We've met," I said.

"Says he'll talk," Vinnie said. "But only to you."

"Okay."

"But here's the deal, Spenser," Vinnie said. "What happens after isn't your call. This is between me and him. I owe Joe that at least."

"Where are you?"

"Gerry's place on the wharf," Vinnie said. "Bamm Bamm and Ennie brought in today's fresh catch."

54

It was night by the time we got back the city, and the wharf was empty and still. I drove my Mustang up onto the pier and sped past the boats up to the end, where I saw Vinnie's Cadillac.

"C-A-D-I-L-L-A-C," Hawk said.

"Bo Diddley taught you to spell that?"

"Ain't no one better."

I parked and we headed to the back entrance beyond the plastic fish bins. The fishing boats creaked along the docks. The lights of the waterfront did their proper twinkling along Boston Harbor. Everything still smelled of fish, the stink permeating everything along the pier.

The door was ajar. We walked into the reception area and were about to head upstairs to the offices when we heard sounds beyond a metal door behind the front desk. We followed the noise and came into a large, brightly lit warehouse with processing equipment. Vinnie and Bamm Bamm Bonzini had Josh Dillon on a conveyer belt with the lower half of his body shrink-wrapped in plastic, his head aimed toward some kind of packing mechanism that clattered and inched him forward.

"He alive?" I said.

"Yeah," Vinnie said. "Just trying to keep him fresh for you."

Josh Dillon was naked under the plastic. His face was a mess and I wouldn't have recognized him except for the fact that Vinnie had told me it was him. I walked over and pressed a big red button to stop the machine.

I looked to Bamm Bamm. He snorted at me.

"Goddamn, Vinnie," Hawk said. "You tryin' to fillet this motherfucker?"

"Okay," Vinnie said. "Okay. Bamm Bamm. Put him back in the cooler."

Bamm Bamm swept up Josh Dillon, tossed him over his shoulder, and marched him off to a large freezer door. I looked over at Vinnie. He didn't look good. His eyes were red-rimmed and I could smell the liquor on his breath. He wasn't taking Gerry's death very well.

"Fat little boy," Vinnie said. "Little snot-nosed kid. He never understood who his dad was and what he did. He didn't understand all the pressures Joe had on him. All the hands out. All the things he had to run to keep order in this fucking town."

I touched Vinnie's shoulder. He had on a blue dress shirt and crisp black pants. His shirt was rolled up to his elbows and his normally perfect hair was scattered across his face. He reached into his pocket for a cigarette and I noticed his knuckles were swollen.

"No bullshit," he said. "From either of you. He killed him. This little crazy punk killed Joe's boy."

I nodded and walked back to the freezer. Josh Dillon hung from a hook reserved for a swordfish or a big tuna. His eyes were swollen shut and his breath was low and uneven. I had to tap at his face to make sure he was alive.

"It's Spenser."

"They're going to kill me," Dillon said. The words not much more than a whisper.

"They won't," I said. "I promise."

"Why?" he said. "Why would you stop him?"

"Because I'm not Bishop Graves," I said. "And I made you a deal."

"It's too late," he said. "Everything is set. You're all too late."

"Where is he?"

"Gone," Josh Dillon said. "All that stuff about a kidnapping and a trial, that was bullshit. We knew Noah had turned. We fed him a bunch of lies and then Bishop killed him."

"He was your brother."

Dillon's head lolled up. One eye slightly open. The other snapped shut.

"So," he said. "He was never committed. He didn't have it in him."

"Bishop Graves is a coward," I said. "He and Cole Buckley want to burn everything down. They don't care about you. Not like your brother or your father. Your father loves you. He'll forgive you for this."

"He's a drunk."

"You can stop it from happening," I said.

"So?" he said. "What does it matter? What's done is done. That bitch is dead."

"No," I said. "You can stop it. You can get through this."

I heard Vinnie and Hawk walk up on my shoulder. I glanced at Vinnie. He wouldn't look at me. He sucked on a cigarette and turned his head to blow the smoke away in the cold storage room. The smoke bloomed into a cloud and hung in the air.

"I can get you protection," I said. "I can get you a deal."

"From who?"

"The Feds," I said. "It's not too late. It's never too late."

Hawk stepped up. He pulled at the hook mechanism and set Josh Dillon swinging back and forth. Bamm Bamm and Vinnie had done a thorough job on the shrink-wrapping. He looked airtight and ready to FedEx.

"Bishop will kill me, too."

"Graves won't be able to touch you."

"Bullshit."

"It's either come with me," I said, "or be left with these guys. I kinda like your chances with me. You come with me and tell me everything Graves wants to do."

Josh Dillon didn't answer. I told Vinnie to take him down. Vinnie didn't move. Bamm Bamm turned to me and grabbed me by my arm. I punched him hard in the jaw with my right fist and finished with two quick jabs to his soft stomach. He fell to his knees.

Hawk lifted Josh Dillon off the hook. He walked to the door.

"Stop," Vinnie said.

He had a gun in his hand. I kept walking.

"I swear to Christ," he said. "I'll shoot you both. He killed Joe's kid. He killed Joe's kid."

Hawk didn't break stride. I turned my back to Vinnie and kept on walking.

Vinnie didn't shoot. I heard a sobbing sound behind me but didn't look back. It was too personal to watch. Vinnie wouldn't want me to watch.

Hawk opened the passenger door to my Mustang and set Dillon against the door. He pulled out a folding knife and cut him free of the shrink wrap. As he began to fall, I caught him and lay him down in the small backseat.

"What now?" Hawk said.

I got in behind the wheel. I didn't start the car. Hawk had the passenger door open. He turned and walked to the end of the pier and stared out across the waterfront.

"Can you really help me?" Josh Dillon said.

"I already have."

"They have two trucks," he said. "And all this shit they stole from this Broz guy."

"What kind of shit."

"Guns," he said. "Explosives."

"And what are they going to do?"

"They're going to kill that bitch," he said. "And everyone that comes to hear her talk."

"When?"

"Tomorrow," he said. "Shit. It's as good as done.

You're too late. They've had this planned for too long. You can't stop them."

"What event?"

"One Boston," he said. "Togetherness and lies. And mongrelization of America. Bishop is right. They deserve this. They all fucking deserve it."

I picked up the phone and dialed Nguyen.

55

Before the sun came up, I stood with Agent Nguyen in Government Center, watching a crew assemble a large stage for the One Boston rally. It was supposed to be an all-day affair highlighting the cultural diversity of the city. There were performances by a Haitian jazz band, dancers from Nicaragua, Celtic music from Ireland, and a group of children with music from the Cape Verdean islands. Today didn't seem a good day for it. It hadn't stopped raining all night, and Nguyen and I stood under our black umbrellas staring out at the empty redbrick expanse by city hall.

"We have her covered," he said.

"I heard."

"No trucks," he said. "No way anyone gets through here. It's a tight perimeter."

"Have you been waiting awhile to say that?" I said. "Tight perimeter?"

"We're professionals," he said. "That is what we do."

"And my job is to make sure the congresswoman gets the chance to speak."

"She will," he said. "No one is stopping her."

"I wasn't surprised by the Minutemen," I said. "But I was surprised by all the other hate she got. She gets mountains of death threats and hate mail every day. And she keeps going. That's why she can't stop today. She stops today and she said it might become a habit."

"You believe in everything she says?" Nguyen said.

"Does it matter?" I said. "I believe in her right to be heard. And for an elected official to be able to do their job without fear."

"These cowards don't see it that way," he said. "You know the kind of weirdos we had down in Georgia. Now they're up here. Hell, they're everywhere these days. People talk about terrorism. Our biggest terrorist threat is in our own backyards."

The streetlamps were on across Government Center, making lovely gold patterns in the puddles along the brick. The T station glowed across the way as a few lights began to click on in the windows of city hall. Boston was waking up.

"If a mouse so much as farts," Nguyen said.

"But where's a mouse when you need one," I said.

I left Nguyen and joined up with Hawk over by Congress. He sat on a concrete stanchion wearing a black hooded poncho over his bald head.

"Carolina open up the show?"

"At ten."

Hawk nodded. He stared out across Congress Street and the glass walls of the Holocaust Memorial. A line of three white trucks turned off Congress and onto Hanover by the Public Market.

"What day is today?" Hawk said.

"Hard for me to remember."

"Saturday," Hawk said. "Lots of folks going to be out strolling the Haymarket."

"True."

"Lots of trucks going in and out," he said. "And most of them are going to look like the ones those Minutemen took off Gerry Broz."

"You think we better take a look?" I said.

Hawk pushed off the stanchion. "We'd be fools not to."

We crossed Congress through the memorial, the glass slick with rain, water sluicing down the names, and over onto Hanover.

"'And as the morning steals upon the night, melting the darkness.'"

"What's that supposed to mean?"

"It means it's early."

Hawk nodded. He looked like a monk under the poncho. But I didn't know many monks who kept a loaded .44 Magnum under their scapular. I had my Browning up under my jacket. Despite the umbrella, the rain dripped off the bill of my Braves cap.

When we got to Blackstone, the market was bustling and alive with tents and awnings as far I could see. Delivery trucks and vans were parked all along Blackstone

Street, bringing in fresh seafood, produce, and flowers to the vendor stalls.

"Think the Feds know about this?"

"Nguyen bragged how a mouse couldn't fart in his tight perimeter."

Hawk shook his head. He walked ahead and turned down the rows of trucks. We checked the cabs and the open trailers. Many of the drivers and deliverymen were black and Hispanic. For most English was a second language, as it had been for sellers and drivers at the market for as long as I could remember. Long before that, it was the Irish selling hay for horses.

I looked for anyone I recognized from the Minutemen rallies or photos I'd taken at Carolina's campaign stops. The rain tapped at the canopies and tarps over the vendors. White string lights and bare bulbs lit up the little kiosks filled with fish on ice, fresh berries, and apples. If I hadn't been searching for domestic terrorists, the sight of all the food might've made me hungry.

"Might need some assistance," Hawk said. "Too many trucks. Coming and going."

I texted Nguyen. And then Hawk and I started searching every truck down Blackstone Street. The rain falling harder now, workers and vendors scattering from the cabs and up under the canopies.

The more trucks we checked, the more kept arriving, spilling out onto the Greenway.

"Like finding a needle in the Haymarket."

"You know they here," Hawk said. "I can smell those peckerwoods."

56

I wandered in and out of trucks and cargo vans, checking open doors and tailgates and scouring faces. No one said a word to us or asked any questions, Hawk moving to another row of trucks parked along the Greenway. The rain was slow and steady now, and I was wet after dropping my umbrella upon entering the market.

I jumped up onto running boards and looked in windows. I grabbed the arms of complete strangers and spun them around. I looked for anyone or anything connected to Bishop Graves and the Minutemen. We were only a block over from Government Center and any of those trucks could break through the barriers and kill a lot of people. Terrorists with a lot less had done a great amount of damage to the city and its people before.

I felt an adrenaline rush as I jogged from truck to truck. Once seeing a man that I was sure was Bishop Graves only to get close enough to learn he spoke German.

I'd lost sight of Hawk in the rain and the sea of tarps and tents. I stepped up onto a running board of a truck to look around and catch my breath. Down the rows, I saw a man in what looked like black tactical clothing. He was bald and clean-shaven, standing by the tailgate of a small delivery truck.

I jumped down and walked toward him. I didn't recognize him. But I did recognize the logo for Neptune's Delight. It was one of Gerry Broz's trucks. I kept on walking past him and glanced in the window of the truck, seeing Cole Buckley behind the wheel.

Hawk appeared on the driver's side. He tapped at the window with his .44.

Buckley started the engine. Hawk shot out the window and pulled Buckley through the broken glass. People were yelling and screaming, the crowd running away from the gunshots.

When I looked back for the man I'd first noticed, I watched another man run past him and toward the stalls in the market. He'd shaved off his beard, but I was sure it was Bishop Graves. I ran after him, and Graves pulled down tables of produce to block my way. People panicked, running in every direction. Graves ran into a tent and out through the other side. I jumped over a table of strawberries and melons and toppled over before regaining my footing and following him through the stalls where the market ended.

I heard a revving engine and looked behind me as another truck plowed down Blackstone Street, taking out car doors and tables, splattering produce and crushed ice, vendors diving out of its way. The truck raced toward the end of the Haymarket and out to North Street.

Sirens wailed as Graves ran toward the parking deck and nearly got hit by a passing van trying to cross the street. I slid over the hood of a car and hit the ground running, focusing on Graves's back as he ran into the Haymarket, which hadn't opened to customers yet.

Graves turned, pulled a gun, and shot at me. I jumped behind a concrete barrier set up near the front steps of the market. He shot at me again. I heard more sirens and he turned back, running away from Faneuil Hall and between Quincy Market and the South Market. He darted behind a shuttered kiosk.

Two patrol cars rolled up onto the opposite end of the pedestrian mall, closing in on Graves. He would have to get out by them or through me. Either way wasn't going to work out so well.

I'd found cover behind a concrete bench. With my Browning in hand, I looked as suspect as Graves did. But until some cops got closer on my end, I'd make sure I blocked the way.

I heard a roaring motor and squealing tires and watched as the white truck came racing into the pedestrian mall toward me. Graves ran out to catch the truck, gun in one hand and a cell phone in the other.

I fired off two shots to change his mind.

The man in tactical gear I'd seen earlier jumped out from the driver's seat and shot at me.

I fired once and he stopped. Graves now ran in the other direction, toward the cops.

He didn't drop the phone or the gun. The officers, I wasn't sure how many, opened fire and dropped Bishop Graves very hard and very fast onto the walkway.

I dropped my gun and raised my hands. A BPD officer who'd shot at Graves ran to me with her weapon drawn. I considered trying to explain who I was, thought better of it, and lay down on the ground like she ordered me to do. I caught my breath lying in a big puddle while the heavens opened up.

I was maybe ten feet away from Graves. He was on his back and writhing. Police officers surrounded him. One cop, a black man, was down on his knees pressing his jacket to Bishop Graves's chest to stanch the bleeding.

The officer over me cuffed me but helped me to my feet. More cops had the other Minuteman on the ground by the white truck.

I heard her radio. They had two people dead back at the Haymarket.

Soon the EMTs arrived and took Bishop Graves away. The patrol officer put me in the back of her unit and drove me to the Haymarket, where dozens of cops had gathered. I spotted Agent Nguyen talking with two agents.

It took about thirty minutes, but finally the special agent in charge vouched for me and the cuffs were removed. I massaged my wrists and joined the Feds.

"Two dead?"

"One was Cole Buckley," he said. "The other was an old man who got clipped by that truck. Lucky. It could've been a lot worse."

I looked around but knew Hawk was long gone. Hawk wasn't much on standing around with cops and answering questions.

"Think you can get my gun back?" I said.

"Don't press your luck," Nguyen said.

"You mind me asking what was in the truck?"

"Would you believe me if I said nothing?"

I looked at him.

"I think the plan was just to plow through the crowd, start shooting, and take out the congresswoman," he said. "If lots of her supporters got killed, so much the better."

"Jesus," I said.

It had stopped raining, but the Haymarket was empty, crime scene tape blocking the entrance. Half of the market a tattered mess of tarps, tents, and overturned tables from where the second truck had plowed through, trying to escape and pick up Bishop Graves.

"What a mess," Nguyen said.

"But it's done."

"For now," he said, adjusting the little flag pin on his lapel. "Keeping these assholes down is starting to feel like a game of Whac-A-Mole."

57

Thank you for coming last night," Kyle Rosen said. "Carolina was thrilled you and Susan made it."

It was ten days after the gunfight at the Haymarket corral and the morning after the congresswoman's primary victory party. We stayed late into the night at the Cambridge Marriott, where I had several cocktails and allowed Susan to take advantage of me later.

"She's sorry she wasn't able to thank you in person," Rosen said. "But she had to fly back today to get to work on some very important legislation."

"She is a very important person," I said. "No thanks needed."

Rosen sat in my client chair while I sat at my desk, running down a few more leads on Hawk's mystery woman. Pearl guarded the entrance to my office door as she snored softly on the couch.

"I wish I could say the threats have stopped."

"So soon?" I said.

"They poured in after the Minutemen were arrested," Rosen said. His curly hair was even longer and wilder, as if no mortal could calm it. "I guess a lot of people look to Bishop Graves as some kind of prophet."

"I tried to make him a martyr," I said. "But missed."

"It was better he lived," Rosen said. "I look forward to his trial and his sentencing."

"He already shaved his beard," I said. "Prison will be a little different than living with his mother."

"Wish we could afford to keep you on permanently."

"Wish I could afford to continue," I said. "But my dog has very expensive tastes."

Pearl looked up from the couch and sniffed at the air. Sensing there wasn't any danger, she lay her head back down and continued to snooze. I leaned forward in my office chair, my elbows resting on my desk. On my computer, I had three possible women who could be Hawk's Dominique. One was dead. One was married. I hoped contestant number three would be the one.

I looked over the desk at Rosen. I smiled.

He smiled back.

I sensed something was on his mind.

"I guess we need to settle up."

I shrugged.

"Your hours exceeded what we'd anticipated."

"You didn't anticipate late hours tracking down white nationalists wanting to disrupt the election and cause mass chaos and dissension?"

"No," Rosen said. "Not really."

I wrote down a figure on the edge of a yellow legal pad, tore off the page, and handed it to him.

"That's it?"

"Consider the rest a campaign donation," I said. "My last case was very lucrative. Hawk ended up adding on to his home in the Bahamas."

"Wow," he said. "Just wow. I don't know what to say. Can I at least get Carolina to take you to lunch next time she's in town? That way we can offer a proper thank-you for everything you did."

"Has the congresswoman ever been to Karl's Sausage Kitchen?"

"I don't think so."

"The Agawam Diner?"

Rosen shook his head. He looked a bit confused.

"We will have to fix that."

I stood and offered my hand. I told him details would be worked out forthwith. Rosen smiled all the way out the door. I worked for another few hours, finally getting some information that I hadn't thought I'd get today due to the time difference. I made some notes and pecked away at some open reports before I snatched my jacket and my cap and walked down Berkeley Street to Davio's.

I found Susan at the bar, wearing her cheaters and reading through the wine selection. She pretended not to notice I'd taken a seat beside her.

"Come here often?" I said.

"Only to pick up strange men and bring them back to my lair."

"'Lair'?"

"Yes," she said. "You think you could handle it?"

"Maybe," I said. "If you promise to be gentle. I bruise easily."

Susan grinned, removed her glasses, and cocked her head at me. She wore a very stylish navy dress that appeared to come loose with just a slight yank of the belt. She smelled of lavender soap and sunshine.

"You're late," she said.

"I had an important call to make."

"More important than me?" she said.

I reached into my jacket and pulled out my phone. I scrolled through to one of the pictures I'd found online.

"Stunning young woman," she said. "Who is she?"

"This may be a lot to process."

I told her about Hawk and the favor. And the dead end on Dominique but a new lead on this younger woman. She was twenty-two, mixed race, and in photos brooded with a singular intensity that seemed familiar. The bartender brought a Riesling for Susan and an Allagash white for me.

"Wow," Susan said.

"You said it."

"When are you going to tell him?"

"So you think I should tell him?"

"Why wouldn't you?"

"I'm not sure Hawk is ready for this."

"Would you be ready for similar news?"

I shook my head. I drank some beer.

"But that's not up to you to decide."

I nodded. I rotated the beer in my hand clockwise. And then back the other way.

"He wouldn't have asked if he didn't want to know," she said. "All of it."

"She lives in Sète," I said. "South of France."

"Who was the mother?"

I told her all I knew and all I didn't.

"And he never mentioned her to you?"

"Nope."

"You men," Susan said. "Sometimes the self-containment must feel like a prison."

58

The next morning, Hawk and I worked out with Sixkill one last time before he headed west. We put on headgear and sparred in the boxing room Henry kept special for us at the Harbor Health Club. As the light came up through the windows of the gym, Henry was quick to offer both criticisms and mild disgust.

"If you keep skipping leg day, you're gonna start clucking, Spenser."

"But at least you and I will finally see eye to eye."

Henry shook his head and turned from the room. I'd soaked through my sleeveless sweatshirt. Hawk removed his gloves with his teeth and reached for a water bottle.

"Been a while," Sixkill said. "I train sometimes with a guy in East L.A. Different kind of style out there. Different way of training."

"Good to meet up with new people," Hawk said. "Learn new things."

"Hawk was lucky to meet me," I said. "I taught him the ancient Celtic fistic arts."

"And I introduced him to speed and quickness," Hawk said. "Eating all those potatoes made him slow."

Sixkill smiled. He had on his old ROCKY BOY NORTHSTARS FOOTBALL T-shirt. The shirt was more worn out than I recalled, with the neck slit and the sleeves cut off. His black hair pulled tight in a ponytail. His face still showing the scars he'd gotten when we'd taken on a crew trying to push Henry out of his condo on Revere Beach.

"Sometimes I wish I could stay," Sixkill said. "This feels like home."

"All those swimming pools, movie stars, women in bikinis?" Hawk said. "Shit."

"And then there is that," Sixkill said.

"We can't teach you any more," I said. "You did right. You got your own world and your own business. Just make sure to send us a cut of the profits."

"Will do," Sixkill said. "Once I turn a profit."

Hawk drank some more water and tossed Sixkill a bottle. Sixkill killed half the bottle.

"See," Hawk said. "He do take after you."

After, Sixkill went back to my place in the Navy Yard to pack. Hawk and I showered and dressed and met back outside by Rowes Wharf and the ferry terminal. We drank coffee and walked along the Harborwalk, cooling off after the workout.

We found a place to stand and rest our coffees on a concrete piling. I reached into my gym bag and handed him a thorough report on everything I'd learned about Dominique and her oldest daughter.

He slit open the envelope and started to read. It was only a few pages long. After he was done, he slid it back into the envelope and put it into his gym bag.

"Wish to discuss?" I said.

"Ain't nothing to discuss."

"Damn," I said.

Hawk looked at me.

"Susan bet me twenty bucks that's what you'd say."

"Susan's a smart woman."

"What will you do?"

Hawk drank some coffee. He looked out at the harbor and the Atlantic beyond. It was cool and windy. A little salt tang in the air. It was a long swim to France.

"Don't know," he said. "Have to figure out that part next."

"Wish I could have found out more."

"So much more," Hawk said. "Maybe I'll tell you one day."

"I'll invoice you later."

"Haw," he said. "Still waiting on that check from Carolina Garcia-Ramirez. But then it looks like she's already back in D.C."

"Rosen told me the threats keep on coming."

"Folks broken these days," Hawk said. "Ain't gonna be happy till they burn it all down."

"At least we won't be out of work."

"You do your thing your way," he said. "And I'll do mine."

"If you need help on this," I said. I gestured down to the file in his bag.

"You'd be glad to fly to France with me and partake in the champagne and baguettes?"

"It's the least I could do."

Hawk tossed the rest of his coffee and stood at the edge of the pier and looked out at the sailboats crisscrossing the harbor, getting that last little bit of sailing in before winter froze all our bits off.

"Gonna get cold soon," Hawk said.

I nodded.

We pounded fists and Hawk walked back toward the wharf. When I looked behind me, he was gone.

Acknowledgments

My great thanks to Mark Arsenault of *The Boston Globe* for his keen insight into the city's political scene, and to my former student and friend Nick Simpson for the terrific conversations about life inside the beltway. I'm also grateful to Angela Moore Atkins and Jack Pendarvis for their close reads and support during production. And, as always, thanks to the Putnam team for rolling out the fiftieth Spenser novel: Danielle Dieterich, Katie McKee, and Brennin Cummings. Cheers to you all.

TURN THE PAGE FOR AN EXCERPT

Just days after their team's biggest win, Paradise High School's star baseball player is found dead at the bottom of a bluff. For police chief Jesse Stone, the loss is doubly difficult—the teen was the nephew of his colleague Suitcase Simpson, and Jesse had been coaching the young shortstop. But as he searches for answers about how the boy died, another body is found, and this time it's former Paradise police chief Charlie Farrell. When threats—and gunshots—appear on Jesse's own doorstep, Jesse and his team must discover the common factor between the two deaths before there's a third.

1

Jesse Stone looked out at the baseball game being played at O'Hara Field, a ballgame on an afternoon like this always a beautiful thing, at least to him, his eyes fixed at the moment on the kid playing shortstop.

Jesse felt as if he were looking at himself, back when he was a high school senior, back when he could see a whole lifetime of baseball days like this stretching out in front of him.

This kid was a little taller. Had a little more range. But not more arm. Definitely not more arm.

Nobody ever had more arm than I did.

Jesse felt himself smiling. Because even knowing what he knew about what had happened once he made it as far as Triple-A, the big leagues close enough to touch, knowing how baseball would break his goddamn heart later, he wanted to climb down out of the bleachers and be this kid's age and change places with him in a heartbeat.

Just for one more afternoon.

Have one more game like this.

"What did you think about when it was late in a game like this?" Suitcase Simpson asked.

Suit was on one side of Jesse. Molly Crane was on the other. The kid at short, Jack Carlisle, was Suit's nephew, his sister Laura's boy. About to accept a scholarship to go play college ball at Vanderbilt, unless he changed his mind at the last second. Jesse didn't follow college ball the way he did the majors. But he knew enough to know that Vanderbilt had a big-ass program, and had sent a lot of kids to the big leagues over the years.

"I wanted the ball hit to me," Jesse said.

He heard a snort from Molly.

"So you could be in control. I'm shocked. Shocked, I tell ya."

Without turning, Jesse put a finger to his lips.

"Don't you shush me, Jesse Stone," she said. "You act like we're in church."

"Baseball is better than church," Jesse said.

Molly, the good Catholic girl, stared up at the sky. "Forgive him, Father." She smiled. "And not just for that."

Jesse turned to Suit. "I feel as if I've been sitting next to fans like her at ballgames my whole life."

"You wish," Molly said.

Suit shook his head. "*I* feel like I've got a bad middle seat on a long plane ride."

The Paradise Pirates were ahead of Marshport, 2–1. League championship game. Bottom of the ninth. Jesse always wanted to laugh when he heard people calling teams "bitter" rivals in sports. Only people on the outside. They had no idea. All they had to do was watch a game like this. Every single one of these kids on this field, both teams, waiting for the ball to be put in play and so much to start happening at once, was exactly where he wanted to be.

Where I always wanted to be.

Wanting the ball to be hit to me.

He had been working with Jack Carlisle a little bit this spring, at Suit's request. Trying to teach the kid some of the things that Jesse had learned on his own. Not teach him everything he knew. Just some of it. Some of the baseball he still had in him, despite landing on his shoulder that day in Albuquerque, his dreams about making The Show crash-landing right along with him.

His father had always been more interested in being a cop than he was in baseball. Or in watching his kid play baseball. Jesse could count on one hand the times the old man had actually shown up for one of his games.

Two outs now. The Marshport center fielder had just struck out swinging.

But the tying run was still at third base.

Go-ahead run at second.

"Move to your right," Jesse said quietly.

As if somehow Jack Carlisle could hear him.

"He pulled one into the hole his last time-out."

Still talking to himself. But tricking himself into believing he was talking to the kid at short.

"What?" Suit asked.

"Nothing" was Jesse's reply.

The Marshport batter stepped out of the box, buying himself some time. Maybe about to win the game, and the championship, for his team with a hit, or end his season with an out.

Across the field Jesse saw Nellie Shofner, from the *Town Crier,* taking notes. She still hadn't moved on to a bigger paper, though she clearly had the talent, and the work ethic. Jesse knew she was working on a feature about Jack Carlisle, one the *Crier* was going to run as soon as he signed his letter of intent with Vandy.

Nellie saw Jesse looking over at her and waved.

"Oh, look," Molly said. "It's Gidget."

Jesse ignored his deputy chief and leaned forward, the pitcher ready to pitch and the batter ready to hit now.

Hit it to short.

He's not afraid the way I never was.

It happened then, exactly the way Jesse had pictured it, or maybe willed it, the kid with the bat hitting a sharp grounder to Jack's right. Crack of the bat unmistakable on a ball you'd just caught clean.

But the damned ball looking like a base hit, for sure.

Except.

Except Jack Carlisle *had* moved over, the way Jesse wanted him to, Jesse had seen him do it right before the pitch, the kid reading the ball perfectly as it came off the bat. So the ball was headed into left field. But then wasn't. There was Jack Carlisle half sliding, half diving to his right, backhanding the ball. Knowing in the moment he had no chance at the kid who'd hit the ball, and was flying down the first base line behind him.

You either knew what to do next or you didn't.

Jack knew.

From his knees, he sidearmed the ball to his third baseman. Snap throw, right on the bag, something on it. *I could make that throw.* The Paradise third baseman, Finn Baker, put the tag on the runner, the runner clearly out. But if the runner heading home crossed the plate before the tag was applied at third, game was tied.

He didn't.

Game over.

Home team had won the title.

After the celebration in the middle of the field, and then the trophy presentation, Jesse stood with Jack Carlisle near second base. Suit was there, too. And Molly. Jesse knew, though, from experience, the kid really didn't want to be with them. He wanted to go be with his teammates. This was part of it, Jesse remembered, that feeling you had in the first few minutes after you won the big game, and you never got those first few minutes back.

"Party tonight," Jack told Jesse. "Over at the Bluff."

Jesse grinned. "Better not be adult beverages involved."

The kid grinned back. A younger version of Suit. Family resemblance impossible not to see. Jesse thought Jack Carlisle looked more like Suit than he did his own mother.

"Can't speak for the boys," Jack said. "But I'm not gonna blow everything by getting drunk and stupid."

Then he ran across the field to where the Paradise Pirates were already posing for pictures.

"There were guys I played with in high school who could have taught a master class in drunk and stupid," Jesse said to Suit and Molly.

"Boy, those were the days, my friend," Molly said.

"We thought they'd never end," Jesse said.

It was right before Jesse felt as if somebody had dropped a bomb on Paradise, Mass.

Two, actually.

2

Spike was at the Gray Gull, which he had owned for a few years now.

He was Sunny Randall's best friend but had become Jesse's friend, too. Spike also owned Spike's, on Marshall Street in Boston. He had just been spending more time in Paradise lately, primarily because his current boyfriend had a weekend place on the water.

Sunny liked to call Spike a gay superhero. Jesse had asked her one time, just in the interest of proper record-keeping, what kind of superhero she considered him.

"An inner-directed one," Sunny had said.

"Anything else?" Jesse had said.

"Hunky one," she'd said.

Back when she still considered him as such, sometimes quite enthusiastically.

"I know you want to ask me how she's doing," Spike said to Jesse when he arrived at the Gull.

Both of them knowing who "she" was.

"I'm fighting it," Jesse said. "The way I do my urge to drink."

"How about if I tell you anyway?" Spike said.

"How about I pop into the kitchen and look for possible health code violations?" Jesse said. "*Or* we could stop talking about Ms. Randall and you could show me to my table."

"Right this way, Chief Stone!" Spike said.

Charlie Farrell, who'd retired as police chief in Paradise long before Jesse had arrived from Los Angeles, was already seated at his favorite corner table, a martini in front of him. White hair, worn long, but he was able to carry off the longish hair, even at his age. Good tan. Bright red V-neck sweater. Charlie was partial to red. Said his late wife used to tell him the color "popped" when he wore it. Red golf shirt underneath it. Charlie didn't look his age, which Jesse knew to be right around eighty. It was his hands that gave him away. They always did. His hands looked older than the town lighthouse. Or the ocean beyond it.

He grinned and put his right hand out to Jesse. Jesse shook it, but lightly, knowing by now Charlie's hands were about as sturdy as leaves.

"Chief," Charlie said.

"Chief," Jesse said.

"I'd get up," Charlie said to Jesse, "but it would take too long."

"We need to get you one of those portable ski lifts you've got at the house to get you upstairs," Jesse said.

"Bite my Irish ass," the old man said.

Charlie and Maisie Farrell had finally gotten tired of

the Paradise winters and moved down to Naples, Florida, after he retired. To live happily ever after in the sun. But Maisie Farrell was diagnosed with Alzheimer's two years ago, died last year from complications. Charlie had sold their condominium almost immediately after the funeral and moved back to Paradise. He told Jesse one time that he thought guys his age waiting around to die in Florida seemed like a cliché.

He pointed to his martini glass and did what he always did, no matter how many times they met for dinner, and asked if Jesse minded.

"Yeah," Jesse said. "Tonight's the night I decided to let *your* drinking finally bother me."

"Well, you never know," Charlie Farrell said.

"As long as you drink responsibly," Jesse said.

"I'm eighty years old," Charlie said. "What the hell's the point in that?"

He drank some of his drink and smacked his lips and put his glass down. He never ate the olives. Said they were more decorative than anything else.

"I never asked," Charlie said. "Were you a martini guy in your drinking days?"

"Scotch," Jesse said. "Lots and lots of scotch."

"You still miss it?"

"Only when I'm awake," Jesse said.

Spike brought Jesse an iced tea without Jesse having ordered it.

"On the house," Spike said.

"Too small to be a bribe," Jesse said.

"Gotta start somewhere," Spike said.

Charlie wanted to know how things were going with the red-haired lawyer.

Rita Fiore.

Jesse smiled. He smiled a lot when Charlie was on the other side of the table. Like he was here with his grandfather.

Or maybe a second father.

"You know how they say in sports that the legs go first?" Jesse said. "I'm starting to think they go second."

Charlie Farrell sighed.

"And the thing you're talking about that *does* go first?" he said. "It just keeps going and going. *South*."

"So it doesn't keep going like the Energizer bunny," Jesse said.

"A battery, maybe," Charlie said. "But a dead one."

"I'll bet Miss Emma doesn't say that," Jesse said.

Librarian emeritus in Paradise. In Charlie's demographic.

"Despite her advancing years," Charlie said, "Miss Emma continues to be aspirational, bless her heart."

Jesse laughed. Sometimes he thought the best part of being in Charlie's presence was just listening to the old man talk.

They both made small talk over filets and fully loaded baked potatoes. Jesse wanted to know how Charlie's grandson was doing. Nicholas. In his late twenties, in a wheelchair since his motorcycle spun out of control one night in the rain on the Stiles Island Bridge. Jesse was the first to the scene. The helmet Nicholas was wearing might have saved his life. But couldn't prevent the damage to the lumbar region of his spinal cord.

"He loves working at that candy store," Charlie said. "They got the kid moving up fast in sales."

It was a lot more than a store. It was the hottest new business in Paradise, Mass., the candy company owned by Hillary More. She had moved here with her teenage son the year before, opened More Chocolate, and it had almost immediately become a sensation, and not just in Paradise. Hillary More had bought the old firehouse at the edge of town, refurbished it, extended it, hired only local people to work for her, making an especially big point of hiring people with disabilities like Nicholas Farrell, who now handled talking to nonprofits using More Chocolate for fundraising. The factory where the chocolate was actually manufactured was up in Nashua, New Hampshire, just over the state line, for tax purposes.

Jesse liked her a lot. He couldn't see himself having a romantic relationship with her, as much as she kept trying to put that into play, and not just because he knew she was a single parent with a son at the high school. What he did fantasize about was her running for mayor in the next election, an idea she had already floated herself from time to time.

It was a piece of a larger fantasy for Jesse, one that involved shooting his current boss, Mayor Gary Armistead, out of a cannon.

Jesse noticed Charlie had gotten quiet when it was time for him to order dessert.

"What?" Jesse said.

"*What* what?" Charlie said.

"Unspoken thoughts have never been one of your specialties," Jesse said. "Right up there with bullshit."

"I promised myself I wouldn't bother you with my niggly problems," Charlie said.

"With you, there's no such thing," Jesse said. "You're family, Chief."

So Charlie told Jesse about the "Grandpa call" he'd gotten the day before. A female voice, young, saying it was Erin. Granddaughter. Nicholas's sister. Traveling in Europe. Telling him that one of the girls she was traveling with in Europe had been arrested with drugs, and that they both needed a lawyer, which is why Grandpa needed to wire money, like right now. Or, better yet, buy some cash cards and read her the numbers over the phone.

"Erin" said she'd call back in the morning.

"What's pissing you off so much about that?" Jesse said. "You're too smart to have gone for it. On top of that, you're a cop."

"What pisses me *off*," Charlie said, "is thinking about other geezers who do fall for this scam, and lose money they can't afford to lose. Or give the scammers an account number from their bank and get themselves good and cleaned out. Or buy into the fact that the IRS is coming after them if they don't come up with some dough, and fast."

He told Jesse then that Miss Emma had even lost a few thousand dollars to a scammer of her own the year before.

The martini was long gone. Charlie was working on an espresso now. And even though Charlie had gotten sidetracked riffing about the scam and spam calls, they both knew they weren't leaving until Charlie got his vanilla ice cream.

"I'd like to have a talk with whatever thief is behind this thing," Charlie said.

"It's the same as looking to get even with telemarketers," Jesse said. "But even if you could somehow stop one of them, it would be like whack-a-mole. There's more of them than there are of us."

Jesse turned and waved for their waiter.

"Order your ice cream," he said. "That always makes you feel better. And let this go."

"Something else that's never been one of my specialties," Charlie Farrell said. "And not one of yours, either, I might add."

"How about this?" Jesse said. "How about we put a tap on your phone? I'll put Molly on it. Next time they call, *if* they call, keep them on the line and maybe they'll slip up."

"I just want one face-to-face with these bums," Charlie said. "Maybe pistol-whip one of them."

"Focus on your next face-to-face with Miss Emma," Jesse said. "And allow your former department to serve and protect that Irish ass of yours."

Spike came over and took Charlie's dessert order.

"Two scoops tonight," Charlie said.

"Good call, Gramps," Jesse said.

"Your ass," Charlie Farrell said.

The Dean of American Crime Fiction

Robert B. Parker